ACCLAIM FOR
THE MOMENT OF EVERYTHING

"Populated with an endearing, eccentric cast of characters, and told with sharp Southern humor, THE MOMENT OF EVERYTHING is a gift for those who believe in the magic of bookstores…and in the power of books."

—Tracy Guzeman, author of *The Gravity of Birds*

"If the cast of *Girls* moved to the Silicon Valley and got tech jobs, if the correspondence in *You've Got Mail* took place in the pages of a used book, you might find THE MOMENT OF EVERYTHING at this hypercool intersection of retro appeal and modern smarts. Shelly King has drawn a perfect heroine for this very moment—snarky enough to make you laugh and yet satisfyingly full of hope and soul. Thoroughly rooted in the now, but achingly in love with the past, THE MOMENT OF EVERYTHING is a book lover's book—a warmhearted illustration of the continuing relevance of books and bookstores in our modern culture that's sure to make readers fall in love."

—Lydia Netzer, author of *Shine Shine Shine* and
How to Tell Toledo from the Night Sky

"In Shelly King's charming novel, a young woman finds love letters in an old copy of *Lady Chatterley's Lover*. Her quest to discover their source leads her in and out of the many worlds of

Silicon Valley, and the surprising twists and turns of love and self-discovery. We're the lucky readers who get to come along for this delightful ride. Ms. King writes with humor, passion, and great intelligence."

—Ellen Sussman, *New York Times* bestselling author of *French Lessons* and *The Paradise Guest House*

THE MOMENT OF EVERYTHING

A Novel

SHELLY KING

GRAND CENTRAL
PUBLISHING

NEW YORK   BOSTON

Grand Central Publishing
Hachette Book Group
237 Park Avenue
New York, NY 10017

www.HachetteBookGroup.com

Printed in the United States of America

RRD-C

First Edition: September 2014
10 9 8 7 6 5 4 3 2 1

Grand Central Publishing is a division of Hachette Book Group, Inc.
The Grand Central Publishing name and logo is a trademark of Hachette Book Group, Inc.

The Hachette Speakers Bureau provides a wide range of authors for speaking events. To find out more, go to www.hachettespeakersbureau.com or call (866) 376-6591.

The publisher is not responsible for websites (or their content) that are not owned by the publisher.

Library of Congress Cataloging-in-Publication Data
King, Shelly.
The moment of everything / Shelly King. — First Edition.
    pages cm
ISBN 978-1-4555-4679-4 (trade pbk.) — ISBN 978-1-4555-4678-7 (ebook)
1. Books and reading—Fiction. 2. Social media—Fiction. 3. Psychological fiction. I. Title.
PS3611.I5858M66 2014
813'.6—dc23
                                        2013044015

For Mama, who always said I should write

THE MOMENT
OF EVERYTHING

Where is human nature so weak as in the book-store?

—Henry Ward Beecher

For Connie had adopted the standard of the young: what there was in the moment was everything. And moments followed one another without necessarily belonging to one another.

—D. H. Lawrence, *Lady Chatterley's Lover*

CHAPTER ONE

To Make You Essential to Me

Love finds for us what we do not know we want.
—Henry

Books don't change people's lives, not like everyone thinks they do. Reading *The Razor's Edge* while flying in first class to a meditation resort or *The Sheltering Sky* on a postdivorce hike to see what's left of the snows of Kilimanjaro won't make you any more enlightened than spinning in the teacups at Disneyland. I'm sorry, but that's the truth of it. And the used books here at the Dragonfly aren't infused with any more wisdom than the virginal new ones at Apollo Books & Music. Our books are just cheaper and more tattered. But people keep coming. They keep asking me for elixirs of paper and words to soothe their disappointments and revive their smothered passions. They come because they believe a book transformed my life. Not one of them understands. It wasn't the book that did it.

Looking back, it's hard for me to pinpoint the moment it all began. I could say it was the day I was laid off by ArGoNet Software, or when I first met Hugo, or even further back when I left South Carolina for Silicon Valley. But I guess the bare truth of it is that everything started on that Friday afternoon with me and Hugo sitting on those two springless armchairs on that creaky wood platform in the front window of Dragonfly Used Books, on Castro Street in Mountain View, the heart of Silicon Valley. The passersby, dressed in shirts with dangling Google, Yahoo!, and Intuit badges attached, saw Hugo, balding and with a long ponytail in back, reading a threadbare copy of the first Waverley novel, next to me, a thirty-four-year-old in terrible need of having her roots done, wearing an ex-boyfriend's holey Rush T-shirt over a pair of jeans that had become too tight with unemployment pounds. It was an odd place to sit, right there on display in front of God and everybody. But it was also the only place in the Dragonfly with enough floor space to fit a couple of chairs. Everywhere else, Lord help us, there were only books.

In Silicon Valley, that summer of 2009 wasn't like the one of 2001, when moaning zombies of dead dot-coms roamed the land. This time, companies didn't fail. They just laid off half their employees, offering "involuntary separation from payroll" to give everyone the chance to "pursue new opportunities." Me, I was hiding in Dragonfly Used Books reading historical romance novels and waiting for the Next Big Thing. I'd been through this before.

But it'd been six months since ArGoNet Software shipped my job to India. I'd given up pedicures, eating out, and, finally, cable TV. Hugo told me I was listening for the universe to present me with adventures I could never have imagined. My mother told me I was loafing.

I was reading *The Defiant*, just one of the romances I'd harvested off the Dragonfly's stacks that week. There had also been *The Redemption, The Bandit,* and *The Pirate Queen's Deceit.* No chick-litty books with cocktails and spiked heels on the cover for me. I wanted swashbucklers, with their virile chests and bursting bodices. I guess I was just old-fashioned that way.

When I'd arrived that morning, I'd picked up *The Defiant* out of a cardboard box full of books by the front counter. ROMANCE, $2 A BAG, read the sign. The cover showcased a stunning redhead with cleavage brimming over the top of an Elizabethan dress. A shirtless man with an '86 Bon Jovi hairdo stood in the distance and glared at her menacingly. Or was it passionately? I swear I just couldn't tell sometimes.

Sure, I read other kinds of books. Lots of them in just about every genre you can imagine. But I loved romances. There was something so comforting about knowing the whole story just from looking at the front cover. First, a political intrigue to keep the hero and heroine apart. Next, conflicting loyalties, hardened hearts, and possibly a forced engagement to an economically advantageous but physically and morally repulsive suitor. Several interrupted encounters, until finally they find themselves trapped in a cave, a barn, or a shepherd's cottage during a violent rainstorm, and then you'd have your general bulging breeches, pink-tipped breasts, and primal rhythm as old as love. It wasn't Shakespeare, but it sure beat LinkedIn as a way to kill an afternoon.

I'd gotten to a climatic duel when I saw the owner of the card shop a block away stop in front of the Dragonfly's window. She beamed at Hugo and knocked on the glass, but he didn't move. I nudged him. He noticed Card Shop Lady, smiled, and blew her a kiss.

"Does she know you're cooking Squid à la Hugo tonight for that real estate agent who was in here earlier?" I asked.

"Maggie, when you reach our age, you'll find that ignorance is often liberating," he said as he returned to the dramas of Sir Walter Scott, balanced on the soft pudge above the belt he'd loosened after a dim sum lunch. I'd never seen him in anything other than jeans and worn cotton shirts rolled up at the sleeves. In his late fifties, he peered through black-rimmed reading glasses that made him look like the headmaster at some faraway boarding school where children in English novels are sent. Mr. Chips in Birkenstocks.

I returned to *The Defiant*. The Dragonfly was an eager dealer for my romance novel habit. I found them everywhere: wedged between an owner's manual for a '61 Valiant and a guide to tantric sex. Under the front counter next to the wooden recipe box where Hugo kept index cards to keep track of customers' accounts for books they'd traded in. In a paperback landslide created by Grendel, the Dragonfly's cat, who didn't maneuver between the shelves as deftly as he once did. The Dragonfly's stacks were a labyrinth of L-shaped sections that curled in on themselves like the shells I used to hunt on the Carolina beaches as a child. You could spend hours, even days, searching the stacks trying to find the one specific book you were looking for. Generally, it was much easier to take what you found rather than to try to find what you wanted.

I could knock out two or three of these romances a day. Reaching the half-blank last page gave me that little meth-y thrill that's the Holy Grail every software coder wants their user to feel, like killing it on "Sudden Death" in Guitar Hero or earning the strawberry cow in FarmVille. "At last," your inner addict says, "I did it. I can stop now and spend my hours solving world hunger." But you don't. There're more fake guitars to play or a neon henhouse to buy or, in my case, a pirate to seduce, and what in the real world can compete with that?

My habit drove my last boyfriend crazy. To Bryan, an iOS coder who wrote a barcode image-processing library that uploaded the nutritional info for packaged food that he sold to a bunch of different diet apps for a truckload of money, romance novels made about as much sense as a PlayStation did to a hummingbird. "You've got to make success a daily habit," he'd say to me. "Finding a job is your new job." That made it hard for me to tell him I was playing hooky from my "new job" at the Dragonfly. So I didn't. Then we'd have sex. It's near impossible for a man to concentrate enough to point out the inefficiencies in your time management when the two of you are going down the horizontal ski jump. We were together two years, until he moved to Austin a couple of months ago without ever bringing up me going with him. He was a nice guy. They're always nice guys. But no one comes to Silicon Valley to fall in love.

I was getting on to my duel when I felt a kick in the back of my chair. I turned around the side to glare at Jason, his black *Babylon 5* T-shirt billowing around his toothpick arms, his finger holding his place in a paperback the size of a hay bale with futuristic knights on the cover. He seemed colorless to me—dark wiry hair, skin like the underbelly of a catfish—and his head looked as though it had been pressed by a vise. Barely five feet tall with a slight limp, his appendages sticking out at odd angles, he had the look of someone who'd been half-trampled by a runaway horse and buggy.

"Done yet?" Jason asked.

"What?"

"Chair. Are you done with the chair?" He overenunciated each word, letting me know exactly how much of a twit he considered me. There were only two chairs in the Dragonfly: the pea-green relic with the fabric worn through in spots on the arms that I sat in, and its partner, Hugo's blue wingchair whose dropped bits of stuffing had become a part of the carpet.

"Three more pages in this chapter." I turned back to my duel.

Jason came around the chair and hunched over me like a gargoyle.

"You've been here all day."

I looked around him at Hugo, who sat focused on his book, pretending we weren't in the same room.

"I'm a customer," I said to Jason.

"Bullshit. You've got to buy something to be a customer."

He had me there. Hugo let me sit around the Dragonfly all day without ever expecting me to buy anything. As my landlord in the small duplex a few blocks from the Dragonfly where we both lived, he had a right to worry that I'd traded in my job search for romance novels. Rent didn't just pop out of pantaloons. But he never brought it up. All that might change after the first of the month if I couldn't stretch out the last of my savings, and if this week's unemployment check from the bankrupt state of California was late again.

"I'll be done in a minute," I told Jason and turned back to the duel I was enjoying at no charge.

Jason yanked *The Defiant* out of my hand, stomped over to

the front counter, and held it out to a woman digging through the $2-a-bag Romance box.

"Got this one, Gloria?" he asked her.

Gloria pressed her armload of finds against the appliquéd cat on her sweatshirt while she read the back cover of my book.

I leaped from my chair and swung around the railing like Captain Blood on a masthead.

"You don't want to read that," I said, landing in front of Gloria. "Seriously, the heroine's got acne and the hero's short. The villain is only mildly disagreeable. I'd say just a bit grumpy really. Doesn't make for a good read. Let me find you something in a surly Irish rebel who's trying to avenge his father's murder while resisting the temptation of his enemy's beautiful daughter."

She blinked at me, while Jason rushed past me and plopped into my chair. I turned back to Gloria in time to see her stuff *The Defiant* in an NPR tote bag already overflowing with other books. She slapped two dollars in dimes on the counter and trudged out the door onto Castro Street.

Hugo hoisted himself out of his chair and gave me a have-patience-and-the-universe-will-provide pat on my shoulder before heading to the counter to add Gloria's change to the till. I grabbed *A Devil's Heart* from the bargain box and scurried over to his vacant chair.

·

I'd gotten about fifty pages into *A Devil's Heart* when my iPhone began to scream, "It's judgment day! Sinners repent!" I slid the phone out of my pocket and saw Dizzy's picture. The name over the picture was "God." I kept forgetting to password-protect my phone when Dizzy was around.

"I'm not saying anything," Hugo said. Having lost his chair, he was sorting through a box of thrillers a customer had brought in for trade that morning.

"Telling me you're not saying something about the government listening in on my cell phone conversations is exactly the same as saying something." I tapped the Sleep button on top of the phone to send Dizzy to voice mail.

"Actually," Hugo said, "I was going to mention the brain cancer."

"It's judgment day! Sinners repent!" my phone screamed again. Dizzy wasn't going to be ignored. Jason jabbed a finger in the direction of a sign he'd written and hung above the front counter:

YOUR CELL PHONES ARE EVIL AND WILL EAT YOUR BRAINS! TURN THEM OFF AND READ BOOKS!

Below those lines, Hugo had added in block letters:

NAMASTE—YOUR FRIENDS IN LOVE AND PEACE AT THE DRAGONFLY

I went outside to the sidewalk and growled to myself before I answered the phone.

"You're at home, right? Drilling for jobs?" Dizzy asked.

I jumped out of the way of a skateboarder headed next door to Cuppa Joe. He popped the board into his hand

and joined the Overly Tattooed & Pierced at the sidewalk tables.

"Yep," I said. "Plugging away."

"Snot waffle."

"Puss bucket."

Dizzy was my best friend. We'd grown up together in the lowlands of South Carolina. He was the youngest of five boys, the gay math genius son of a pig farmer. I was an only child, the chubby, freckled daughter of a beauty queen. We really had no other choice.

"According to Foursquare, you checked into Dragonfly Used Books two hours ago. Why are you the Mayor of Dragonfly Used Books?" he said. "Look across the street, sugarbritches."

I turned my eyes to the café right outside Apollo Books & Music, where Dizzy sat with his phone to his ear, lifting a wineglass to toast me. Built like a fireplug with shaggy red hair down to his shoulders, he was a little shorter than my five foot six, though no one could ever get him to admit by how much. Today, he was wearing long cargo shorts—which on his stubby legs came halfway down his calves—and a Red Elvises T-shirt. He pointed to a tall coffee drink on the hubcap-size table where he sat.

"That better be a triple shot latte," I said.

"With extra foam," he purred into the phone.

I waited for a break in the slow-moving traffic down Castro Street and then scurried across to join him. For years, this Mexican-tiled courtyard led into an abandoned movie theater, but now it was the mandatory café that came with the chain bookstore. The town had gone all cattywampus when Apollo wanted to convert the closed theater to one of its stores, but all that fussing soon died down as Apollo won everyone over with its wide, well-lit aisles, where people in matching polo shirts looked up inventory and escorted you to your book like liverymen in a fairy tale. Hugo imagined himself to be in competition with Apollo, but I wondered if Apollo Books & Music even knew Hugo's store existed. The Dragonfly had no advertising, no displays, and hardly even a sign to speak of. It would be fair to call it just a great big pile of books and a cash register. Yet Hugo insisted it was on the good side of the fight for the soul of a community that had no idea it was in peril. So we inhabitants of the Dragonfly stepped foot in Apollo only when in dire need, such as when the Dragonfly's plumbing wasn't working or when a friend had already paid for a latte. But I had to admit I wasn't immune to Apollo's appeal. I found a certain corporate comfort in the bags and mugs imprinted with the store's name. They dovetailed nicely with my collection of clothes embroidered with logos of software from all the companies I'd worked for, companies with products that didn't actually exist that were being sold to people who did not actually have money to buy them.

"I was so looking at jobs. I needed a break," I said, punching Dizzy in the arm. Dizzy worked more than eighty hours a week. His hobbies were developing open source software, trying to get his car to run on French fry grease, and providing tech support for a group of astronomy students in Brazil who thought they'd discovered a comet. For Dizzy, time was a unit to be traded in for output. Not using it efficiently didn't make a whole lot of sense to a software engineer whose job it was to make things faster with fewer resources.

"But you looked this morning, right? Did you see that Martin Wong gave you a recommendation on LinkedIn? He just landed at WebEx."

I hadn't seen it because I'd been too busy reading about tawny lasses and virile lads. What could Martin, a sales rep at ArGoNet I'd worked with for two seconds last year, have to say about me?

As I fired up the LinkedIn app on my phone, Dizzy reached into a canvas Apollo bag stuffed with technical books with pencil drawings of animals on the front covers: a baby elk for HTML 5, a fox for iOS. I also saw *World War II: The Definitive Visual History*. Once, at an ArGoNet company meeting, Dizzy had screened the first twenty minutes of *Saving Private Ryan* to inspire the troops. "Beachheads!" he screamed. "We need beachheads!" Everyone put their heads between their knees to keep from throwing up. Dizzy said it was the best quarterly meeting we'd ever had.

The book he pulled out of the bag, though, was a novel, a trade paperback in earthy tones with sharp corners and a stiff, steady spine. I could even smell it from where I sat, the pine bark scent of freshly cut paper. My fingertips tingled, thinking of the unblemished cover. It was a small, delicate thing, a newly hatched bird. Unlike the books that lived in the Dragonfly, it was unweathered by overstuffed purses, spills from morning coffees, and teething puppies. It was *Lady Chatterley's Lover*.

"You've read it, haven't you?" Dizzy asked. "I mean they don't give you an English degree unless you've read D. H. Lawrence, right?"

"Yeah, I've read it. Our freshman English lit survey. You were in the same class."

"Well, who the fuck remembers? Listen, I've got pure gold for you. We're getting another round of funding from Wander Fish. Remember Avi Narayan?"

"Sure." I didn't really, but it was easier to just pretend.

"She's got this book club and wants the two of us to saddle up," Dizzy said, holding up another copy of the novel. "We're all supposed to have the same edition."

"I don't do book clubs. My mother's in a book club."

"Yeah, the same one as mine. But we're doing *this* book club. Silicon Valley Lesbians with Advanced Degrees or some shit like that."

"We're not lesbians, jackass."

"I'm texting you the URL for their blog."

Christ on a cracker. Mama's book club couldn't even agree on how much sugar to put in the iced tea, but this group had a blog? I opened the text message and tapped on the link. Silicon Valley Women Executives Association Book Club, the SVWEABC for short. They had a logo.

"Uh, Dizz, you're not a woman."

"Yeah, I know. They're expanding, just haven't rebranded yet. I'm their first dude."

"They're starting with you?"

"Yeah, can you believe it? I'm totally saving her ass. I'm in her office today and she's got this *Lady Chatterley's Lover* on her desk, and she starts telling me about this book club like I give a fuck and how two people just dropped out and there's only eighteen of them now. So anyway, I saddle up for this thing. Then I remind her of you. How you were this hotshot English lit major and how she should invite you to her jamboree. They meet up at Avi's place in Woodside. We'll probably need a sherpa to get up there. They do this every month. Nothing modern. Only dead writers."

"Dead?"

"Yeah, that's their criteria. That and your shit can't stink."

"Why am I supposed to want to do this?"

"I'm not jumping ship anytime soon, Mags. We've got a chance at ArGoNet with the new funding. And Avi's on the board now. She can bring you back in."

We'd been through this before, me and Dizz, since that day ten years ago when we skipped grad school commencement and drove his '86 CRX from Columbia to Palo Alto. It was the late nineties, Dizzy wanted to tap into the vein of Internet gold before it dried up, and I wanted to be with Dizzy. So we packed up our freshly minted master's degrees—his in computer science, mine in library science—and headed to Silicon Valley. I figured I could work in a coffee shop while I looked for a library job. But Dizzy got me in at his first start-up company as the admin at a ridiculously high salary, twice what I'd make as a librarian. And in start-ups you're never just one thing. The next thing I knew, I was in front of a customer being introduced as the head of Professional Services. I didn't write code, but I understood how information fit together and how to make it pretty. Engineers loved me because I made them look good. The execs loved me because I could make the tech talk sound like *The Velveteen Rabbit*. I felt like a comic book orphan who'd just learned that all of her oddities were really signs of her superpowers and that there was a bunk reserved for her at the Hall of Justice. Then the tech bubble burst and planes flew into buildings. The bottom fell out of everything. Dizzy and I took a hit, but we sucked it up for a couple of years at the only companies that were hiring. Then the next wave came and it was called social media. VC funding bounced around the valley again, like a pinball lighting up little companies all over the San Francisco peninsula. Dizzy met some angel funders at a Meetup for entrepreneurs and came up with the idea for ArGoNet.

You could think of ArGoNet as Facebook and Twitter meets corporate intranet. The idea was that we would create a secure hosted environment where employees could communicate and connect with one another and the company could serve up internal communications to everyone, safe and secure from the outside world. Dizzy and I cashed out everything, hired a Stanford MBA as our CEO, then rented a six-hundred-square-foot windowless office space over a Chinese travel agency just down the block on Castro Street. Four years, six hundred hires, three CEOs, and five rounds of layoffs later, the board sent my position to India. On TV, people tearfully leave a job with hugs and good-byes, carrying a box with a plant sticking out of it. In reality, you show up one morning to find a check for two weeks' salary with your name spelled wrong and a security guard waiting to inspect your purse on the way out.

"Are you serious about getting me back in?" I asked.

"Was Erwin Rommel the Desert Fox?"

I had no idea, but I figured that was a "yes" because he didn't look at me when he said it. That usually meant he was serious. And worried. We were in uncharted waters. We knew what to do at ArGoNet, where to sit and who to talk to when we needed something. I knew the code Dizzy and his team had written as if it were a book I'd read so many times the cover would fan open whenever I laid it on the table. I understood the logic and illogic of it, the quirky behaviors that frustrated and delighted me, the little workarounds I'd discovered that made it do things even Dizzy didn't know about.

"You can do this," Dizzy said. "You show, you wear something nice, you say something brilliant. Bam! You're back in the game, sugarbritches."

"When is the book club meeting?" I asked.

"Tomorrow afternoon."

I unfurled copious amounts of curse words.

"You'll be fine," Dizzy said. "You can talk the flowers down off wallpaper when you want to."

I pictured my copy of *The Defiant* sitting on Gloria's countertop, probably next to a bag of fat-free cookies and last month's *Redbook* with the Lifetime network playing in the background. There was a chance I may have lost my touch.

"Wait, weren't you going to Napa with that Apple hardware engineer tomorrow?"

"Nah, we broke up at that sushi place in Cupertino night before last. Didn't you read my Yelp review?"

Reviews were Dizzy's personal diary. Reviews of movies, restaurants, crap he bought on Amazon. And Dizzy didn't just leave his thoughts on the thing he was reviewing, but wrote long narratives about what happened at the place or with the thing and why it happened and who it happened with. I used to love reading Dizzy's reviews. Sometimes I'd comment on them, pretending like I didn't know him but hated what he had to say, and we'd get into a fake rant that usually got us escorted out of whatever site we were on, like kids ramming too hard on the bumper cars. I hadn't looked at his reviews for a long time. It wasn't as much fun when I didn't have the money to share in whatever he was evaluating.

Dizzy downed the rest of his wine, looking like it was causing him pain. Then he held the glass away from him, examining its emptiness. "Bear piss," he said. He grabbed the back of my head and kissed me on the part in my hair. "Gotta run. I'm meeting the code monkeys down the street at Finnegans Wake for drinks. Wanna come? I'm buying."

Dizzy always paid for the drinks. It was his best leadership quality.

Finnegans Wake was a faux Irish pub that was big with the Orson Scott Card and *Red Dwarf* crowds. I truly used to love going to the FW with the gang from work after another fourteen-hour day. We'd eat jalapeño poppers, drink Guinness, and quote *Real Genius* into the early hours of the morning. Then I'd stumble the few blocks home, sleep a couple of hours, then get up and do it all over again. It was my place of triumph, my reward for turning bellowing customers into fluffy bunny rabbits. If things were still the same as they were this time last year, I'd be the person everyone would order drinks for, the one they all wanted to talk to. But tonight I would just be the boss's unemployed friend.

"Homework," I said, holding up *Lady Chatterley's Lover*. And with that he left me, on my own, with only three hundred pages of post-Victorian literature standing between me and gainful employment.

"I see you have a new book," Hugo said when I went back to the Dragonfly to collect my things.

"Don't freak out. I can explain." I told him about the book

club while I zipped up *Lady Chatterley's Lover* in my leather back-pack with the ArGoNet logo. I also threw in my unfinished *A Devil's Heart* along with *The Fortune Hunter* and *Daughter of the Game* just for grins.

"I'm sure we could find you a copy here," Hugo said, scur-rying toward the stacks. "I think I remember seeing one just the other day."

The Dragonfly was about as neat as a trailer park after a tor-nado. I'd be there all night waiting for him to find the book he thought he remembered.

"I think I saw one in Sports and Recreation!" Jason shouted after him. A lady looking through coffee table books glared at him and put her finger to her lips. "What!? It's a bookstore, not a library."

"Hugo!" I called. "I think we're supposed to all read the same edition!"

"Fascists!" I heard him yell as I walked out the door.

.

If you thought of your hand as the peninsula, San Francisco at the tip of your middle finger and San Jose at your wrist, Mountain View would be in the center of your palm. Unlike San Francisco, we didn't have hipsters in granny glasses and turtlenecks coding in refurbished warehouses. And even with Google as a resident, the Mountain View address didn't carry the same cachet as Palo Alto or Menlo Park. If Silicon Valley brimmed with carpet or paper mills instead of computer com-panies, Mountain View would be where all the line workers and their middle managers lived. Only the 1,500-square-foot houses from the fifties had solar panels and structured wiring and went for just over a million.

Despite the cost of living, I loved many things about Mountain View, like the old-fashioned iron lamps that lined the streets. They were right out of Dickens, except for the electricity and all, and allowed me to read on my walk home. It usually took me between seven and eight pages to get home from the Dragonfly, which was two less than it took to get a Savage Hammerhead Mocha at Cuppa Joe and three more than it took to get a to-go order of moo shu pork from the cheap Chinese place around the corner. And the walk home was quiet, uninterrupted reading time when I didn't have to fight Jason for a chair. The only sounds on the tree-lined streets were of families tucking themselves in for the night: the clinking of dishes in the sink, the missed piano notes from one more practice round of "On Top of Old Smoky," the unmistakable fit of giggles that can come only from a toddler being tickled.

I'd spent most of the last three hours at Cuppa Joe determined to conquer *Lady Chatterley's Lover*. I was just going to finish my chapter in *The Devil's Heart* before getting to it. But when I left Cuppa Joe, I was done with *The Devil's Heart* and sixty pages into *The Fortune Hunter*. For once, Lady Chatterley was going home untouched.

With the twenty-dollar bill I had to get me through the weekend, I stopped by the Asian grocery for a couple of packs of soup and a lottery ticket. Then it was just a few blocks to the duplex Hugo and I shared. The smell of a backyard grill made my stomach rumble. Hugo's dinner date appeared to have turned into a party. I could hear laughter from behind our duplex and the rubber-fingered guitar chords of a Fleet-wood Mac song.

I clomped up the four steps to the porch that connected my apartment with Hugo's and saw that my screen door was ajar. Between it and my front door, I found a paper plate covered in tin foil with a note taped to the top.

Asparagus wrapped in prosciutto. And I found your book for you. Come join the party.

Yours,
Hugo

I looked down again in the dark corner behind the screen door. There was indeed what could be described as a book. It was not a twin of the book Dizzy had given me. This one looked like it'd been kicked into doomsday and spit back out again. The spine was missing its cover, exposing open weave and glue beneath. Waxy cloth, frayed at the corners and stiff from the sun, stretched over boards warped with water dam-age. The yellowed pages creaked when I turned them, like they were registering complaints at having to move in their decrepit condition. It was the book version of the rusted-out '62 Ram-bler that Dizzy used to drive in high school, the one I refused to ride in out of fear for my life. It wouldn't have surprised me if the book, too, belched black clouds of exhaust. I took the poor thing inside. If I could have given it warm milk and a bed of its own, I would have.

My apartment was not a mirror image of Hugo's two-bedroom palace on the other side of the wall, but rather a one-bedroom add-on, an afterthought with a small breakfast bar that separated the suggestion of a kitchen from a living room that was just big enough for a love seat, a papasan chair, a forty-seven-inch flat-screen, and five Ikea bookcases, stuffed with the books that chronicled my life. *The Great Gatsby* that suffered a Dr Pepper explosion. A *Pride and Prejudice* that never recovered from a nosedive into a puddle. And the only book my mother ever gave me: a B. Dalton edition of Hans Christian Andersen's fairy tales, the one with the Little Mermaid on the cover, its pages brown and crisp and fragile with wear.

I loved that book and its terrible stories. For an entire summer, I read and reread the horrors that happened within. While my friends plunged into childhood fascinations with *Dracula*, *Frankenstein*, and *Sweet Valley High*, I delved into the severed lives and unhappy endings of those fairy tales. In the pages, I found the story of a mermaid who sacrificed her voice for legs and slept on the doorstep of the prince she loved. While each step felt like knives slicing into her feet, she danced for him whenever he asked. In the end, he married someone else and the Little Mermaid drowned herself in the sea. My mother loved the singing crab and the dancing fish in the movie. But it was the original mermaid I loved.

I'd always wanted to be the girl whose mother bought her lots of books. I imagined her patting me on the head and writing a blank check so I could order from the *Weekly Reader* at school. I imagined my walls covered floor to ceiling in brimming bookshelves with a shelf ladder on wheels that I could climb up and propel myself back and forth, stopping where I liked to inhabit whatever magical world seemed perfect for that day. Our house did have lots of books, untouched Harvard Classics from *Twice-Told Tales* to *The Sun Also Rises* that stood like centurions in my mother's living room. The coffee table books—reverent photographs of Southern farmlands or South Carolina football—were always polished and clean of fingerprints. And in her kitchen were cookbooks as neat as the day Mama excavated them from the *Southern Living* shipping box. No *White Fang* or *Treasure Island* or *The Lion, the Witch and the Wardrobe.* Those, I found on my own at the library.

When I was eight, my mother was horrified when I told her I wanted to be a librarian. I could see how she pictured me, a matronly stack-dweller with comfortable shoes and hair in a bun looking over her glasses at people with a dour expression full of contempt for past-due fines. Nothing I said could convince her that her vision was not my future. The librarians I knew were superheroes of data. Like the Old World explorers, they navigated uncharted oceans of information, drawing maps to get anyone anywhere. And they were the keepers of things other people forgot, archiving the incidents of life and piecing them together.

In high school, I'd started volunteering in our town's library, a small yellow house close to the square. My parents' house had endless quiet rooms where an only child could hide away with a book, but the quiet of the library quivered with life, those searching for what they needed and wanted. And I could help them find it. I pushed carts of books up and down the aisles, the wheels squeaking under the weight of words. I pounded due date stamps on lined cards I slipped into books' paper pockets. And after my shift was over, I stayed and crouched on a Kik-Step stool in the distant corner of the Reference section and read books my mother would never have let me bring in the house—Judy Blume's *Forever...*, *Song of Solomon*, and lots and lots of historical romances with wind-swept hair and overflowing bodices on the covers.

As an undergrad at the University of South Carolina, I learned from the librarians how to understand what people wanted and how to navigate their way to what they needed. All the skills I needed to land at Internet start-ups, like building content management systems and the interfaces that drove them, I learned in a library. I understood that every pile of information has a pattern, a thread that runs through each nugget. Give it a tug and everything falls into place. "The knowledge imposes a pattern, and falsifies," T. S. Eliot wrote in *Four Quartets*. "For the pattern is new in every moment."

I still paid my grunt dues shelving books at the college library, the 8 p.m. to midnight shift, bowing to the dictates of the Library of Congress's numbering system. It was meditative, scanning the spines along the shelves and finding just the right spot for a book. And each night, as I pushed my cart of books down the rows, returning what had been borrowed to their home, I'd come across a pair of lovers in one form of embrace or another. Sometimes it was simply leaning into each other against a wall while reading or catching a nap. And other times, from the other side of the shelves I could hear a couple in the throes of passion that only people without their own rooms could conjure. At night, the stacks were like the forest in *A Midsummer Night's Dream*, with mischief and passion hanging in the shadows.

I set Hugo's *Chatterley* down on the breakfast bar and opened it to the title page. At the top, someone had written a date—

April, 1961. And then my eye traveled down the rest of the page, resting on what wasn't supposed to be there. The entire title page was a patchwork of handwriting.

I turned on the lamp above the bar and looked more closely. It looked like a man's handwriting, a mixture of script and print, utilitarian but with an elongated elegance. The *t*'s were crossed with bold strokes and the *i* dotted with a short upward dash, like the flame on a candle.

Love finds for us what we do not know we want.

And under that was a second bit of writing in a different hand, the letters full and looped together, flowing and feminine, and I thought of summer green grass and swirling skirts.

And I have found you here.

I picked up the book, holding it tight to keep it together, but my grip was too much and the pages exploded all over the counter. As I scooped them into a pile, I thought about how much I loved Hugo. I loved how he thought I could take a book like this with me to the meeting tomorrow. He reminded me of my great-aunt Trudy, who always carried half a grapefruit in her purse and never understood why you didn't want to share it.

I munched on the asparagus and then settled into the papasan chair I kept by the window, cracking open the spine of the unblemished *Lady Chatterley's Lover* Dizzy had given me. I was ready. This was going to be good. I was going to will it into being good. I turned to the title page, the crisp, unwritten-on title page, but my eyes drifted back to the pile of pages on my breakfast bar.

Love finds for us what we do not know we want.

I turned back to the book in my hand. Chapter 1, page 1. I forced myself to concentrate. I was going to finish this book tonight, and tomorrow at this book club, socks would be blown clean off and into the dryer. At page two, I felt an uncontrollable urge for a Diet Coke and some Pirate's Booty.

A few minutes later, crunching down on a piece of cheese-powdered puffed rice, I found myself gazing again at the pieces of Hugo's book. Nearly every page was tattooed with notes in the margins, written in the same two hands as the scrawls on the title page. I angled the book toward the lamplight. At the beginning of chapter one, I found this:

Hello? I am Henry. Who is there?

Hello, Henry, it is Catherine.

Catherine, thank you for writing. I grow curiouser and curiouser. —Henry

No more than I. Why Lady Chatterley's Lover? *Why start writing in this book? —Catherine*

I don't know really. I just saw this poor, ravaged book, felt sorry for it, I suppose. I thought I might keep it company. I've always liked the novel. Did you know the original title was Tenderness? *I love the gentleness of their love. Especially Mellors's letter in the end. 'If I could sleep with my arms around you, the ink could stay in the bottle.' —Henry*

I sat there—Pirate's Booty halfway to my lips—wondering what the hell was going on. I picked up another random page from the pile. Page 156.

Catherine—

You haunt me, tempt me, prickle my senses. I want to breathe you in and carry you around in my lungs, to make you essential to me. I want you to know what it is to feel my hands on you and to hear my voice say your name.

—Henry

I looked down at the paper that was now scattered all over my kitchen. Of all the questions that buzzed in the hive of my brain, this is the one I heard the loudest. What the hell had happened between "thank you for writing" and "to make you essential to me"?

I shoved the loose pages aside, trying to find a note on a later page. 389, nothing. 335, nothing. Even in the high 200s, there wasn't any correspondence. But then, at last, I turned to page 249.

Sunday is the first day of summer. Meet me in Pioneer Park, by the fountain, noon. —Henry

I felt like I'd arrived home from a trip to find I'd picked up someone else's suitcase at baggage claim. I scanned the sheets in front of me. Words seemed to expand and contract in Henry's and Catherine's writing, words I'd seen all day long in the romances I'd been reading at the Dragonfly. *Embrace, desire, longing.* They were words from books, not real words that real people used, not anymore. They were meant for parchment and quills and pots of ink, to be sealed off with wax and hand delivered by men riding desperately through the night. Yet there they were, looping characters written in ballpoint in the margins of *Lady Chatterley's Lover.*

I gathered the explosion of pages toward me, tenderly returning them to where they belonged. Whoever Henry and Catherine were, they were in my care. I don't remember how long it took for me to go through and reorder all those pages. I only remember the sounds of Hugo's party seeping in through the closed window, and how I tried to ignore them as if they were the sounds of lovers in the next room.

CHAPTER TWO

The Silver Needle

This is a book of passion. She sheds her skin. She is
reborn through desire.

—Catherine

Thank God for the UPS man. If it weren't for the doorbell, I'd
still be asleep. When it woke me up, I found myself halfway sliding off my sofa with a loose page drool-glued to the side of my
face. I scrambled to the door, signed John Lennon's name on the
pad the UPS guy handed me, and held the door as he wheeled
the box inside. Then I looked at the clock. The SVWEABC
meeting started in an hour. Dizzy would be here any minute to
pick me up. I dove into the shower and then ran to my closet.
I could either go for the Cisco marketeer look in an outfit a
saleswoman at Nordstrom picked out for me, or I could go for
the T-shirt and jeans look of a Googler. I chose the latter, pulling
on a pair of jeans and a T-shirt that said *Schrödinger's cat is dead*
on the front and *Schrödinger's cat is not dead* on the back. I was sure
Dizzy would be in his usual cargo shorts and T-shirt, too. We
are geeks. Best everybody know that up front.

Just as I heard Dizzy's biodiesel convertible pull up outside,
my cell phone rang. Mama.

"Did you get the package I sent you?" she asked. "I just got a text from UPS that it was delivered. What do you think?"

There was no point opening the box now. I knew what it was. Another piece of furniture. There was never a problem in the world my mother didn't think could be solved by a Tiffany lamp. Before I moved to California, I didn't have a place of my own for her to redecorate. But she'd had no problem driving more than thirty miles to my college apartment, charming one of my roommates into letting her in, and replacing my T-shirts and torn jeans with linen skirts and Ann Taylor sweater sets anytime she wanted. Now that I was three thousand miles away, she could only send stuff, and furniture was her stuff of choice. Bulky, cumbersome, pain-in-the-ass-to-get-rid-of furniture. In my working days, I'd speed-dialed the Salvation Army to haul away marble-topped kitchen carts, leather wing chairs, and baroque console tables that Marie Antoinette would have considered a bit over-the-top. Lately, I'd turned to Craigslist and managed to pay my Internet bill for several months thanks to Mama's largesse.

"I can't talk right now," I said. "I'm on my way to a meeting."

"You can't be on your way to a meeting. You're unemployed."

In the world I grew up in, only people of a suspicious nature were asked to leave a job. When I told my parents about my layoff, they insisted I return home and live out my unemployment shame under their careful watch. If I were only to come home, marry, and have children, then the Lord would provide. There was a time, I suppose, that I thought the same would be true of ArGoNet. If I were only to do everything I was asked, ArGoNet would give me a wealthy and secure future. But no matter how much I worked or how good I was, it didn't matter in the end. It came down to numbers, and the numbers were smaller when they came from India. The sea judges not whom it swallows. Savior or sinner, it's all the same to the tide.

"Mama, I can't explain right now, but I have to go. It's important."

"More important than your family? Okay, go to your meeting. And your father and I might die right here on the road to Hilton Head, but what do you care about that?"

My parents were married a week after they graduated from college. My father, a track star. My mother, a runner-up for Miss South Carolina. The pictures of their early life together are full of smiles and the ease of two people who would have their connect-the-dot lives paid for by the people who brought them up. They did not ask questions. They didn't even know there were questions to ask. I knew exactly how their Saturday had gone so far. Daddy, as he'd done since before I was born, would have gone to meet his fraternity brothers for breakfast before returning home to Mama, who would already be dressed in a sherbet-colored golf outfit, complete with ankle socks and matching sun visor. Their golf bags would be leaning against the banister in the foyer, and she would be sitting on the curving oak staircase, hands clasped around her stubble-free knees, waiting for him. When I was a kid, they would golf closer to home, getting a babysitter for Friday and Saturday afternoons and evenings at the club. But as soon as I hit my teens and was able to stay on my own, my parents, newly untethered, discovered the world of golf resorts. These places were my parents' Six Flags, a land of primary-colored evening wear and perfume that smells like fresh-cut grass. I'm not sure Mama even liked golf. But Daddy loved it and that was what mattered to her.

"Okay, Mama, I'm going to open it right now."

With a kitchen knife, I sliced open the top of the box and pulled out a mission-style oak end table, a surprisingly understated choice for a woman with stuffed mallards on her kitchen wall.

"Have you opened the card?" she asked. "Open the card while I'm on the phone."

"I don't see a card."

"It's in the drawer. Why don't you ever look inside of things?"

Outside, Dizzy tapped on his horn a couple of times while I opened the drawer to find a piece of my mother's stationery adorned with tiny lilies, her favorite flower. "For new beginnings," she had written on the envelope.

My mother was a beautiful woman who tried to make everything around her as beautiful as she was. But to me, there was nowhere that she succeeded more than her handwriting. Her letters looked as if they'd practiced walking with unabridged dictionaries balanced on their heads until their posture was perfect. The *o*'s were never too fat and the *l*'s were never too skinny. It was the handwriting of a woman who had never doubted where she belonged and woke up each day knowing what it held in store.

My heart jolted when I opened the card to see a check for $10,000. I stared down at the four beautiful zeroes all attached to one another at the top as if they were loops in lace. My mother was finally helping me in a way that was actually helpful.

"Mama, I don't know what to say."

"Well, we decided to give you your inheritance early."

Now I was a bit stunned. Those zeroes suddenly looked very tiny. My parents were loaded. This was, for all practical purposes, a disinheritance.

"Well, it's not all you're getting," she replied to my silence. "Just a bit to cover your move back home."

And there it was.

"I'm happy here," I said, hearing Dizzy honk his horn again. I grabbed my bag and ran out the door with Mama still in my ear.

"You don't know what happiness is. You're unemployed and unmarried. You gave this California thing a try and it didn't work out, which I seem to recall telling you would happen before you went to all the bother of moving out there. It's time, Margaret Victoria. Time to come home."

As I slid onto the bench seat of Dizzy's car, I thought about my parents' house. A big colonial revival near the downtown square, built by my great-great-great-grandfather after the War of Northern Aggression with money he siphoned from the carpetbaggers. I always felt pushed out to the corners of that house, which was too full of my parents' deliberate joy with each other to leave room for me. As I pictured it, I could smell my mother's lilac soap. She'd wait until just an hour before my father's arrival at home to bathe, washing away the scent of the day spent out of his presence. Her longing for him frightened me. Our home was not enough for her. I was not enough for her. If I had ever lost my father, I would have been an orphan.

"Do you know what your uncle Jamie said to me the other day?" Mama went on. "He asked me if you were one of those funny kind of girls. Then he tells me that it's okay if you are because he accepts your 'alternative lifestyle.' He says this to me right by the Vidalia onions at the Winn-Dixie. I cannot have a gay child, Margaret Victoria. That's all just fine about Dizzy. His mama has four more boys. But not me. It's just you, and if you're gay...Well, that's just too much to ask of me."

I looked over at Dizzy and remembered telling Mama he was gay. To her credit, she never said a bad thing about him or treated him any differently, in that she still expected him to kowtow to her every desire in exactly the same way she did with everyone else. But every time she was around him, I could see the effort in her eyes as she reconsidered everything she said or did, as if instead of gay, he was from a foreign country. It wasn't the matter that Dizzy was gay that bothered her. It was the inconvenience of it.

"It's because we let you read too much isn't it?" she asked. "I never should have let you quit the tennis team. If you'd gotten more sun you wouldn't be like this."

"Mama, I'm not gay."

Dizzy spewed his mocha all over his steering wheel.

"Then come home and get married like a decent woman," Mama said. "Bill Cumberland just got divorced."

"He's as old as Daddy."

"He's single."

"I have a life here."

"Do you have a husband? Do you have a family?"

Again, I answered her with silence. Marriage had always seemed like some distant event to me, like that extra ten pounds people always say they're going to lose.

"Margaret Victoria, please explain to me what the point of all this is. You've been out there for ten years. *Ten years.* Now, you have gotten neither rich yourself nor married someone who is. I saw on *Oprah* the other day that there're so many single men in Silicon Valley that they call San Jose 'Man Jose.' Apparently you can't swing a dead cat without knocking over a dozen single men. With those kinds of numbers, what's wrong with you, Margaret Victoria?"

I could tell her about my last blind date, a couple of weeks ago, who canceled twice because of work then took me skydiving because he'd read a study online that doing something physically exhilarating on a date activated pheromones that led to attraction. I'm sure he was very interesting, but I was too busy throwing up from all the exhilaration to pay attention to what he was saying.

"The odds are good, Mama. But the goods are odd."

"Then what is the point of staying out there?"

I looked at Dizzy, hands on top of the steering wheel, thumbs tapping at a song in his head. I wanted to tell her that I came out here to be with my friend, that Dizzy and his family became my family when I realized I really had none of my own. I came here to prove something to myself, and that I was still trying to figure out exactly what that was.

"Thank you for the table," I said. "But I can't accept it, and I can't accept the money."

"You're going to starve to spite me? They're hiring secretaries at the new Mercedes plant in town. Men like secretaries. You could live here and drive to the plant every day."

"I'm not keeping the check, and I'm not keeping the table."

"You have to keep the table. It belonged to your grandmother."

I looked at the shipping invoice taped to my mother's envelope. "It's a Pottery Barn floor sample."

"Don't be smart."

As I tore up the check, I felt anything but smart.

.

The SVWEABC blog announced the June meeting would be held at Avi Narayan's house in Woodside and asked members to inform the hostess of any dietary restrictions due to allergies, religion, weight-loss plan, or politics. (The post's comments included grumblings about the non-UFW grapes at the last meeting.) The blog also included entries for highlights from a biography of D. H. Lawrence, links to books of critical analysis on Amazon, and the PDF file of a paper one club member's daughter wrote on Lady Chatterley for her Sex and the Social Order class at Smith. A clip art drawing of a finger with a string wrapped around it pointed to a reminder for all members to "support your local bookstore" and purchase the Penguin Classics edition of the book from Apollo Books & Music with the club's discount.

"Sometimes I think we put more effort into the blog and the nibbles than we do reading the book," Avi said, her British accent whispering over her *r*'s as she escorted Dizzy and me into her living room.

I had first guessed Avi to be in her mid-forties, but now I noticed the loose skin at the neck and puffiness around the eyes that made me add a few years to that number. Regardless, she was what we would describe back home as a "well-preserved woman." Next to her red sundress, her skin was the color of toasted sugar. She had her thick black hair tied in a leopard-print scarf that would have looked like a discarded candy wrapper on my head. I'd bet Avi had never fallen asleep drooling on her sofa in her entire life. She probably emerged from the ocean each day in a seashell while cherubs adorned her hair with flowers. She was as close as I was ever going to get to Oprah.

"Yep, it's a very effective use of clip art," I said, to which Dizzy gave me a look that said he was sure, if I'd tried, I could've come up with an even lamer line, like, "The wallpaper is nice" or "I like cheese."

"Well, you two stay right here," Avi said, "and I'll fetch you both a cup of tea."

"You read the book, right?" Dizzy asked, after she stepped away. "Please tell me you stayed up all night and wrote down all kinds of brilliance that will blow the panties right off this crowd."

The truth was that I'd just read over the SparkNotes before I fell asleep in the wee hours of the morning. I'd stayed up most of the night reading, but not the novel.

Catherine,

Where are you? It's been a week now with no reply. You are of-

ten in my thoughts and I wish to hear from you. But if you don't want to continue this conversation, I understand.

—Henry

And on the opposite page,

Catherine,

Another week has passed and still no word from you. I would think that perhaps I've imagined you all this time but for the notes you've left in this book. I will check back in another week. If you haven't replied by then, I will wish you well, but I will miss you.

—Henry

And then, at last, on the following page, I'd sighed with relief when I saw Catherine's handwriting.

Henry,

I am back. I am sorry for being away. I will not go again.

Yours,
Catherine

Thanks to SparkNotes, I knew a bit about Connie Chatterley and Mellors's goings-on, but for high drama, I was throwing in with Henry and Catherine.

"I'll get by," I said. "What about you? You're looking a little too well rested."

"Oh, I'm good. Remember that *Lord of the Rings* junkie I dated last year? Dude was fucking obsessed with Sean Bean, who is also in a British *Chatterley* miniseries. I sat through that man showing his vitals about eighteen million times."

Inside, I was smacking myself for not thinking of BitTorrenting a movie version last night.

"Mingle time," Dizzy said, shaking out his mane of red hair. "You take the left flank and I'll go right."

And before I could stop him, off he went to a group of women examining the labels on wine bottles at the bar. I attempted mingling. It was not successful. All the other women bunched into tight whispering circles of three or four. I'd drift close to one, expecting to be caught in a tractor beam of conversation, but that didn't happen. All I got were overheard snippets about "finding more blocks of time," "college admissions coaches," and "spa-ing in Miraval." Then there were the ones on their own, in a corner, texting or talking on the phone. I employed the strategy I used to survive my childhood by retreating to a corner and hoping no one would talk to me.

"I saved you a bit of the Silver Needle," Avi said, reappearing and sitting next to me. She handed me a teacup as delicate as a glass slipper. "Dizzy mentioned you were fond of white tea."

I looked over at the bar to see Dizzy refilling the wineglass of the woman next to him, then sniffing a canapé before tossing it into his mouth. Fond of white tea? I drank Trader Joe's chai with Hugo from clog-size coffee mugs. What other stories had Dizzy told her about me?

I took a sip. Silver Needle tasted like tree bark, and I feared I'd forever lost the power of speech.

"They harvest it once a year," she said. "In the first few days of spring. I think it has a sweet and delicate yet airy fragrance."

Perhaps on Avi's home planet tree bark tasted sweet, but here under our sun it had a bitter, woody taste of, well, tree bark.

"Nice tea," I said.

Avi smiled and looked at me with expectant eyes. I knew that look. She wanted me to dazzle her. But in that room full of employed people, I had nothing but the feeling of not sleeping enough after months of sleeping too much.

"Well," Avi said with acrylic politeness. "You'll have to excuse me while I play hostess."

Whatever grip I was trying to get to pull myself back into the life I wanted felt miles beyond my reach.

I looked over at Dizzy, who was tossing a chocolate truffle into his mouth.

"This is...don't tell me...these are those truffles they sell at the Clos Pegase Winery in Calistoga." The woman next to him nodded, and Dizzy laughed. I loved his laugh. Geese flying overhead would soon descend in search of missing gaggle mates. He may have gotten his teeth capped and whitened and become a snotty cork dork who brought his own wine to restaurants, but he would never ever be able to get rid of that laugh I adored.

He refilled the wineglasses of a couple of women around him, then headed tipsily to the chair beside me and plunked himself down.

"So I got the whole scoop on why they needed replacements," he said. "First there was Harriet. The official story is she was reassigned to the East Coast, but she really had a stress-related breakdown. She went out for a bike ride at lunch, and they found her two days later eating fried chicken and waffles. At a truck stop. In Fresno."

"Chicken and waffles are about the only thing that could get me to ride a bike for two days," I said.

"Yeah, me too," he said. "But let's keep that to ourselves. Then there was Jill, whose start-up tanked, so she joined a clothing-optional intentional community down in Bonny Doon."

"Wow," I said. "That's...wow."

"We got this, Mags," Dizzy said. "We are so in here. If the bar for membership were any lower, we could slide over it on our bellies."

He slapped my knee, then strutted back to the group at the bar like he lived in a house like this instead of a shared rental whose centerpiece was a Carolina Gamecocks blow-up chair and a 340-bottle wine refrigerator. I was left with the word *membership* still lingering and the dread that there would be more of this.

I reached into the tote for my book, but I didn't feel the sharp pages of the Penguin Classic edition that Dizzy had bought me. Instead, there was only the stiff worn cover of Hugo's dilapidated version. Panicked, I dug around, practically sticking my whole head in the bag like it was Sylvia Plath's oven, finding only its nylon-lined insides. Two hours of sleep had given me not only rings under my eyes big enough to start my own circus, but also an impressive level of idiocy. I'd brought the wrong book. I looked around the room at all the Penguin Classics clutched in hands and resting on chairs. Not only had I not read the novel, I'd never used *spa* as a verb, and

I'd brought a copy of the book that I had to hold together like an overstuffed sandwich.

"Ladies, please, shall we get started?" Avi said, calling the room to order, before sitting gracefully in the chair next to me. Dizzy, sitting on my other side, gave me a look that said, *Maybe you could spend the rest of the afternoon hiding in the trunk of my car* when he looked down at my tote bag and saw the book I'd brought.

"I think I speak for all of us," Avi said, "when I say we'll miss Harriet and wish her well on her reassignment back to the East Coast. And the same to Jill, who has decided to take a leave of absence to pursue new opportunities."

I looked over at Dizzy, who hid a laugh behind a cough.

"Some of you have met our guests and potential new members. I think we're all especially happy to welcome our first *male* guest, Dizzy Gordon. Dizzy is the CTO at ArGoNet. I recently spent a lot of time in a conference room with him and the rest of the exec staff going over strategy, and with Dizzy in the room it was a lot more entertaining than that sounds. I can't wait to hear what he has to say about this book."

There was a little applause, mostly from Dizzy's barmates, but to Dizzy it might as well have been a standing ovation. He stood and gave an exaggerated bow while rolling his arm in front of him until it dropped toward the floor.

"And this is Maggie Duprés," Avi went on, resting her freshly manicured hand on my arm. I curled my fingers to hide my ragged cuticles.

"Maggie was recently the director of information architecture at ArGoNet. But what impressed me most about Maggie was her life before Silicon Valley. She has a master's in library science and studied English literature as an undergraduate. I'm sure you will all understand why I have her sitting next to me. I need someone who can help me make sense of this book!"

They all laughed. I'm sure everyone in the room knew this was the first time anyone had professed awe at my English degree. It was a trick I'd noticed most successful people used. Make yourself the joke, and the little people will love you all the more.

"Since we have two new guests, I want to take a moment to remind everyone of our process," Avi continued. "We go around the circle and everyone takes a turn telling us what you think of the book. Remember, one at a time."

"The novel is a paradox," began a woman in a pink sweater set on the other side of Avi. "Simultaneously progressive and reactionary, modern and Victorian."

Everyone else had their books neatly in their laps, while mine was locked up in my bag like Rochester's wife in the attic. When the woman in pink regurgitated the main analysis from SparkNotes.com, the one I had planned to use, any notions I still held on to of pulling off this little caper without embarrassing myself disappeared.

My mind scrambled back to the freshman English literature survey course where I'd first encountered *Lady Chatterley's Lover*. What was it? Something about the class system in English society?

"It's all about class," said the next woman. "The whole affair of Lady Chatterley and the gamekeeper is a microcosm for the British class system."

Strike two. I tried to remember other things the professor had said. It wasn't Lawrence's best novel. It was problematic. It was a prosy thumbing of one's nose at society rather than a thoughtful work of literary merit. Lawrence was pushing boundaries to see what he could get away with, just because he could.

"Mellors overwhelms her in the woods," said the next woman. "He's always the dominant partner. This is women's liberation?"

"There are no sympathetic characters," said the next woman in the circle. "I didn't like any of them."

"The profanity got old."

I remembered Dizzy whispering passages to me in the library study tables, while I tried not to giggle at the absurdity of a stuffy, bearded, old man trying to shock people by using four-letter words we used every day for dismay at having our bikes stolen to elation about pancakes for breakfast in our dorm. Yes, the novel was sorely outdated by modern standards. I could use that.

"Everything is dated. What relevance is this to our lives today?"

I could *not* catch a break.

"Clifford's a bastard. I hate her for marrying him," said the next woman. "She's an idiot."

Avi sat stoic in her chair, her face impassive as she nodded with each comment, before patiently directing the next participant to speak.

Even Dizzy got into the mix when it was his turn.

"The coal pits sucked," he said. "Reminded me of my first job in the Valley."

By the time we reached him, no one had had anything positive to say. It was only because I was sitting next to Avi that I heard her sigh. It was a sigh filled with frustration and anxiety, much like the one that seeped out of me every day when I checked my in-box to find it empty of interview requests. I looked past her to the bookshelves that lined the opposite wall. They were inlaid oak shelves with carvings of vines and leaves winding around the edges. And on those shelves were thick mass-market paperbacks with spines cracked like an old crone's face and hardbacks with dust jackets worn white on the edges. I'd seen the shelves of people who did not love books. Avi's books, though, were nearly broken from being loved. Avi was a book geek. She wanted everyone to like *Lady Chatterley's Lover*. She was waiting to hear how it moved them, how it got under their skin. But everyone hated it, and Avi was taking it personally. I decided then that I liked Avi Narayan very much.

As Dizzy clipped along about coal pits being a metaphor for choking despair of being matched with the wrong CEO, I reached into my bag and pulled out my book. The notes had all sorts of tidbits about the book. I'm not sure the SVWEABC would have approved of Henry and Catherine, but I was also pretty sure Henry and Catherine would not have approved of the SVWEABC. H and C loved this book.

Did you know the original title for the novel was **Tenderness?** *I love the gentleness of their love. Especially Mellors's letter in the end. 'If I could sleep with my arms around you, the ink could stay in the bottle.' —Henry*

Henry, what a hopeless romantic you are. **Tenderness** *does not suit at all. This is a book of passion. She sheds her skin. She is reborn through desire. It is about great sex and what that does for you.* —*Catherine*

"And so later when…"

"Dizzy, I'm sorry, can I interrupt for a moment?"

Dizzy screeched to a halt and glared at me, while the rest of the group stared at me like I'd just grown a second head. Avi looked at me with polite quiet. I held her gaze for another second, and smiled at the surprise on her face when I gave her a wink. I was going to save this meeting for Avi Narayan.

"I think everything everyone has said here today is exactly on target," I said, "except that we're not talking about what we should be talking about. No one has talked about the sex. The good, old-fashioned, in-the-woods, in-front-of-God-and-everybody sex."

Wineglasses stopped in midair. Avi nearly spit out her tea. I had their attention. I felt Dizzy staring at me, willing me to shut up. I didn't dare turn back now. My heart spun like a hyperactive third-grader without his Ritalin.

"I've been sitting here listening to all of you," I continued. "And I'm so impressed with all the well-read and thoughtful opinions. And I can't disagree with a single point any of you've made about the society and the social order and the book's place in literary history. But I don't think that's why anyone reads this book, do you? It's about the sex. I don't think people were particularly worried about the social order when they banned it. They banned it because of the sex."

I looked down at Catherine's note again. I placed my hand over it, as if shielding it from the plagiarism I was about to commit.

"It's about shedding one's skin and being reborn through desire. I don't know about the rest of you, but I think that's really something. Don't you?"

The room was still. But no one was looking at me. They were looking to Avi for direction.

"That's an excellent and insightful observation, Maggie," Avi said. "Thank you. It's a perfect lead-in to some discussion questions I'd like to pose to the group."

I turned to look at Dizzy, who was straining to hold in a laugh. His leg bounced like a jackhammer with the effort and the grin on his face threatened to burst open into actual guffawing at any moment.

Just as she did before the meeting, Avi reached over and laid her hand on my arm. And she was smiling. I felt anointed. The Indian goddess of the SVWEABC had blessed me and accepted my offering. I would live a life of enlightened goodness and go forth and read the classics.

Avi asked her book group questions and the responses were more positive this time around. I will have to say one thing for the members of the SVWEABC. They adjusted their trajectory in response to market conditions.

After the meeting, Avi guided me through the room, introducing me to people who actually wanted to talk to me now. Everything I said invoked sparkling splashes of laughter, and I again floated on the current of a charmed life. It'd been a long time, and it felt like a thousand Christmases. Best of all, I'd somehow managed to misplace my cup of tree bark tea.

When an opening presented itself, Dizzy nudged me over to the bar.

"Holy shit on a Frisbee!" he said. "I don't know what was in that tea, but holy shit! She loves you. Everyone loves you." And then he stopped and leaned in close. "You know what this reminds me of? Remember our Microsoft pitch, how they started asking all these questions about user studies and I didn't even know what they were talking about? Then you started telling them about this study and that study. They were in awe of you. Then we got in the elevator and you turned to me and said, 'Now I'm going to have to go find studies that back up all that stuff I just made up.'"

I slapped him in the stomach to shut him up.

"This is the greatest day ever," Dizzy said, downing his wine. I had a feeling I'd be driving us both home.

With that, I nudged him in the direction of his wine buddies, because Avi started coming our way.

"Maggie, why are you here?" Avi asked, pouring me a glass of cabernet.

"Trying to suck up to you, so I can get my job back."

Avi laughed. Pay dirt.

"Why do you want your old job back?" she asked. "Why not move on? That's the way of the Valley."

That pitch at Microsoft with me and Dizzy was still in my head. I remembered what that was like, to be hungry for that big deal and to feel like we could do anything.

"I started that company. Me and Dizzy and some angel funders. I know that software better than anyone alive, even the guys who wrote it. They know how each individual part works, but they don't know how the whole beast moves and thinks.

Ask any coder. There's no price high enough for a power user like me. And the customers love me. What I did today in your living room? I can do that on any day of the week in any conference room."

Avi poured a glass for herself and took a sip.

"Dizzy talked like a carnival barker to get you into this book group. Now I see why. Tell me, what have you been doing with yourself since the restructuring at ArGoNet?"

Restructuring. What a polite way of describing the uprooting of my life. But I pushed aside the petulance and did a quick dig for an answer.

"I've been doing some pro bono consulting at a small used bookstore my neighbor owns." *I've been wasting time at the Dragonfly and learning fifteen hundred new ways to describe a man's privates.* "Sales have been soft with the downturn in the local economy." *No one gives a flying frog's butt about the Dragonfly with Apollo across the street.* "I'm working with him to improve his margin." *I'm sitting in a dusty window reading trashy novels.*

"How interesting. What are some of your ideas?"

Ideas? I didn't think moving the boxes Jason deposited around the store like air-dropped supplies would count as an idea. My thoughts went back to Henry and Catherine.

"It's not just a bookstore, it's a mystery," I said. My mouth was wandering off without much thought to propel it. But in my mind, Henry's and Catherine's notes played like a tune I couldn't get out of my head. "You never know what you'll find. Apollo is predictable, like a planned subdivision. The Dragonfly is a medieval city without a map. Each turn brings something unexpected."

She smiled and reached into the pocket of her dress and pulled out a business card.

"I'd like to hear more about what you're doing at this bookstore of yours," she said, writing a phone number on the back of the card. "And I expect to see you and Dizzy at our next meeting. I like your pluck. It's a shame ArGoNet lost you. But I would be impressed if you could make a retail outlet like a used book shop profitable in this economy. I like to help people who impress me."

She gave me the card and told me to call her at home anytime. And then she left me alone with my wine and a heart that was beating out of my chest. I'd done it. Screw the pleading cover letters and dumbed-down résumé. I held the Golden Ticket in my hand. I was going to get my superhero cape back.

.

My legs were stiff as I set my laptop beside me on my bed and tried to get up. After the SVWEABC meeting, I was wired. But two nights in a row without sleep caught up with me and I finally crashed in the early gray of Sunday morning. I stayed under the covers for the whole day in that heavy kind of sleep that comes only during the day when you don't want it. It was just past midnight now. I'd thought all that rest would make me feel better. But I still felt an odd brew of adrenaline behind my sternum, bubbling thicker in the dark.

I church-keyed the cap off a Rolling Rock, and sat on my kitchen counter, too awake for sleep, but too tired for anything else. There was something about the blanketed sounds of the night that made me just want to be still for a bit. The whirling of my ceiling fan, the refrigerator clicking, Coltrane playing on KCSC from Hugo's radio outside, all these whispered sounds you can hear only after the neighborhood turns in. Even the sound of pulling out *Lady Chatterley's Lover* from my bag was louder than it normally would be.

I paged through the book, watching the notes in the margins shift from Henry's handwriting to Catherine's until they came alive like the figures in a flipbook. *In the soft night, I wonder about you*, Henry wrote near the end. *What color are the dishes you eat from? What pictures are on your walls? What books are on your shelf? All these definitions of who you are. But mostly, I want to assure myself that you are in the same world I am, that you aren't just my hopes appearing on this page.*

I tried to remember the dishes Bryan had had at his home, but nothing came to me. Were they white, perhaps? Or maybe blue. I do remember that there were no pictures on the wall. He liked minimalist interfaces. And no books. None. *All these definitions of who you are.* Bryan had never left anything behind in my apartment. The night after he said good-bye, I'd gone through the ritual of looking for bits of him. But there was nothing. No pictures, no clothes, nothing. Nothing for me to claim I'd never found when he would ask for it later.

I thought about Catherine, sitting in her kitchen on a night like this all those years ago with Henry's words fresh in her mind. I tried to picture her, thinking she must have looked like her letters, willowy and graceful. How did Henry's words make her feel? Did her smiles come more easily? Did people wonder what was different about her? The Catherine of my imagination would keep her secret close. She wouldn't like the way people watched her the way they do when someone is in love, thinking they know you, snickering at your joy. She would know that love makes you conspicuous.

I looked down at Henry's words and wondered what it was about them that made her trust him with her heart. I wanted to pry open Henry's notes and see how they worked, try to understand the mingling of passion and longing that compelled Catherine to reply. The two of them had only these fragile marks on a page that formed words and that led them to this. The words that Henry and Catherine wrote to each other were ones I'd heard a thousand times in books, but I never knew people really said such things to each other. At least I'd never said them.

Where were they living when they started writing to each other? The Dragonfly would be little help. Hugo didn't keep track of where his books came from. Though he and Jason wrote down sales in a large leather ledger at the front counter, if customers asked for a receipt, Hugo gave them a pen and pad so they could write one. It drove his accountant Robert mad, which I suspect was his primary motivation, along with the desire to be a bad capitalist.

Hugo had owned the store since the eighties, but it was a used bookstore long before that. I stared at the "April, 1961" at the top of the page, trying to tell which one of them, Henry or Catherine, had written it there, but there wasn't enough to go on. Henry's first notes led me to believe it was his book, so probably him. But then why would Catherine start writing in someone else's book? No, the book must have been in a place where they both could get to it, i.e., a library or a bookstore, but there wasn't any sign of the book having belonged to a library. The book could have arrived at the Dragonfly with the notes, or it could have all happened at the Dragonfly.

It could have happened at the Dragonfly. It all happened at the Dragonfly. It sounded like something that belonged on a sign in the store window, or a tagline on a website. I could see people walking by on the street, looking up at the sign, wandering in to ask, "What? What happened here?" And lost in the haze of Henry and Catherine, they would browse. They would buy books. I thought about my talk with Avi that afternoon. Maybe I had a project after all. I needed to talk to Hugo.

I pulled on a pair of yoga pants, a sweatshirt, and shoes and headed outside with the book. As usual, Hugo was in the backyard, his legs crossed at the ankle and propped up on the patio table, blowing silvery clouds of smoke from a hand-rolled cigarette into the patio umbrella he'd set up next to him. He was bent over a *New York Times* crossword in his lap, lit by a lamp strapped to his head as if he might go mining for ore later in the night. Sharing the table with him was a guy I'd seen around the store buying old bicycle manuals. He, too, had his feet propped up, the index finger of his right hand curled around a cigar.

As I approached them, Hugo looked up from the puzzle, blinding me with his headlamp.

"My Georgia peach."

"I'm from South Carolina. You know that."

"There's a difference? Okay. Six letters. Alabama's Bear."

"Bryant, you heathen."

"Alabama has a bear named Bryant? Whatever do they do with him?"

"He was a football coach," said Hugo's friend. "In the sixties. They called him Bear."

"Really?" Hugo said. "Never heard of him."

Hugo's friend grinned, clamping his teeth around his cigar. Even though he was sitting, I guessed him to be a little taller than me. He had skin the color of nutmeg, and his dark hair fell in small curls that brushed the shoulders of a linen saffron kurta that had faded and softened with years and wear. Frayed jeans half covered the green rubber flip-flops, and I noticed little tufts of black hair on the tops of his feet and his big toes. His smile made me self-conscious about not having put on a bra.

"How is it possible," he asked, "that the Indian guy and the chick know more about football than you do?"

"Incredible luck, I suppose." Hugo turned to me. "You know Rajhit, don't you?"

"Mary, right?" Rajhit asked.

"Maggie," I said, dropping down in the chair next to Hugo.

"Would you like one?" Over the table, Rajhit held up a leather case housing three cigars. I slid one out and took a whiff of the tobacco's burned candy scent. The last time I smoked a cigar was the night we'd gotten the first round of funding from Wander Fish and Dizzy took the entire company to La Bodeguita del Medio in Palo Alto. I drank too many mojitos and ended up draped over a system architect at PayPal on one of the oaky leather couches in the humidor room in back, passing a cigar back and forth as I listened to Dizzy go on about how all our lives would change now. He talked of value position, return on investment, and new paradigms. I didn't care. We were drinking single malt scotch, warm and aged with sin as if we'd stolen it from Daddy's liquor cabinet, and I sipped away, sinking into the warm pool of Dizzy's certainty about our future.

As I slid a cigar out of Rajhit's case, he handed me a clip. I snipped off the cigar's end and leaned over the table while he held a lighter for me. I placed my hand on his to steady it, and circled the end of my cigar in the flame for an even burn. I looked up to see him looking at me instead of the lighter.

"Good?" he asked.

I nodded and leaned back, puffing, feeling the earthy smoke tickle the back of my throat, hugging *Lady Chatterley* and the secret lovers against me.

"Hugo, I have an idea," I said.

"You've decided to become a Navy SEAL," he said, writing in another answer to his puzzle. "No, no, I've got it. You're going to move to Nepal and herd yaks."

"Close. I think I'm going to try to make the Dragonfly profitable. Pro bono, of course."

Hugo looked up and turned his headlamp off. Out of the corner of my eye, I saw Rajhit trying not to laugh.

"Well, there goes my opportunity for yak butter. Why would you want to ruin my perfectly unprofitable enterprise?"

I told him about Avi and the book group meeting. He listened, nodding his head, looking as serious as he did when he examined the ginger at the Chinese market down the street for freshness. I trusted that he'd get the weirdness of my plan. Hugo had never gone anywhere on a straight path. At nineteen, he'd left his family's Idaho farm with *On the Road* tucked under his arm like a counterculture Baedeker and hitchhiked to San Francisco. But he soon deserted the flophouse on Haight Street were he'd crashed. "The sex and drugs were as advertised," he told me once, "but the personal hygiene was nonexistent." So he hovered around the city docks in a navy surplus jacket, unloading ships and reading Jack London, until he followed a blonde across the Bay Bridge to Berkeley. There he followed a former prom queen from Texas into a physics classroom and an Asian activist into political science. After years of following women around campus, he had several degrees, including a master's in math and in comparative religion. He had several patents and had attended Le Cordon Bleu in three countries. So, of course, he owned a used bookstore.

"So this profitability thing is just temporary?" he asked.

"After I'm employed again, you can go back to losing money by the fistfuls."

"I've got a better idea," Hugo said, taking another drag from his cigarette.

"Does it involve crystals and the sacrifice of a small animal?" Rajhit asked.

"Small animal? Really? I'm a Buddhist."

"You're a Buddhist who wraps his asparagus in prosciutto," I said.

"Why don't you forget about the start-up world and work for me at the shop? Then you don't have to worry about profits and such. You could just spend time doing what you've been doing. You've seemed happy enough with that."

For half my life, I'd been aware of my capacity to disappoint the people I loved. Instead of telling my mother I didn't want to join her sorority, I told her I chickened out before the rush mixer. In the same way, I didn't know how to tell Hugo that I preferred the company of the J. Crew–clad clients of ArGoNet, who were looking to think outside the box after doing a deep gap analysis to determine the result-driven best practices that would leverage their bandwidth to a more satisfied, strategic fit. I didn't know how to tell him that working in the Dragonfly would feel like failure, that I would be dealing with people who got angry because the store didn't have a copy of *Larry's Guide to Better Knot-Tying*. And then there was the just plain weird. Earlier that week, I'd been told by a little old raisin of a man decked out in a camouflage Utilikilt that, on the advice from the local wizard who lived over on Villa Street, he had invested in a company that made penile implants. He'd just sold off his entire portfolio for a killing. "Forget high tech and real estate," he told me. "Always invest in technology for better sexual performance. Those stocks never go down." This was not how I wanted to spend my days.

"Hugo, I—"

He grabbed my hand and pulled it to his lips for a quick, exuberant kiss, absolving me from having to answer him. He was the only person I knew who could get away with such a cheesy move. He was also the only person I knew who seemed incapable of being disappointed in me, and so he was the one I worried about disappointing the most.

"You may change your mind yet," Hugo said. "In the meantime, you have my permission to do in the Dragonfly anything that will make you happy." He stood to leave, stretching his arms high above his head. "But start tomorrow. Late in the day tomorrow."

As he ascended to his apartment, I thought Rajhit would

take off as well. But he settled deeper into his chair, smiling at me like he knew something I didn't.

"I always liked that novel," he said, nodding toward the *Lady Chatterley's Lover* I still held against my middle. "Did you know Lawrence's original title for the book was *Tenderness*?"

I laughed before I could stop myself, thinking of the day before and my performance at the book club. I laughed because he probably remembered this detail from some freshman lit class and had it tucked away in his catalog of factoids that would impress women he met in the middle of the night. And I laughed because it felt good to flirt a little. It'd been too long.

"It doesn't really fit though, does it?" I said, pulling Catherine's words through my memory. I was eager to see if they would have the same effect on Rajhit that they had on Henry. "It's really a book of passion. Lady Chatterley sheds her skin. She is reborn through desire."

He caught a deep breath through a wide grin, and I knew then these notes were magic.

We lit two more cigars, I grabbed a couple of beers from my apartment, and we drank and talked the kind of nonsense that substitutes for philosophical musings in the early hours of the morning. When the beer was gone, I felt that familiar impulse to invite him in for whatever else I had in the liquor cabinet. For the first time in too long, I felt young and endless.

But then I remembered the dishes piled in the sink and the ring around the tub and the copies of my résumé scattered all over my living room floor. And more than that, I anticipated the simple heartache that I could see if I fast-forwarded through the next few months in my mind. Rajhit was trouble. Possibly the best kind. But it was still time to call it a night.

I held out my hand to shake Rajhit's and my stomach somersaulted as he held my hand a little longer than was necessary.

"I'm glad to have met you, Maggie," he said. Then he disappeared into the darkness, leaving me alone still feeling his fingers wrapped around mine.

CHAPTER THREE

Closer Than We Thought

> We settle and settle more and all the while we tell
> ourselves we are being practical. We're not. We're
> being cowards.
>
> —Henry

It all happened at the Dragonfly...

It was the perfect headline. Intrigue? Check. Promise of a good story? Check. Name of the business? Check. Yes, all together, it was quite clickable. And then people could come to the Dragonfly and find their own mystery. At least that was my good intention, path to hell be damned.

It was midnight, and I was alone in Suds and Surf, a Laundromat a few blocks from home in a tiny row of shops that also included a Salvadorian restaurant, a pet-groomer, and a florist who also did taxes in Vietnamese. Thanks to the free WiFi, I'd been working on the Dragonfly's website for a couple of hours, stretching out the geeky muscles I hadn't used in way too long. The Dragonfly was like software that had been sitting around for decades that no one wanted to take the time to rewrite. Building a website was just like putting pretty icons on that dated, inefficient code. It might be pretty, but underneath was still disorder, dust, and JavaScript held together with a little chicken wire.

There were no funds for a website hosting service, so I was on my own. I had a spare computer at home, so I set up a Web server and a database and now here I was at Suds and Surf building out the pages with free and awesome open source software. I registered a domain for ten bucks, downloaded a template with a book theme, and within a couple of hours, the Dragonfly had a website. That afternoon, I'd dusted off a scanner I hadn't used since Mac OS 9 and scanned Henry's and Catherine's notes and posted them on the pages of the website. Looking at my work on the screen, I wondered what Henry and Catherine would think of my posting their romance here. How would I feel if I were Catherine? I closed my eyes and tried to put myself in a time when men wore suits and hats to baseball games and women carried clutch purses in gloved hands. I tried to imagine finding Henry's first note and pulling a pen out of my purse to write a reply. But no words came. Catherine was fluent in a language I couldn't even pronounce.

Movement along the street caught my attention. The streetlight showed the silhouette of a bike that looked like something from the fifties that Wally and the Beav would have ridden. A rocket-shaped headlight was strapped on top of the handlebars and a wicker basket hung on the front. The rider looked my way and stopped, and I got nervous. Then I saw it was Rajhit, and got nervous for a whole different reason.

He propped the bike against the open glass double doors and stepped into the fluorescent light of the store, his hands in his pockets.

"I was just by your place," he said.

"Hugo's got a date tonight," I said.

"The real estate agent or the antiques dealer?" He stood in front of the washing machine opposite me and lifted himself to sit on it.

"Not sure," I said. "But I think he was making tofu cheesecake this afternoon."

"Probably the golf pro then. I think she's vegan."

He was in a faded pair of jeans, a white button-up shirt with the tail out, and those green flip-flops. I could see his torso moving under the shirt.

"Actually, I wanted to see you," he said.

"At this hour?"

"You're up, aren't you?"

"You didn't know that."

He fiddled with the sweet-gum leaf he'd detached from the bottom of his green flip-flop. I stretched, hoping I came across as someone who entertained here every night. We both seemed to be deciding what to say or not to say.

"I'm glad to see you," I said. It was true. I was. But he looked a little too happy, and I felt the need to justify what I'd said. "I'd like to know what you think about something."

He followed me to the table where my laptop was open next to the copy of *Chatterley*. He bent down to look at my screen.

"Is it wrong?" I asked. "Putting the notes out there."

He looked at me like he wanted to ask me something, and for some reason that made me a little anxious again, the nice kind of nervous that happens when you're alone with someone you're attracted to, afraid he will say exactly what you want to hear and then you won't be able to help yourself. But there was something else, a shiver under my skin from the possibility that anything could happen, as if the slightest breath could topple castles.

"No one knows who they are," he said. "It's anonymous. And you're trying to help Hugo and the Dragonfly."

"Yes, but I'm mostly trying to help myself."

"I don't think that's a bad thing."

I walked over to his bike to put a little distance between us and climbed onto the leather saddle. It was a little tall for me, and I held the doorframe for balance.

"You know about bikes?" he asked.

"I had a ten-speed in high school."

He told me how he'd found the frame on Craigslist a few months ago, painted the white lines with a brush intended for model airplanes, ordered the tires special from eBay.

"Is that what you do? Restore bikes?"

"I have no occupation, if that's what you mean. Other than being a layabout."

"How does that pay?" I looked down at the candy apple red of the frame.

"Terrible, but it comes with the added bonus of being a consummate disappointment to my parents." He hopped down and walked toward the bike. I thumbed the bike's bell like I hadn't noticed. It sounded like the doorbell in my grandmother's house. He straddled the front tire and held the bike near the center of the handlebars, balancing me. He told me how his father once paid a thousand people in India to pray for him to get into MIT, how he worked hard in school and grad school, worked his way around the Valley until he landed a chief technology officer position, but how the only time he was happy was riding his bike back and forth to work. "My parents used to send my picture to their friends trying to find me a wife. Now they send my résumé to executive search firms."

"So you're going to restore bikes all day instead?"

He started walking backward, pulling the bike with him down a row between the washers and dryers. I rested my feet on the pedals and let myself go with him.

"I like working with something I can touch. Look at her lines, the way she curves just right to sustain you and propel you at the same time. It's engineering you can touch. I like that. I don't know if I can make a living with it, but it feels good for now."

He ran his hands along the handlebars to the edge of the handgrips where I held on. Even though he stopped short a few centimeters away from my skin, I could feel him. "She had qualities no one could see at first. Much like the Dragonfly."

He let go and stepped away.

"It was good seeing you, Maggie. Tell Hugo I'll drop by the store later in the week."

"What about your bike?" I was still on it.

He turned and slid his hands back in his pockets like he was trying to keep them there.

"The bike is for you."

Harmless flirtation was one thing, but this was something else. I tried to conjure a line using my mother's finishing school charm or Rosalind Russell's snappiness.

Instead, I said, "I'm not going to sleep with you because you gave me a bike."

"It's a nice bike," he said.

"Even so."

I couldn't tell if the thought had never occurred to him and he was humoring me, or if he was just flat-out busted. Either way, he was enjoying himself. And what worried me more was that I was, too.

I watched him walk down Calderon Avenue through the circles of light from the streetlamps. Two houses away, he turned and waved, knowing I would still be watching him.

.

"What the hell is this?"

I looked up from the bottom shelf of the Dragonfly's Romance section to see Jason standing over me with a box of books. He hadn't expected to find me here. He especially hadn't expected to see me next to empty shelves with a bottle of Windex and a handful of paper towels.

"This section's a disaster," I said, continuing to wipe down a shelf.

"This section was fine the way it was," Jason said, glaring at me as if I'd suggested we turn the place into a Walmart. He'd complained loudly the day before as I posted signs in the store window announcing, VISIT US ONLINE AT WWW.DRAGONFLYUSEDBOOKS.COM.

"It was a rat's nest the way it was. Relax." I thought it best not to mention that Hugo had given me a key. Knowing I had free access to his domain would probably send Jason into catatonic shock. But then again, maybe that wasn't so bad. "I talked to Hugo about it. He said I could do what I liked."

I knew Jason cared only about the Sci-Fi/Fantasy section, and it showed. It was a mosaic of perfectly ordered book spines. The mass-market paperbacks were housed separately from the trade paperbacks, which were merged with the hardbacks. British editions sat in their own section—apparently a Sci-Fi/Fantasy book sold better if it was the same version that Douglas Adams had had on his shelf. But Romance was stuffed in the back corner of the store, where the books looked as if they'd been shot out of a cannon to lie where they fell. I knew the Romance section ranked nowhere on Jason's very short list of important things, and that this outrage of his was just dick-wagging. I was on his turf, even if it was the part of his lawn he hadn't watered in weeks.

"Hugo said you could do this?" he asked. "Hugo?"

"Yeah," I said. "Remember him? Balding? Beard? Pays you?"

His eyes became slits. Veins poked out of his neck. He made Khan in *Star Trek II* look like the Dalai Lama.

"Hugo!" He turned away from me and disappeared around the corner. "She's changing shit!"

I jumped up after him. "Jason, it's okay. Hugo's cool with it."

"Bullshit!" He pushed his way past a couple of browsing customers. "Hugo!"

A man examining a biography of Churchill pointed to the men's room. "I just saw him go in there."

Jason pushed the restroom door and stood there, holding the door open. The Churchill reader did a double take and then headed toward the door of the Dragonfly, leaving the book behind. I halted my pursuit of Jason, but not before I caught a glimpse of Hugo's feet under the first of two stalls.

"Hugo, do you know what she's done?"

"Jason," I heard Hugo say, his voice bouncing off the tiles.

"I'm imagining my Place of Peace, where the grass is green and soft and birds sing and all the bathrooms have padlocks."

"What's next? Flowered wallpaper? Doilies? You gotta be honest with me, man. This place is going to start smelling lemony fresh, isn't it?"

"Negative energy, Jason. We've talked about this."

"She's got Windex. Books are supposed to be dusty. They smell good when they're dusty."

"Hugo!" I kept myself at a safe distance, about halfway down the aisle from the open door. "I tried to explain to him!"

Something rubbed against my leg and I was hit with a stench that could curl steel. I looked down to see Grendel, the Dragonfly's cat, walking by me. He was long-haired and black, with a bite taken out of his right ear, and he looked more like a runty bear cub than a cat. Usually, Grendel perched on top of the stacks and swatted at customer's heads as they passed by. This was a rare ground appearance. I wondered if he always smelled this bad and if the stench just usually drifted upward, which might explain why the office space above the Dragonfly had been empty for two months. You can blame only so much on the recession. Grendel sauntered past me, carrying something in his mouth, and headed toward the open men's room door.

"I had that section just the way I wanted it," Jason said. "She doesn't have any experience with this. We haven't trained her. What's she doing messing with our stuff?"

"Grendel's here," Hugo said. "Grendel smells like last year's garbage. Grendel's dropping a bird carcass on my foot. I'm in my Place of Peace. I'm in my Place of Peace."

"I quit!" Jason slammed the door shut. A moment later, I

heard the bell over the front door ring and the commotion of Jason trying to maneuver his bike out of the store. The few customers left in the stacks all looked at me.

"I don't actually work here. I'm just helping."

I scurried back to the Romance section and sat on the floor, hiding from the scene up front. The thing about the Dragonfly, to pile onto its load of idiosyncrasies, was that there were only two places in the whole store where I got decent cell phone coverage, near the window in the chairs and in the very back, where I was now. So as soon as I sat down, my phone started to vibrate in my pocket, signaling an alert from an app I'd installed to track how many views the website got and how many times the Facebook and Twitter posts had been shared. When I saw the numbers, I nearly dropped the phone. Henry and Catherine had gone viral.

CHAPTER FOUR

Savage Hammerheads and Other Temptations

I try to go on with my day, doing what is required
of me, but I find myself here again and again, wondering where you are.

—Henry

"That's fucking *gold* you've got there," Dizzy said, pointing his spatula at me. "One hundred thousand views in twenty-four hours for a shitty little bookstore? Fucking gold."

Sitting at my breakfast bar, I yawned in delight as Dizzy stood at the stove and made us the fried bologna sandwiches he'd long ago perfected. Growing up, Dizzy and I would watch his mom, Miss Velda, as she made us these sandwiches—greasy, goopy glorious pokes in the eyeball to every fitness guru who ever insisted we should all give up carbs or examine our poop. It wouldn't have surprised me if she'd fed them to us just to piss off Jane Fonda. For years we watched Miss Velda and memorized each step. She'd slather Duke's mayonnaise onto Sunbeam white bread, sweeter than molasses. She'd press down on the bologna with her spatula when it domed up on the heat of the cast-iron skillet to make sure the center part had that nice scald on it just like the edges. She'd peel off a slice of American cheese and melt it over the bologna until it oozed like lava. Then she'd scoop it all onto the Sunbeam, and we were just a bag full of Lay's potato chips and a dill pickle away from heaven.

Dizzy and I carried on this tradition in our dorm's basement kitchen at Carolina. Even the greatest of disappointments had the silver lining of fried bologna sandwiches. A lower-than-expected test grade, a broken heart, or even a bad weather forecast would become an excuse to further Dizzy's birthright of the best fried bologna sandwiches in all creation. It was then he became an artist at Picasso levels. He'd slice the bologna himself into a thick disk that carpeted the bread even after shrinking up a bit on the skillet. Then he'd double up on the cheese, draping one square angled over the other so the corners fully covered the circle of bologna and left no rounded edges exposed. And after placing all of this on the bottom slice of bread, he revealed the inspiration that is the mark of true genius. He layered potato chips on top of the bologna and cheese before covering it with the second slice of lavishly mayo-ed bread. The result was a Fourth of July explosion of sweet and salty and savory that surfed waves of cholesterol. We could feel our arteries clogging with each bite.

"Jesus wept," Dizzy said. "Who would have thought you could get those numbers out of a few love letters? Fuck me sideways. Any local retail outfit around would love to have that kind of traffic. Your reporting system must be spinning like a slot machine hitting the jackpot."

"I had to turn off the tracking app on my phone," I told him.

"Jason hates the sounds a cell phone makes, so I was on vibrate, but it was like walking around with an angry hornet in my pocket."

Most of the hits were from the Dragonfly's Facebook page I'd created. But then other traffic came in from different pages, such as other used bookstores, blogs about romance and dating, blogs about books, blogs about the lost art of letter-writing, Twitter feeds from a romance novelist and grad student at Northwestern. The fifty or so people I'd e-mailed the site URL to the night before had shared it with another fifty or so people. But a few of those people had a much wider audience, so the numbers jumped to the hundreds and then the thousands quickly. My in-box for the info@dragonflyusedbooks.com account I'd set up twenty-four hours ago already had more than a hundred e-mails. I scanned the subject lines. People wanted more, lots more. They wanted to know what happened to Henry and Catherine. Did they get married? Are they still together? It was a collective lunge toward a happy ending, and I wished I had one to give them.

"Have you told Avi about these numbers yet?" he asked.

I shook my head. "It's so new. And I'm not sure what the best approach is."

"Food is always the best approach," Dizzy said. "Call her up and ask her to lunch."

"I don't think I can just call up someone like Avi and ask her to lunch. Besides, I'm broke. Where am I going to take her to lunch?"

He reached into his back pocket for his wallet.

"Here's fifty bucks. Chase around that Korean food truck that only tweets its location. She'll think you're original. If she likes finding talent in unusual places, wait until she tries the food."

"And how are we supposed to chase down this mystical food truck? I sold my car, remember?"

Dizzy stopped for a moment and then started digging in his pocket for his keys.

"Dizz, it's okay. I'll ask her to meet me someplace near the bookshop. And thanks for the loan."

"It's a gift," he said. "A thank-you for saving that sorry-ass book club the other day. Sugarbritches, I'm already mentally redecorating your office for when you come back."

Dizzy dropped another slice of bologna in the hot skillet on my stove and tipped his spatula in the direction of my bike, which was parked in the living room.

"That really is a nice bike. Hell, I'd sleep with him for that bike. So you think this Rajhit guy is the next ex–Mr. Right Now?"

"Is your pessimism meant to be reverse psychology?"

"Nah, it's pretty much genuine. What are you waiting for?"

"I don't know. There's just something so kind of earnest about him."

"Yeah, we don't want any of that. No fucking forthrightness either. And that honesty bullshit is just asswipe for the lame-minded and gullible."

"Do you have a point here?"

"My point is this," Dizzy said. "If you're going to rule some-one out, it's got to be for a bigger flippin' reason than he's got some exceptional quality that requires a nineteenth-century adjective to describe it. Look, I know Bryan messed you up a bit when he went to Austin…"

"It's not that," I said.

"Bullshit it's not that," he said.

"I mean it's not that he left. It's what it was like when he was here."

Dizzy shrugged. "You were with him for two years and he still introduced you as 'my friend Maggie.' You don't get heartbroken over a guy like that."

"It just all seems like more trouble than it's worth," I said.

"Then you're not doing it right."

"I'm not talking about sex."

"Neither am I," he said. "Mayo the bread."

"What about you?" I asked, taking the bread out of the bag. "The Apple guy didn't work out?"

"He wanted to order Philadelphia rolls. At Sushi Maru. Can you believe that? You're in this palace of authentic... *authentic*...sushi and you order a fucking Philadelphia roll. Let's just go to South Legend and order lemon chicken while we're at it. And you know the goddamn heathen cut his linguini with a knife. A knife!"

"I take it I can read up on the details online?" I asked.

"Yeah, yeah, it's all over Urbanspoon," Dizzy said, sliding the cheese-carpeted bologna onto the bread. "Fuck 'em. We'll stay single forever and shack up in a nursing home for gay gods and their favorite fruit flies."

"To wiping drool off each other's chins," I said and held my beer bottle out for him to clink, but he left me hanging as an explosion went off in his pocket.

"Shit," Dizzy said. He dug around for his phone and looked at the text message. "It's after lunch in New Delhi. I've got to get into the office. Wander Fish has the whole company by the balls. We've got to put together a demo for them by Monday."

Demos meant hours and hours of late nights knitting together parts of the product to give the impression the software did more than it could. They were brutal, like running a marathon at a full sprint. They would need him tonight in the worst way.

"You know what? I'll come with you."

"What was that?" Dizzy asked, getting up.

"Give me a minute."

I slid past him and waded through the flood of clothes on my bedroom floor to the corner, where I was sure there was a reasonably clean pair of jeans I could trade in for my sweats.

"You don't work there anymore," he called from the kitchen.

"Maybe not, but I'm still a stockholder. What are they going to do? Throw me out?"

I was tingling at the thought of the night ahead. The adrenaline of a deadline, the dull ache behind my eyes, the self-inflated sense of importance, the primal joy of seeing the Starbucks across the street open at five o'clock tomorrow morning. I'd gotten a hundred thousand views of the Dragonfly's website in twenty-four hours. I was a goddess. ArGoNet so deserved me.

"It'll be great. Just like it used to be," I said, sniffing sweatshirts and pulling on the least offensive one. "You'll see. I'm the empress of demos, remember? You used to say that all the time. They laid me off because they couldn't afford me, right? Okay, I'm not asking for money. I'm just helping."

Dizzy stood, leaning against my bedroom door with his arms folded.

"You want me to come with you, right?" I asked.

"You know I do."

"Okay, so, what's the problem?"

He just stood there and waited for me to answer my own question. I could feel the corners of my eyes heat up with traitorous tears. He wrapped his arms around me. For a long moment, one of those that lasts longer than others, I thought he would say it. If they didn't want me, then he didn't want them. But from the living room, I heard his phone announce another text message.

"We're going to get you back," he said. "Call Avi. Go have lunch. It's going to be just like before."

He looked at me expectantly. Had he said the right words? Was I okay? Could he leave now?

"Helping out at the Dragonfly is temporary," I said. "I just need something to impress Avi. You know that, right?"

"Of course," he said, heading for the door. "We're getting you back. You'll see."

I watched from the doorway as he drove away in his French-fry-grease convertible with a wave. I looked over at Hugo's windows. They were dark and his old Volvo was absent from the driveway. I'd have to wait for him and our chai tea from Trader Joe's. I was now in the business of waiting.

.

The next day, Hugo stood at the window of the Dragonfly, arms folded, glaring across the street at the sign in front of Apollo Books & Music: ASK US ABOUT OUR USED BOOKS.

"Fascists," Hugo muttered, pacing around the reading

chairs. He yelped when Grendel swatted at his ankle. Jason scooped up the cat in his arms, scratching him behind his ear, the one with the bite taken out of it. He bent over and whispered to the cat, probably something along the lines of, "Be patient, we'll get them when they're sleeping."

"It's not just across the street," Jason said. "They're all over."

I'd seen them myself. Big beautiful signs in minimalist font announcing Apollo had one other way to sell books on the cheap.

"Robert, can we sue them?" Hugo asked the man behind the counter. Robert was Hugo's accountant, a friend from his Berkeley days. He appeared each month to mumble new curse words over Hugo's bookkeeping. I'd always thought of accountants as hobbits in short-sleeve dress shirts, fat ties, and Buddy Holly glasses. But Robert looked like Shaft in a Hawaiian shirt. He'd been married to the same woman for twenty-five years, had a son starting at MIT in the fall, and had just bought a vacation home in Tahoe. Hugo would never say either way, but there was a lingering suspicion in the Dragonfly that Robert could be a Republican.

"Sue them? You break your neck on their wet bathroom floor? Sure," Robert said. "But I think Apollo can sell some damn books."

"Can we talk about this again, please?" I tugged on Hugo's sleeve and held *Lady Chatterley's Lover* out to him. "You're absolutely sure you have no idea where this came from?"

Hugo looked at me over the rims of his reading glasses.

"Maggie, I'm old. I have a double-decker pill case. I drink martinis made with pot-infused vodka. It's Tuesday, right?"

"Monday."

"You see my point."

"You're not old."

Hugo grinned and rubbed his belly.

"I went by Henry for a while," he said. "In college, I think. A young lady I was seeing at the time thought Hugo sounded like a communist's name."

"She was right," Jason said.

I stood in front of Hugo and pointed to *Lady Chatterley's Lover*.

"Comrade, please. Focus," I said.

I told him about the e-mails and Facebook posts and the questions on Twitter from people wanting to know what had happened.

"Everyone wants answers," I said.

"Sometimes it's the questions that are a lot more interesting," Hugo said, sliding the book from my hands and giving it to Jason. "Jason, what about you? Do you know anything about this?"

Jason took the book from me, held it to his head, and squeezed his eyes shut. "Yes, I see something. It's becoming clearer. There it is. It's a snowball being thrown through the gates of hell."

"You're not helping," I said, taking the book back.

"Wasn't trying to." He got up and hoisted himself onto the counter to sit next to Robert's laptop, which Robert then moved away from him with an annoyed sigh. "Look, people write all kinds of crap in books. Doodles, reminder lists, the names of slutty girlfriends crossed out and replaced by the names of other slutty girlfriends."

"Negative energy, Jason," Hugo said.

Jason reached for a stack of books in front of the counter. He thumbed through the first one, put it aside, and then riffled through a second, Lonely Planet's *Paris*, stopping every few pages.

"Check it out," he said. "All the best places to kiss underlined with little hearts as a ranking system. It doesn't mean shit. It's just people using books for things that they can't fit on a highway overpass. Go ahead. Pick one."

I lifted *Wild Orchids and Trotsky* from the stack near the counter. On the back of the softcover was a note starting just above the bar code and written diagonally across, the lines getting shorter the closer the writer worked toward the corner of the book.

Dad, please wake me up if I am not up by 9:30. I do not have an alarm on my clock. Actually, come to think of it, 10 o'clock is okay, too. —Thom

"See what I mean?" Jason said as he yawned and stretched.

"It's not the same thing," I said, picking up *Lady Chatterley's Lover*. I wanted to say, "Henry and Catherine fell in love." But I didn't. The phrase felt uncomfortably trite. It was something my parents said all the time, telling tales of their college sweetheart years to dinner guests on a current of laughter. As a child I was awed by their fairy-tale story and believed them when they promised it would happen to me as well. I expected it and feared the moment when I'd meet my love and my life would click into place and all would be decided. I felt a heaviness around my heart just thinking about it now.

I was about to walk away from Jason when I noticed the

small wooden recipe box that Hugo kept by the leather sales ledger. Inside the box, I knew I'd find tattered index cards with the names of all the Dragonfly's customers with book trade credit. Some of those cards had been in there probably as long as there had been a Dragonfly. Maybe someone in that box knew something about the book. Maybe it was worth a few phone calls.

"Hey, give that back," Jason said, grabbing the box out of my hands and holding it tightly against his T-shirt, right in front of the print of a bicycle proclaiming, TWO WHEELS. ONE DARK LORD.

"That's confidential information!"

"What confidential information?" I reached for the box, but he turned his torso away from me and all I got was a fistful of black T-shirt. "We're not talking state secrets."

Jason pushed by me, tucking the card box in the crook of his arm like he was sprinting for the goal line.

"Let her take a look. It won't hurt anything," Hugo said. "Right, Robert?"

"Do I look like a man who wants to get involved in whatever it is you people are talking about?" Robert asked without looking up, his fingers dancing over his calculator.

"Jeez," Jason said. "If we had another 9/11 and the FBI came in here wanting to look through our files to see who'd bought *Martha Stewart's Guide to Home Bomb-Making*, you'd tell them to go to hell. But *she's* got a free pass?"

"It's hardly the same thing," I said. "You don't keep records of what books people buy."

"Bollocks," Jason said. "It is the same thing."

"He has a point, Maggie," Hugo said.

"You've got to be kidding me."

"It would be different if you worked here," Hugo said. "Actually—" he walked over the cash register, pulled out a twenty, and handed it to me.

"What's this?"

"It's your wages for the last two hours," Hugo said.

Robert stood and reached across the counter to snag the twenty from my hand and put it back in the cash register. "She'll get a proper check just like Jason does." He riffled through his papers and handed me a blank timecard.

I stared at it. A timecard? I hadn't filled out one of these since my work-study job in college. "But I haven't done anything but nag you about this book. You're going to pay me for that?"

"Jason nags me all day, and I pay him."

"You're seriously going to do this?" Jason asked.

"Seems I already have." Hugo leaned back against the counter, stirring his tea. "Solves all kinds of problems. You're always complaining about Maggie doing things in the store without actually working here. And now she's an employee. She can look through the customer files without any ethical quandaries."

I'm not sure who was more disturbed by this proposal, me or Jason. I looked over at him, his breaths coming out in short puffs, the fingers of his pinched hands wiggling like they were playing scales on an invisible keyboard. He was already feeling bits of his fiefdom slipping away. And me? What was I going to do here? I was already having a hard enough time finding a job between romance novels. When was I going to find time to do any work?

"Look, you're around all the time anyway," Hugo said. "I'd say you've completed our training program. Next thing you know you'll be on the fast track to serious screwing around like Jason." He wrapped his arm around my shoulders and squeezed me against him as if he understood what a consolation prize my life had become. "Nobody panic. It's just until Maggie finds a new job."

Jason looked back and forth between Hugo and me in disbelief. He walked up to Hugo, lifted the spoon out of his mug, sucked on it like a lollipop, then plunked it back in the tea. Then he slammed the recipe box on the counter and disappeared into the stacks.

"That boy's not wrapped too tight," Robert said.

"He'll come around," Hugo said, looking forlornly at his mug. He paced back and forth in front of the counter, unsure of what to do with the germ-infected thing.

"I won't take handouts," I said, "If you're paying me, I mean to work."

"That'll be a change around here," Robert said.

"Fine. Do whatever you think ten dollars an hour requires," Hugo said. "I trust your judgment. Just don't sit on the floor. Jason's bare feet have been there."

.

With two hours of work already under my belt, I treated myself to a coffee break. Next door at Cuppa Joe, a lanky teenager pulled himself away from the Overly Tattooed & Pierced around the outside tables to come inside and take my order.

I knew the chalkboard menu at Cuppa Joe by heart. The four-dollar drink names were straight out of a witch's book of spells.

"Savage Hammerhead Mocha?" the kid asked.

I never gave my usual order a second thought. I'd given up just about everything from my working life except this. But at $10 an hour before taxes, how long was I working for a Savage Hammerhead Mocha?

"Small coffee with room."

"Nifty," he said, looking at the cash register as if he couldn't decide which one of the poles on a car battery to attach the jumper cable. Squeezing his eyes halfway shut and rubbing one hand over his shaved head, he poked at the keys and looked relieved when it rang up the right amount. I didn't blame him. Mrs. Callahn, the owner of Cuppa Joe, was beyond particular about how things ran in her shop. While Hugo's management style was a laughing brook, Mrs. Callahn's was a full-force fire hose.

I handed over a buck fifty plus a quarter to the tip jar, which was papered over with cartoons enticing you to give money to the underpaid. The kid handed me my coffee, which I milked up before settling in with the recipe box at the large round table in the middle of Cuppa Joe. Around me, at the smaller tables, several coders on laptops sat with headphones to save them from music that sounded like grumpy mating wildebeests. A group of medical residents pored over big three-ring binders, ignoring the two clean-cut khaki-clad guys next to them discussing "new paradigms." In the corner, a middle-aged couple was fighting. Not yelling fighting. Leaning in and whispering fighting, which is actually worse.

A familiar pickup pulled up to the curb. Years ago, it must have been white, but now the orange rust stains gave it the look of a wild Pinto. Mrs. Callahn had arrived, her truck stacked with bags of beans from an organic supplier up in the Santa Cruz Mountains that only she seemed to have ever heard of. Petite and willowy with a marine buzz cut, she wore an orange broomstick skirt with a tank top, denim vest, and turquoise earrings large enough to eat dinner off of. Mrs. Callahn always looked like she should be running the gift shop of the Georgia O'Keeffe Museum instead of a coffee shop in Silicon Valley. As with most Japanese women, I had a hard time telling how old she was, but Hugo knew her in college when he helped organize peace marches in the early seventies, so I figured she was about his age. There were rumors of an unhappy marriage deep in her past. It was said that her ex-husband had offered her $50,000 to take back her maiden name, and that she'd turned him down. As much as Mrs. Callahn might have struggled to keep Cuppa Joe going, she was rich in spite and resentment.

Mrs. Callahn maneuvered the Overly Tattooed & Pierced off their chairs and had them carry the dozen fifty-pound canvas bags into Cuppa Joe, following after them like an elephant herder.

Stopping at my table, she reached for my glass mug and held it up to the window light.

"Wrong! Very, very wrong! Not dark enough!"

"Mrs. Callahn...," the kid said.

"No excuse. The Hammerhead should be darker. You know better. This is no good."

The kid blinked three times, then ran into the storage room to hide.

"It's not a Savage Hammerhead," I said. "Just drip coffee today."

Mrs. Callahn arched one eyebrow, thin as a whip. With no apology, she set my coffee back on the table and sat down next to me.

"Why so much milk?" she asked. "It's good coffee. You cannot taste it with so much milk."

Everyone knew Mrs. Callahn burned her beans. Most of her customers swore they liked it that way, but they were lying to themselves like the people who say they run marathons to relax. Hugo claimed the coffee at Cuppa Joe scared off the toxins and was the best colonic in Silicon Valley. Jason asked for it in an IV during gaming all-nighters. But I came here because at Cuppa Joe you didn't have to learn a whole other language to order your coffee. Small, medium, large. That's it. And there weren't any mugs for sale or teddy bears or greeting cards on recycled paper with microchips so that cartoon penguins could sing "Happy Birthday" to you. Cuppa Joe was all about the coffee, no matter how foul. You could probably grind up the table I was sitting at and get a decent pot out of it. But honestly, the woman burned her beans, and I needed milk to get it down and that was the truth of it. But if Mrs. Callahn wanted to live in her own little fantasyland where Microsoft Windows ran like lightning and she served great-tasting coffee, far be it from me to ruin it for her. So I gave her the classic, one-size-fits-all answer that got me out of just about anything.

"It's a Southern thing."

Her face relaxed into understanding that I was a woman reared by java heathens and deserving of her sympathy.

"What are you doing with Hugo's box?" she asked.

I told her about getting accidentally employed at the Dragonfly.

"No more hotshot jobs then?" she asked.

"The Dragonfly is temporary."

"Temporary has a way of becoming comfortable, and comfortable becomes permanent."

"It's not going to be that way," I said. "It's a stopgap solution."

"Keep talking like that," she said. "It will keep you out of the Dragonfly."

I opened my backpack to put the box back in, when I saw her eyes light on *Lady Chatterley's Lover*. As I watched, too shocked to stop her, she reached into my backpack for the book and laid it on the table.

"It's not very pretty," I said, feeling like I was small-talking a hostage taker. "Hugo's going to show me how to put it back together. There are these notes in the margins. See? I want to preserve it."

She tapped the cloth cover. "Forget about these people. All of these fireworks end up like that." She nodded toward the fighting couple in the corner. "Get a real job. No one is going to take care of you but you."

She got up and left without a *good-bye* or *hope to see you soon*. I would have taken it personally, except she did this to everyone. So it was kind of comforting, just like the lumpy seat of the green reading chair in the Dragonfly.

Even though Mrs. Callahn was a bit scary, I appreciated the order she commanded. As she returned to her rightful place at the espresso machine, the kid came out of the storeroom and the music switched to a cool jazz. I stared down at *Lady Chatterley's Lover* and thought of the Dragonfly and the burden of books that lay ahead of me, thinking of the story of Psyche, who was forced to sort a mountain of poppy, wheat, and millet seed in a single night before she could return to her true love. Ants came to her rescue. I wondered if I could rent some.

.

"I just don't understand all this bookstore business," Mama said.

It was nearly midnight in South Carolina, and I could picture my mother in one of the Quaker rocking chairs on her front porch, a jelly jar in her hand. The sparkling clean brick-heavy crystal tumblers she kept on the wet bar were for company. A jelly jar was for drinking vodka alone. She would have turned the outdoor light off. She'd say it was to keep the bugs away and the temperature down. But it was also so the neighbors couldn't see her. In the dark she'd rock and sip vodka from that jelly jar until she was stirred up enough to call somebody.

"I'm just helping out a friend," I said.

"Some friend," she said.

I poured two fingers of bourbon into a blue Solo cup and went outside to sit under the umbrella in the backyard. The fog had made it over the Santa Cruz Mountains that separated the valley from the coast, and I could smell the tomato plants Hugo was nursing in large terra-cotta pots on the patio.

"Where's Daddy?" I asked. I tugged down the sleeves of my sweatshirt. The wet air felt cold, even though it was nice.

"Surgery," she said, as if it were the name of a country where men went when they didn't want to be found.

I pulled my knees to my chest. Even through my jeans, I could still find the hard line of a scar on my right knee. One Friday afternoon in eleventh grade, I'd ridden my bike to my father's office to swipe some office supplies for a science project that was due Monday and which I hadn't started yet. The office was dark, which was no surprise—Daddy always cleared everyone out early on Fridays. But I knew that he kept the spare key in the soil of the hanging fern in front of the window in his private office. I stood on my tiptoes on the edge of a knee-high brick planter overflowing with the petunias my mother planted every year. I could feel the edge of the key sticking up in the soil hidden by the canopying blossoms. As I slid the key from its hiding place in the dirt, my eyes fell into my father's darkened office.

My father had taught me about adrenaline, how it shocks you into a fight-or-flight response. But the jolt I felt in my heart when I saw the movement in his window didn't do either one. It made me clumsy, and I fell off the edge of the brick planter and onto the stone walkway, cutting open my knee. I pulled myself up against the planter and stared at the crimson rising out of the tear in my jeans. Behind me, I heard murmurs and some rustling about. When I stood, the blinds were closed in the window. It didn't matter. I knew what I'd seen. My father between the legs of Mrs. Celia Collins, whose ACL seemed to have healed nicely.

I felt warm blood running down my leg as I biked home, but I had a possessive need to see my mother. I could never envision my father with anyone but her. All I could think then was that my mother must be gone, that their house would be absent of her forever. No matter how separate I felt from them, I had believed in their happiness. I needed to believe that feeling absent to them was the sacrifice I made for the great love they had for each other.

I was out of breath as I abandoned my bike and let the screen door slam behind me. I stood inside the house, panting in the unlit foyer, disbelieving that my mother was really there, sitting on the third step of the stairway next to the golf bags, her fingers entwined around her knees. Her grandmother's clock chimed 3:30.

I sat beside her on the step. I was crying. I hadn't noticed until just then.

"Mama."

She stood up and folded her arms, walked to the screen door, and looked up at the patch of sky beyond the front porch, away from my tears and my bloody leg.

"Smells like rain," she said. "We probably won't be able to go at all now."

"Mama, I was at Daddy's office," I said. How could I say the words? What words were there to say about this thing I knew? "Mama, I need to tell you something—"

Her hand cracked like lightning against my face. My head knocked against the wall and shook the pictures above. Pain flooded my brain, and I saw nothing but spots and her silhouette in the light from the door.

"You have nothing to say to me," she said.

I smelled the scent of her face powder and lipstick and the whiff of alcohol on her breath.

I jumped up, and she didn't try to stop me as I rushed past

her. I picked up my bike and rode to Dizzy's. Miss Velda sent Dizzy for his car.

"Georgine knows," she said in the backseat of Dizzy's Rambler, her arm around me as Dizzy drove us to the emergency room, where I'd get my knee stitched up. "This isn't the first time. But she can't talk about it. If she talks about it, it makes it real. And then she'll have to do what she can't bring herself to do."

The Rambler's windows were rolled down, and I lay my face against the cold metal of the door. Dizzy woke me up when we got to the hospital.

"Your father will be home soon," Mama said on the phone as I sipped from my blue Solo cup. "I should warm up his supper."

My mother—above all, Mrs. Mason Duprés—dancing for her prince.

CHAPTER FIVE

I Will Find You

We cannot be as we are in the flesh, only in this book.

—Catherine

"No, no. I remember. I'm Henry."

This came from one of a group of three older gentlemen, regulars who came in on their lunch break to stock up on Terry Pratchett or to look for that one Isaac Asimov they'd never read. His name was Mike and so was his friend's. The third was named John. Two Mikes and a John. They called themselves the CIA Bathroom.

"You're not Henry," said the other Mike. He was wearing a *Maker Faire* T-shirt and a NASA security badge. He stood behind the first Mike, who was going through a shoe box of pegs for the bookshelf rail slots. "You didn't even move here until 1974."

They'd been at this for twenty minutes. I'd been trying to fix a broken shelf in the Self-Help section, around the corner from Sci-Fi/Fantasy, when the three of them placed their books on the floor and took over. Chivalry was not dead in Silicon Valley. It just masqueraded as engineering prowess.

"It could have happened in the seventies," I said.

"Mike, I've known you thirty-four years and I've never seen you write with a fountain pen," said John, shorter than his friends and with the wiry build of a late-in-life runner; he sat on the floor holding up the shelf while his two friends took their time relieving him. "Henry's notes were written with a fountain pen."

"I remember distinctly," said Mike #1, rubbing his belly over the logo from a chili cook-off competition.

"No one remembers anything distinctly about the seventies," said Mike #2.

"Okay, say you are Henry," said John, still holding up the shelf. "Why did you start writing in a book? Why did you call yourself Henry?"

"It's not like we had Match.com back then," Mike #1 said.

"So you just start writing in a book…," said Mike #2, still holding the box of pegs.

"With a fountain pen," said John, who had by now stacked two columns of books below the broken shelf so he didn't have to hold it up any longer.

"What is it with you and the fountain pen?" Mike #1 asked.

"…hoping that some beautiful woman would start writing you back," said Mike #2.

"Calling yourself by some other name," said John.

"Well, it worked," said Mike #1.

"It worked for Henry," said John.

"Precisely," said Mike #1.

All week, men had been coming into the Dragonfly claiming to be Henry. They all seemed to have some sort of collective memory of this wildly romantic version of themselves—after a heartbreak, a divorce, a particularly good acid trip—when they did such things as start a correspondence in a book with a woman they'd never laid eyes on.

"Nineteen sixty-one," said John. "The date above the first note says 1961. Did you time travel during the seventies as well?"

"Apparently, I'm not supposed to remember," said Mike #1.

They went on and on, taking three times as long to fix the shelf as I would have on my own, while I gazed up at the Self-Help section for guidance.

It was my second full day as a Dragonfly employee, but having spent so much time here, it felt like much longer. The Dragonfly catered to a broad clientele, who occasionally showed the charming eccentricities of Dickens characters. There was Miss Miranda, as tall as she was wide, who was overjoyed when Hugo found a copy of the cookbook her husband kept throwing away in hopes of never having to eat that meatloaf recipe again. And the woman with a pug she carried in a front-facing baby carrier who liked Janet Evanovich and Ian McEwan and had taken up with Steinbeck on Hugo's recommendation. There was the man who sat on my Kik-Step in the back corner, reading through the stacks of sheet music like they were novels. Hank, another regular, who only last Wednesday bought *How to Win at Craps*, *A Cultural History of Masturbation*, and four Agatha Christie novels. And, of course, there was Gloria, who came in twice a week with her NPR tote bag, Tuesdays for Mystery and Fridays for Romance. She always paid in loose change she kept in a plastic bag. And the CIA Bathroom, who had to constantly remind one another of what books they'd already read.

After Mike, Mike, and John finally finished with the shelf, I accompanied them to the front of the store and wrote up their purchases in the big leather binder Hugo kept at the counter.

"So Mike," I said. "If you're Henry, where did you ask Catherine to meet you in the last note?"

"That wasn't on the website," Mike #1 said.

"I know," I said. "I didn't post that part. For just this reason."

Mike #2 and John turned toward him, looking smug and hopeful at the same time.

"The bar at the Fairmont Hotel in San Jose," Mike #1 said.

"Enjoy the Cherie Priest," I said, smiling and handing him his books. "If you run into the real Henry, send him my way."

"Working here has turned you into a cruel woman, Maggie," Mike #1 said as his two friends pushed him toward the door.

"Just the way you like me," I called back.

Jason came out of the stacks to drop an empty box by my foot before disappearing back into the stacks. As far as I know, he and Hugo had never exchanged a word about his indignant resignation. He had just come back into the store yesterday, grabbed a stack of books, and started up where he left off.

I looked up at Hugo, who was sitting in his chair reading another of the Waverley novels.

"Sorry about Jason," I said.

Hugo waved me off. "He quits every couple of months or so. He spends a day in Pioneer Park reading comic books and waiting for his friends to get off work. Then he comes back here out of boredom."

Pioneer Park.

Sunday is the first day of summer. Meet me in Pioneer Park, by the fountain, noon. —Henry

It seemed odd that the scene of Henry and Catherine's meeting would also be the spot for Jason's sulking.

I took a left at Biographies, a U-turn around Twentieth-Century History, and a sharp right at Poetry to get to Romance. In my first cleanup project, I'd arranged the Romance section by genre—bodice-busters in Historical Romance, cosmos-on-the-cover titles in Chick Lit, vampire cowboys along with demon lovers in Paranormal Romance—with a special display section of eighties classics from Harold Robbins and Jackie Collins. I'd spent days finding them all over the store, behind and between diet books, astrology books, biographies, even Ellery Queen mysteries. Books to make you thin, to take away the pain in your back, to teach you spells, to make you mad or make you cry. Then I picked up an autographed 8 x 10 glossy of Johnny Depp at a garage sale and hung it beneath the Romance section sign. It wasn't like I'd found a cure for cancer, but getting the Romance section together felt like progress. If anyone were to actually stumble into the Dragonfly, make their way through the obstacle course of boxes and books at the front of the store, and navigate the labyrinth of stacks to the far back corner, I'm sure they'd show their appreciation for all my work by buying many, many romance novels.

I'd moved a Kik-Step stool back here, anticipating moments like I had now where I could spend a little time with the book. A chapter here, a few pages there. I felt like I owed it to the novel to actually read it again after all these years. I could see why people were so critical of it. It wasn't very lyrical, and you could tell Lawrence had an ax to grind, which always bugs me. But I could also see why so many, like Henry and Catherine, embraced it. It wasn't just the sex, it was the stark longing that drew me in. Wanting someone, thinking of him all day, and then letting yourself be in love. I wanted that kind of longing. The dull nothing of losing Bryan was beginning to feel like torture beyond any heartache. I was bored with it.

I was in the middle of a chapter when I felt another presence. I slowly looked up to see Grendel on the shelf above Johnny Depp, looking down at me as if to say, "You mere mortal." We stared at each other, our eyes locked in an epic battle of human encroachment in the wild animal's habitat. I'd removed his favorite pile of books, a mountain of Sue Graftons, from a spot in Hugo's office that got a strong patch of sun between four and five in the afternoon. And ever since he'd lurked, following me along the heights of the bookshelves, like one of Stephen King's ghosts, waiting for his moment of revenge.

Yowling, he launched himself at me. I jumped up, trying to avoid him, but he got me on the shoulder. I screeched and dropped *Lady Chatterley's Lover*, while he bounded from my shoulder to the top of the bookshelves across from us, but not before leaving four deep scratches on my skin that started to bleed through my white T-shirt.

I felt a hand on my arm and looked up to see Rajhit standing next to me.

"Are you mortally wounded?"

"I'll make it back to base, Captain."

He reached around to his back pocket, and pulled out a

crisp, white handkerchief. I tried to remember the last time I'd seen one. Leaving it in a quarter fold, he slid it under the collar of my T-shirt and pressed it down on my wound. I could still smell the heat of the sun in the cotton of his shirt. He leaned his head in closer to examine the scratch. Around us, I could hear the sounds of people moving through the stacks and sliding books off the shelves. An image of the store came to me, as if someone had lifted the roof off. I looked down at the maze of stacks, watching people moving to and fro, gazing at the shelves, their heads slightly tilted to read the spines. And there were Rajhit and me, in a dark corner, close and still.

"I was hoping I'd find you here," he said. "Though maybe not bleeding."

"Hugo should give me hazard pay."

We both smiled and did that small puff of air thing that substitutes for a laugh when you're trying to be quiet and unseen. We stood there, my cheek near enough to his to feel warmth from him. He blew a tender breath on my wound through my shirt. It was a small, quiet gesture, one I could have easily ignored as if it had never happened. But the quietness of it moved me.

"I wanted to talk to you about the bike," I said.

"Is something wrong with it?"

"No, it's great. It's awesome actually. It's just..."

He smiled and looked away. "You don't like me."

"Oh no, I like you. That's the thing."

"You don't like getting gifts from people you like? You're an odd woman."

"You're making this difficult."

He smiled.

"I don't think I'm the one making this difficult." Without looking up at me, he whispered, *"I try to go on with my day, doing what is required of me, but I find myself here again and again, wondering where you are.'"*

My eyes closed and everything in me seemed aware of everything in him. My hand came up and fingered the end of one of his curls. And as if that was what he was waiting for, he pressed his lips along my collarbone. The wet heat of his mouth permeated the cloth. Around me I could hear the daily business of the Dragonfly while back in my dark corner, Rajhit knelt in front of me and spread his hands over my hips while he kissed the top of my belly through Hanes cotton. His hands slid under my shirt, his fingers spreading over the small of my back, pulling me tighter against his mouth. I sank my hands into his downy curls and held on. Then I felt his fingers on the front of my jeans. He unsnapped them and peeled open the zipper. The first time I felt his lips and his tongue against my skin, it was right below my belly button.

Then he was standing, leaning against me, his arms shielding me. Someone else was here. I heard the shoes squeaking and, around his shoulder, I spotted Gloria's porthole glasses scanning the titles as if we weren't there, like one of those dinosaurs who could see you only if you moved. She slipped several books into her bag without giving them much of a glance and rounded the corner.

We were back as we were before, our faces side by side, our lips next to each other's ears.

"I want to see more of you," he said.

"I think you've just seen plenty of me."

"You know what I mean."

"I like it when you find me."

When he kissed me, he tasted like green tea and cinnamon.

"Okay, I will find you," he said, pulling away.

After he was gone, I dropped to the Kik-Step behind me and took a deep breath. The air still held the scent of him. There was no way something that felt this good was going to end well.

From somewhere in the store I got a whiff of Vietnamese takeout, and I remembered walking with Bryan to the little Pho Hoa around the corner and how he held my hand like it was a bag of groceries and how we spent the meal looking at our phone screens instead of each other. Whatever this was with Rajhit, it was better than that.

I stared at the shelves in front of me, the section I'd worked so hard on. Here was order, control. This was the one place in my life where things made sense. But as I looked at the perfectly ordered rows, the last names of authors jumped around the alphabet. Vampire cowboys were sharing shelf space with Mr. Darcy types and bare-chested pirates. Everything was out of order. I didn't understand. It had been fine the day before. Dismayed, I leaned back on the shelves behind me, looking at the section as a whole, and realized that all of my hard work had been reassembled. The book spines were now organized by color.

"Jason!"

From the front of the store came a trollish laugh.

.

I sat in the dark, curled up in the papasan chair by the open back window, listening to the party next door. The notepad

I'd been doodling on for the last hour was resting on my lap. I'd been trying to figure out how much longer I could survive on my minimal income. Hugo had lowered my rent by a couple hundred dollars, bless him. So now I had $400 after rent for food, utilities, phone, and anything else that came along. Movies were out. So were lunches for the most part. And there was only so much instant ramen a girl can stomach. I could move, find a shared house on Craigslist, but moving was expensive, too. By the time I came up with first and last month's rent and a deposit, I'd be in the hole deeper than I was now. And I wouldn't have Hugo next door. No, moving wasn't an option.

My phone dinged, and I picked it up to see a text from Dizzy. It was the fourth message in an hour telling me he was at Finnegans Wake, and it was Friday night, and I needed to come over there pronto. Only he didn't say "pronto" and he used a lot more curse words. I watched the clock on my phone. *At 8:00, I'll go over,* I told myself. But the top of the hour slid by and the bottom, too, and I was still sitting on my Pier 1 cushion.

Along with worry over my bank account, my last conversation with Dizzy was weighing heavily on me. I knew I should call Avi and ask her to lunch. She'd given me her number, after all. It just felt so tenuous. My life had hinged on Dizzy and ArGoNet. I'd become dependent on expectations that had come to nothing. I didn't have much to show for my years in Silicon Valley. Not much of a career or any money, a busted relationship, a shabby bookstore I was putting way too much time into. I'd been to too many business meetings thinking all my hard work was going to pay off, only to be denied for some grand reason like some exec didn't like the blue button.

I picked up *Lady Chatterley's Lover* from where it lay on the side table and thumbed through it, the pages giving off the smell of used sheets and stale promises. The notes had saved me that day at the book club meeting. Maybe they offered some wisdom now.

Henry, we can only exist as the people we are in these pages. We cannot be as we are in the flesh, only in this book. It is here where we can belong to each other. —*Catherine*

I know you're afraid. I'm afraid, too. But fear isn't real. It's just emotion mixed with memory. Fear is only dangerous if it keeps us from what we want. And I want you. —*Henry*

Emotion mixed with memory. Who talked like that? Maybe Hugo. Okay, Hugo and Henry. I thought about that day at Avi's, the last time when I felt like the world was mine for the taking, even for just a few moments. I took a huge risk that day. Henry was right. It's not the fear that's dangerous. It's not getting what you want because of it.

I wasn't going back home. If ArGoNet was done for me, so be it. But I wasn't out yet. I had a network, though it was a network of one. I'd walked away from the SVWEABC with only one business card, but it was *the* card.

I pulled out the bag I'd carried with me to the meeting, with Avi's card still inside. I popped open my laptop and typed in her e-mail address. Then I stopped. E-mails were too easy to ignore. When you're climbing the ladder, you answer every message like it's from Jesus Christ or Steve Jobs. When you're at the top like Avi is, answering messages right away whiffed of a need to please. It was downright unchic. No, I wasn't going to wait for an e-mail. On the back, she'd written her home phone number. I was going to call her.

But first, I had to pace around a bit and practice what I was going to say. I was just touching base to see how I might help the team to deliver the best book group experience for my fellow members. Sure, I'd say, I had a lot going on, but when the group was successful, I was successful, no matter the personal sacrifice of time and effort. When I had it just right, I dialed, imagining Avi gliding across the floor in a feather-lined silk robe and slippers like Eva Gabor on *Green Acres* to answer it. And then she did.

"Slutlees.com, Jade? Did you seriously not think I would find out you posted a video of us on Slutlees.com, you stupid little twat? I own this valley. Do you not think I know how to use a computer? Or you think I'm too old for that, too? You know what else I know how to do? Call a lawyer. Jake is going to hunt you down and make you wish you never learned to click a mouse. Now stop calling every thirty seconds to remind me of yet another reason why you're leaving me!"

The few seconds that passed felt long enough for new galaxies to have formed. I stared into the nighttime shadows of my apartment and listened to the anger-fueled huffing of my one and only VIP contact on the other end of the line. What the hell was I supposed to do now?

"If you're going to stay on the line, you can at least say something."

I remembered the picture on Avi's bookshelf, the one with her arm around a tall blonde about my age. However rich and powerful Avi was, she obviously cared for this Jade. If I hung up now, she'd think it was her ex hanging up. I'd be off the hook, but where would Avi be? I squeezed my eyes shut and took a big breath of air.

"I'm so sorry, Avi," I said. "This is Maggie Duprés. From the book club? This is an understatement, but I'm guessing this is a bad time."

There was silence on the other end as I waited for a torrent of swear words. But they didn't come. Instead, all I heard was Avi Narayan hanging up on me.

I held my cell phone in my lap. I couldn't seem to get my brain to do anything. It was frozen shut. I just sat there and listened to the party next door. If I'd picked my sorry ass up at 7:30 and gone over there, none of this would have happened. If I'd sent Avi an e-mail like any other sane person would have, this wouldn't have happened. But no, I had to be fearless. Thanks a lot, Henry.

I picked up *Lady Chatterley's Lover*, still open at the page with Henry's note. This was all his doing. Was I so desperate that I was taking advice from a guy who fell in love with a woman by writing to her in a book? Meet me in the park by the fountain at noon? Are you kidding me? It could have been raining that day. Or city workers could have been repaving the sidewalk. Most of all, he made this invitation in the pages of a book in a bookstore. Slather me in honey and call me a biscuit, but there's always a chance, even in the Dragonfly, that someone may come in and actually buy the book. There were about a hundred million things that could have gone wrong with his plan. A hundred million.

The phone rang. I recognized the number as the one I'd just dialed. Avi. I could see her, winds of wrath stirring her Eva Gabor robe around her as she conjured spells that would turn me into a frog and send lightning bolts through the phone. I didn't know what to do, so I stuffed the phone under a cushion. This was it. The end of any hope of staying here. I had just pissed on the boots of one of the most powerful women in Silicon Valley. I was going to hell. Or even worse, I was going home to my mother.

I pulled the phone out. What the hell? If this was my last stand, at least I was going out all memorable-like.

"I'm the most terrible person alive," Avi said. "How incredibly rude of me."

"No it's my fault—"

"No, no, I should never have answered the phone that way, or should have at least looked at caller ID."

We continued to stumble over each other, trying to outdo the other one with our apologies, all of which seemed to be completely unnecessary. And when the apologies trailed off, we were left with silence.

"Bad breakup?" I asked.

She laughed, and I heard a sniffle.

"Is there any other kind?" she asked.

Again, I pictured her on the other end, but this time I saw her in baggy sweats (okay, they were cashmere) with drips of Cherry Garcia dried on the front. Her hair was a mess. She was wearing outdated glasses. She had a pimple on her cheek. I wondered if the picture of her and Jade was still there on her bookshelf or if she'd run over it with her Mercedes.

"She really posted a video of you two? How bad is it?"

"You can't see me," she said. "Or at least not enough to tell that it's me. She wasn't interested in anyone seeing me. Only her."

"But still…," I said.

"But still…"

It turned out Dizzy was right. Avi was a someone just like any other someone. So we talked for a little more and made lunch plans for Thai food on Monday. After we hung up, I sat for a while with that little burn of loss and joy. And then I got up and walked over to Finnegans Wake.

.

The next day, June 27, it rained. I remember this because for months afterward people used the date as a milestone for describing the events in their lives as in, "I know I had my oil changed on June twenty-eighth because it was the day after it rained." In the Bay Area, we get all our rain in the winter. Rain in early summer, while not unheard of, is rare. And such an occurrence, in Hugo's world, required a party. But then, the miracles of a sunrise and sunset seemed significant enough for Hugo's people to break out the cocktail shakers and swizzle sticks.

I had reason to celebrate, too. I'd just set up the Dragonfly's eBay store that very day and sold our first book online—a signed first edition of Walker Percy's *Love in the Ruins*, which had been sitting up front with the other first editions for as long as I'd been in the store, and was now on its way to one Miss Winifred Johnson in Wichita. (There's no love for the Southern gods of letters in the heathen world of Silicon Valley, with distractions such as smart phones and dual-boot operating systems.) Hugo suggested we have the book blessed for Miss Winifred, it being our first online sale and all. So he called his friend Jesse, who was a second-degree Wiccan priest, and asked him to come to the house. Jesse brought over salt water to sprinkle on the invoice (sparing the book), incense to burn in the store, and dried lavender to fold in the pages. Jesse, conveniently, was also a butcher at Andronico's, so he brought five pounds of lamb shanks, to Hugo's extreme delight. When the rain started, Hugo got to work on the phone. People came. People brought more food. People brought drinks. My insides were very happy.

Even on ordinary days, Hugo's apartment had a mellow, day-spa-waiting-area vibe to it. But tonight, there was an undertow of enchantment. His friends draped themselves around his place with the leg-dangling lethargy of Tennessee Williams characters. When Hugo lifted the lid of a deep skillet on his stove to stir something he was calling Hugo's Mysterious Moroccan Dish, the room filled with the scent of saffron and apricots. A young redhead in a cowboy-patterned sundress strummed a harp and sang something in Gaelic. A man with a lute—an honest to God lute—joined her, along with a woman with flowers in her hair tapping lightly on a bodhran drum. Somewhere, a Renaissance festival was in want of minstrels.

Hugo didn't own anything you could actually sit on like a normal human being. Pillows of all shapes and sizes were strewn about his floor so that his apartment looked much like the fifty-nine-year-old male version of the bottle in *I Dream of Jeannie*. Half buzzed from Jesse's Lower Chakra Martinis, I laid myself out flat, molded to a series of huge ruby-colored pillows, feeling like I was in that place you go to when you fall asleep on the beach listening to the waves. That's when I heard Rajhit's whisper in my ear.

"I've been looking for you."

I opened my eyes and found myself staring up at his smile, that corner of his mouth turned up just like the night he gave me the bike. He hovered over me, his hair loose around his shoulders. I reached up and flicked one of his ringlets behind his ear. The party had just gotten a thousand times better.

He sat on the pillows at my feet, took my bare right foot in his hands, and started rubbing my sole. Two martinis earlier, I might have been able to keep a stone face and ignore the fact that my nether regions were going all Madame Bovary–like. Instead, my head fell into the pillows and my eyes rolled back into my head. I can't say absolutely, but I'm fairly certain there may have been moaning. I was all fine with the world.

"Nice foot," he said. "Attached to a nice ankle at the bottom of what I believe would be a very attractive leg if I ever got a look at it."

"Am I merely a sum of my parts?"

"*'We have never met, yet I do not believe there is any part of you I do not want.'*"

I laughed at hearing Henry's words quoted back to me. Rajhit smiled and slid his hand under the hem of my jeans, running his warm palm up my leg. For the second time in two days, I started thinking about wearing skirts.

And then I heard a *woooo* sound and opened my eyes to see Jason standing over Rajhit and blowing softly into a beer bottle. I tried to shoo him away but he wasn't paying any attention to me.

"Yes, Jason?" Rajhit asked without looking up.

"Dude, you're Dungeon Master for next week and you haven't even sent out the invitation yet. No one knows where we're meeting. Is Deborah even coming anymore? We don't even know if there's a snack theme."

Rajhit's hand slid out from the leg of my jeans and he sat up straight.

"Can we talk about this later?" Rajhit asked, turning to look up at Jason.

"Dude, we let you be Dungeon Master this time because you've been begging us ever since you joined. It's a lot of responsibility. Don't let us down."

My vodka-soaked brain was swimming with any number of questions. I settled on "What the hell are you talking about?"

"Dungeons and Dragons night," Jason said.

I lifted myself up on my elbows to look down the length of my body at Rajhit, who was holding his head in his hands. Now, I'd never partaken of D&D myself, but I'd known enough gamers in my day to understand that only a very few matched the stereotype of pasty-faced losers with long stringy hair, bad skin, and refrigerator privileges that came with renting their parents' basement. Most were completely cool people. But even so, I was a bit shocked. Not about Jason, that was a no-brainer, or even Hugo. But Rajhit?

"What's the big deal?" Jason asked. "Me, Hugo, Rajhit, Mrs. Callahn, and a few other dudes on Monday nights."

"All of you? Really? I never knew that. Great. Exhibit number 746 that you hate me."

"Like we'd let you play."

"Like I'd want to play."

"First of all," Jason said. "I bet you've never even played D&D. Second, when did you turn twelve?"

"Three drinks ago," I said.

Jason bent one knee to poke Rajhit in the back. "So what's the deal for Monday?"

"I need a drink." Rajhit stood and walked into the kitchen. I rolled over, my eyes following him. He stood next to Hugo, facing me but not looking at me.

Jason bent down, his elbows on his knees, hulking over me.

"Don't you want to know about Deborah? From our group?" Jason asked.

"What?" I had no idea who he was talking about.

"He's not exactly Mr. Commitment, you know," Jason said. "Every time there's a single woman in the game, he goes all horndog. They mess around for a while, then it's all 'I can't commit to one person because that'll fuck up my inner pink unicorn.' Then we're out a player. The last time I saw Deborah she was in the store looking for *Eat, Pray, Love* and she looked like she already had the *Eat* part worked out for herself. I don't know why all the women are so into him. He's not even that good of a player."

"Whatever there is between me and Rajhit is between me and Rajhit," I said.

"I just don't want to be involved with all the drama. Okay? No drama."

Jason moved over to the minstrels and sat on the floor behind them, leaning against the wall and accepting another beer from the lute player. I lay where I was and tried to figure out exactly how this evening had gone so wrong.

I got up to fill my glass from the pitcher of martinis Jesse had put in the fridge, but there were two twentysomething girls standing between me and my alcohol, lost in Hugo's set of Magnetic Poetry—Shakespeare Edition. The blond girl, who had a pixie cut and lizard tattoo on her shoulder, had just finished YOUR PECULIAR PURPLE GROAN. Then the red-headed harp player scanned the words across Hugo's freezer door and made TONGUE GODDESS SATISFY SMOOTH LUST. Pixie Cut looked at her with a cocked eyebrow. She moved NIBBLE to a blank space. Redhead added QUAKING. Pixie Cut moved DESIRE. They glanced around them and snickered, like they thought they were getting away with something. Redhead reached behind Pixie Cut and tucked the tag in the back of her tank top that had been sticking out. And when her hand ran back along Pixie Cut's shoulder, she reached for it and kissed it.

I looked around to see if anyone else was seeing this, or if anyone was seeing me see this. I couldn't take my eyes off them. I'd seen them both arrive separately, noticed them being introduced to each other. How long ago was that? An hour? Two? And now they were here—flirting, blushing—and my body started to remember how easy all that used to be.

As I stood there, someone took my hand, which had been resting on Hugo's counter. It was Mrs. Callahn. She took my other one as well and peered down at them.

"It's your turn now."

For a second, my thoughts still so focused on the two girls, I thought she meant it was my turn to find someone. But then she turned my palms up and rotated my thumbs around in their sockets and pressed down on the fleshy parts of my hands, staring down at them through tortoiseshell reading glasses with a beaded chain. She'd meant it was my turn to have my palms read.

She ran her fingertips over the lines in each palm. They felt like cactus spines, and I instinctively jerked my hand, but it only made her hold on tighter. She leaned in, peering at my hands, tilting them toward the light above Hugo's stove. Then she closed my palms and held them together. She stood straight and let her glasses drop so that they hung between her breasts.

"Your heart is made of paper," she said. "Water can dissolve it. Earth can bury it. Wind can blow it away."

I felt my stomach lurch. In the shadows, I could finally see the lines of age in her face, like cracks in hard brown earth that had seen little rain. The vise of her hands pressed mine tighter together. I jerked my hands away.

"That's a terrible thing to say to someone."

She reached over the counter and handed me a cocktail glass.

"Protect it. Find another job. Find another boyfriend. Life at the Dragonfly is not for you."

She toasted me and walked across the room to fill someone else with dread. I stared at my drink and felt I'd had my fill. I stepped over to the sink and poured my drink down the drain. Hugo reached over from his post at the stove and circled his palm on my back in a worried way.

"Too many cocktails," I said.

I stumbled down the hall to the bathroom and splashed some water on my face. A bit of light came in from outside through the small window over the bathtub. The water made my skin feel brittle. I sat on the edge of the tub and hugged my knees until I could breathe again.

Turning off the light behind me, I saw Rajhit in the hallway. He was near the living room, his back to me, leaning against the wall. I stood in the dark and looked at how his body curved, how he stood just out of the light of the room. I thought of all those boys in my past, the ones with sea salt skin, most of them as eager to please me as much as they were pleased with themselves. How easy it had been, how little it took. A whisper in an ear, a touch on the arm. Before anyone cared what I did for a living or what my life goals were. Before I started calculating how long it would take for a relationship to get tired. Back when I was younger, there were just bodies and need, raw and necessary. Each breathless moment before a first kiss, I'd think, *Please don't let him be "the one." I'm not ready yet.* I wasn't ready to sleep at a prince's doorstep and lose my voice, like my mother. And with that, I'd clung to my impermanent heart that expected so little and gave so little in return.

I lay my fingertips against his back. He turned and held his arms out to me, as one is prone to do after several cocktails, and I slid into his hug. His hands ran up and down my back in a reassuring, friendly sort of way and for a moment I thought that would be the end of it. But we went past the time limit for platonic separation and his hands slowed, resting on the small of my back. I exhaled and felt myself go limp against him.

"What Jason was talking about—" he said.

I cut him off with a shake of my head.

"I want this to happen," he said. "You and me."

I reached up and touched his face, touched the Henry-ness of him. His arms tightened, and my body pressed against him. I'd taken one step too many to go back. I brushed my lips against the small triangle of skin above his collar and heard the breath rush out of him. Then he kissed me, more cautiously than I would have expected. My fingers ran along his waist until they found skin beneath his shirt. *I want to know what it's like for you to feel my hands on you, to hear my voice say your name.*

"I thought you weren't going to sleep with me because I gave you a bike," he said.

"It's a pretty nice bike."

CHAPTER SIX

The Venus Glove

I would ride a whale across an ocean just to sit next
to you and hold your hand.

—Henry

I'd made a deal with myself as I watched the sun peek in
through the small window in the Dragonfly's office. When the
edge of the sunlight reached the corner of the desk, I'd roll
off the sofa and get back to work. That was half an hour ago.
The sun was well past the corner and I was still on the office
sofa, my head resting on the store's earthquake emergency kit,
which consisted of a blanket, cat food, and vodka. I couldn't
afford this lying about. I had stacks of books to move, Grendel
the deranged cat to avoid, oh, and my lunch with Avi later in
the day. I just needed to rest a decade or two and then I'd be
fine.

It wasn't really a hangover. It was sitting in that sunny
spot, thinking about the night before, and feeling that warm
middle-of-the-cookie feeling every time I thought of Rajhit.
He had been the lover I'd imagined him to be, even with the
first-time-together fumbling. It was sweet and exciting being with someone new. And afterward, he snuck back over

to Hugo's and returned with cheese, apples, and Belgian beer. With impish dramatics, he replayed his recent dinner at a restaurant up in Napa where all of the menu items were phrased as affirmations, so when he ordered he said things like, "I'd like Radiance Filled with Healing and Light with a side of Endless Joy." I don't know if it was Rajhit or the sex, but at that moment, I felt like I could say words like that in all seriousness.

He'd gotten up around four in the morning, and I'd walked him to the door. There was more kissing at the threshold while I imagined how good my bed would smell—full of him and me—when I got back to it. And then he was gone, and I was alone with all the leftover sweetness.

The door to the Dragonfly's office squeaked open, and Hugo slipped through, walked slowly and deliberately over to me, and set down a highball of light brown liquid.

"Hair of the dog?" I asked.

"Apple cider vinegar and honey in water," he said. "Best hangover tonic there is."

"I'm doing pretty good," I said, stretching and then scratching my belly with both hands like I'd seen him do a hundred times.

Hugo walked over to his desk and leaned back into the chair. Stretching his legs straight out and crossing at the ankles, he started sorting through the mail. I'd sat in a lot of desk chairs in my life, and I can say with no hesitation that the Dragonfly's desk chair should be branded a crime against humanity. But somehow Hugo looked like he was seated in a hammock between two palm trees.

"I take it we're talking about Rajhit," he said.

"I know he's a friend of yours. Are you weirded out?"

He smiled.

"Maggie," he said, "if I had a problem with my friends sleeping together now and then, I'd be a very lonely man."

Hugo opened a letter and spent a moment reading it before stuffing it in his shirt pocket. He rubbed his hand over his beard, his thoughts somewhere else.

I wondered what was in the letter. I'd started handling all the bills and paperwork lately. Robert played it cool, but I could tell he was doing his accountant's inner happy dance every time we talked. He and I had given up on convincing Hugo and Jason that a used computer and retail sales software would be the way to go. Instead I brought my laptop in every day and totaled up the day's sales to enter into the online accounting app Robert used. While I was entering the income, Robert was entering the expenses, so I could see the whole money picture for the Dragonfly. And what I was seeing was encouraging. Before my arrival, the balance sheet for the Dragonfly was about as uplifting as *Angela's Ashes*. But lately, I'd seen an uptick. It was small, but it was definitely there, a tiny tadpole of hope.

I pointed to the envelope. "I can take care of that for you."

"No, no," Hugo said, patting his pocket. "This one's just for me."

From the sofa, I could make out the logo for our building management company. I let it go. We were fine on the basics: rent, utilities, and such. Paychecks were always iffy, but the money was always there somehow, appearing from an owner's equity account. I asked Hugo about it once, and he told me that was from income he received for some patents he'd gotten back in his student days at Cal. He wasn't crazy rich or anything, but he wasn't depending on the Dragonfly to keep him afloat. But I also didn't want the Dragonfly to bleed him dry. I now had another reason to turn the store around.

"Maggie," Hugo said. "About Rajhit…"

"Jason told me," I said.

"Jason? About what?"

"About Deborah and the others," I said. "So he's a lothario. I think I might try that for a while. What's the female version? Lotharia? I like it."

"Maggie."

"What?" I asked. "An uncommitted lifestyle seems to have worked out well for you. You seem happy."

His eyes widened for a second as if he seemed surprised that I would think that, and that, in turn, surprised me. If you asked me, or practically anyone who had ever stepped foot in the Dragonfly, Hugo was quite possibly the most well-contented person in existence. But now his face softened and looked a little distant and I realized how foolish it was to think you understood anyone else's state of being.

"Better drink your tonic," Hugo said, patting the envelope in his shirt pocket. "Jason's going to need you."

When he left, I sat up on the sofa and looked at his vacant chair. The room had felt quiet before he came in, but now it felt empty.

·

"So, how does this work?" Avi asked. "I cry a bit, tell you what a bitch she is, that sort of thing."

We sat at one of the sidewalk tables in front of Avi's favorite Thai restaurant on Castro Street.

"That's what they do in the movies," I said.

I didn't really know what to expect from this lunch. But Avi seemed revved up and ready to go. She'd even ordered for us before I got there, saying that the panang curry here was the best on the peninsula.

"Don't you do this kind of thing all the time? Girl time?" she asked.

I took a long sip from my water glass and wished it were vodka.

"My best friend is *Dizzy*. He looks at relationships like an intramural sport, so there's not a lot of 'that bastard' and 'you deserve better.' There's just a lot of moving on."

"So, the other night's supportive woman thing…"

"You're my first," I said.

Avi's finger tapped her upper lip.

"God, I wished I still smoked."

"So not a lot of women friends for you either?"

She told me women friends were always difficult. They always wanted something from her. Having seen the crew at the SVWEABC, I could understand why she felt that way.

"I'm not any different," I said. "I want something from you, too."

"Yes, but you're honest about it. That makes you different."

We asked for the wine list and soon a cabernet arrived. Avi pulled out a small bottle of hot sauce she carried in her bag for the extra spicy catfish curry she'd just ordered.

"You know what I don't understand about all of these

movies about women's friendships?" she said. "How do they have time to spend that much time together?"

"I know," I said. "They have time for all those brunches and cocktails. Don't they ever have to do the laundry?"

"Or go to the grocery store?"

"Or scrub the toilet?"

"Exactly," she said, in a way that made me think Avi hadn't seen a toilet brush in years, if ever.

"To real women," she said, holding up her wineglass for a toast.

And then the bonding began. I filled her in on Rajhit.

"So no phone numbers, no texting? He just shows up? And the sex was great?" she asked.

"Well, yeah, I guess you could say that."

"I don't think I could ever get a woman to do that," she said. She didn't elaborate beyond, "I really need to stop dating such young women." But that was fine with me. We were eating curry and drinking wine under an umbrella instead of slaving away in an office. And then my office came to find me.

We were on our second glass of cabernet when I looked up to see Jason.

"What the hell? You're still here?" he started.

"Keep it down," I said. People at other tables turned to look at us.

"You were out most of the morning, and now you're thirty minutes past your lunch break."

Hugo had taken the afternoon off, and I'd told Jason I'd be back at the store in time for him to meet friends for a marathon of the original *Battlestar Galactica* on the Syfy channel.

"Just lock up and take off. I'll be done soon."

Jason glared at me with a look that said that I was ruining his life. He'd hardly had any time in the reading chair since I'd started working in the Dragonfly and he really hated that. But now we were peers, comrades in the great adventure of turning the Unwanted books into the Wanted. Damn it, I'd dusted the entire History section in the short time I'd spent in the store that morning. That earned me the right to whichever springless sinkhole of a reading chair Hugo wasn't planted in, and I wasn't giving that up for anyone. As for today, so what if Jason was going to miss the initial Cylon attack and disco scenes from a seventies sci-fi show? Life was hard.

"I can't leave now, dumbass. My whole freaking day just blew up. There's too many people in the store," Jason said.

"What are you talking about?"

"Customers! You know, people who buy things. The store is packed. And it's *your* fault. I had to get the CIA Bathroom to watch over things just so I could come here."

Indignant, he headed back toward the Dragonfly, yanked open the door, and disappeared inside. I watched as half a dozen people followed behind him. Half a dozen.

"Avi, I think I need to go."

"I think I need to go with you."

She tossed some money onto the table next to our unfinished plates and we hurried down the block and a half to the Dragonfly. My jaw dropped when I stepped inside. The Dragonfly was abuzz with business. John of the CIA Bathroom emerged from the stacks carrying an armload of books and trailing behind two high-heeled, overly perfumed women I'd seen pictures of on real estate ads in the *Mountain View Voice*. The two Mikes were adding up purchases and putting cash in the till. And for each person they were helping there was a line of three or four more customers with at least a dozen or so books.

"I thought you said this store was failing," Avi said. "This isn't what failure looks like."

It was like that for another two hours. Customers came and came and books disappeared and cash stacked up. Jason's recruits manned the cash register. Avi walked through the store taking pictures of happy customers with her cell phone. "Good for the Facebook page," she said. Jason and I scurried all over the store trying to find people's requests. In Jason's perfectly ordered Sci-Fi/Fantasy section, this was no problem. But for the rest of the store, it was just me and lots and lots and lots of boxes. I'd never worked so hard. My brain was fried from trying to find the books people asked for, and my body ached from moving boxes to be able to uncover these treasures.

And then, just two hours after it began, it was over. The store was quiet again. I added credit to the CIA Bathroom's store accounts for their help and then settled into the chair across from Avi with a paper cup of wine that had appeared from nowhere.

"I made a dash to the market across the street," she said. "I thought maybe you could use it."

Jason appeared from the stacks, walking his bike toward the front door.

"I *hate* Meetups," he said, pushing his bike out the door. "Some over-forty singles group saw the store's website and got all gooey and decided to blow up my afternoon."

"So you're working in the shop now, not just volunteering time?" Avi asked after he left.

"Yeah, that was an accident."

"This is marvelous. I wish I'd done something like this in my thirties. You're taking this time to do what you love."

"I don't *love* this. Seriously, look at this place. It's…it's exhausting."

"Maggie," she said, leaning in toward me. "It's a book shop. Who wouldn't want to spend their days in a book shop?"

"Someone who understands what hard work it is. I love reading. I love Hugo. But I don't love the Dragonfly."

I told her about how people would carry in boxes of books that I suspected had been rejected by the local landfill. These boxes had been sitting in their garages on top of motor oil stains and soaking up the leaks from the water heater. There was one box that provided a home for a silverfish colony and another that was the last earthly stop for a possum. The books held the smell of cheap cigars, broken liquor bottles, and even residues of the family barbecue. Their owners wanted top trade-in value, which we weren't giving, and they wanted it in cash, which we didn't provide. And I had the honor of running frantically to the Chinese herb store for Fire Dragon incense sticks that were guaranteed to cover any smell.

"And then there's the books," I said. "There's no way to describe to you the mountains of books here. And they just keep coming."

"The more customers you have, the more books will walk out the door."

I drained my cup of wine and dropped my head in my hands.

"And I am all kinds of broke," I said. "You saw what it was like today. I'm doing this for ten dollars an hour. Avi, I need my ArGoNet job back. I'll take a salary cut. I don't care. I just can't do this."

Avi slipped the wine bottle from my fingers and set it down on the table.

"The board is looking for a buyer for ArGoNet," she said. "This last infusion of funding is just to keep it going until someone comes along to buy it."

So it was over. ArGoNet was just like all the companies I'd worked at before. Only I hadn't started the others, just jumped on the merry-go-round when it was already turning. With ArGoNet, I put the ride together, picked out the horses and the music, and flipped the On switch. Me and Dizz.

"I'm sorry if I've given you a shock," she said.

I shook my head and fought the sob in my throat that the one cup of wine had paved a path for. I guess I'd known for some time that this would be ArGoNet's eventual fate. I just couldn't own up to it.

"Dizzy will land on his feet," Avi said. "People like Dizzy always do. The buyer will want him and the engineering team. Everyone else, we'll have to wait and see. But they'll get good severance packages, Maggie. I'll see to that."

I thought about how long ago my own layoff package was kaput.

"And me?"

"You have to move forward, Maggie. There's no going back. And it's best you don't say anything to Dizzy."

"He knows, doesn't he? He's the CTO."

"Of course. But you probably shouldn't know. I should have said, it's best for me that you not say anything. To anyone really."

We finished the wine, and then I snagged a half bottle of gin from Hugo's office and mixed it with a can of sugar-free fizzy lemonade that probably belonged to Jason. At the front of the store, we turned the reading chairs away from Castro Street so we could survey all that was Dragonfly Used Books.

"Are you *sure* you don't love this place?" Avi asked.

"Okay, maybe a little."

"Give it some time," she said. "It's good that the community has a place like this. Keep it going."

She reached into her Prada handbag, which probably cost as much as my monthly rent, and pulled out a yellowed page from my *Lady Chatterley's Lover*. I recognized Henry's handwriting in the margin.

This morning I stood on the path and listened to the water. I closed my eyes, thinking I'd sensed you. Your words hum on the page, so the air must vibrate around you. I felt a breeze and heard the flapping of wings. I opened my eyes, certain I would see your face. There were flowers and the air smelled of apricots. Perhaps only a part of you found me there, a part I can't touch. But it was enough. For today, it was enough. —Henry

I turned it over and there was a reply from Catherine.

I dreamed of you last night. I could not see you, but you came to me and spoke in a voice soft with promise.

—Catherine

"I found it under the chair you sat in at our last book club meeting. I should have given it to you earlier. I just wasn't ready to let it go."

When she left, I was still in my chair holding the page from *Lady Chatterley's Lover* with the notes on it. I grabbed my backpack from behind the chair and reached into the large pocket where I kept Henry and Catherine's book. But the pocket was empty. The book was gone.

.

The following Tuesday morning, Hugo and I were alone in the Dragonfly. Jason was out of the store for a rare day off. Now was my chance. It'd taken me two days to put the Romance section back together after Jason's rainbow connection. At this point, I was sure Jason was lulled into thinking I was just going to roll over and take his abuse. He was wrong.

The Sci-Fi/Fantasy section lined the west wall of the store, stretching all the way to the back corner and to the door of Hugo's office. While the rest of the store resembled a medieval street grid, Jason's SF/F section could have been designed by Roman engineers. Trade paperbacks were separated from the mass markets, and the series books—*Star Trek*, *Star Wars*, *Conan the Barbarian*, *Sanctuary*, *Thieves' World*, and on and on and on—had their own section as well.

I didn't know much about the SF/F world, but I'd spent enough time in the Dragonfly with Jason to know one thing. You had to respect the series. Books of a series were expected to be found together, which is not a big deal if they were all written by the same author. But some series, like *Star Wars*, were written by many different authors but still grouped together because they were part of the same series. Today I would set them free.

The *Star Wars* books were hugely popular with the Dragonfly clientele, so you'd think Jason would have them displayed right up front. But Jason tucked them away on the bottom row in the farthermost corner of the section from the casual browser's eyes. If people asked him where they were, Jason would slowly start toward the stacks while asking questions like "What does the TIE stand for in TIE fighter?" or "What was the purpose of the Cloud City?" Answer correctly and he'd take them directly to his treasure and give them a discount. Answer incorrectly and he'd motion in the general direction and ignore their cries for help when they got lost. And then there was Grendel, whose favorite napping place was somewhere along the way, so they had the possibility of losing a limb to look forward to as well.

But I had an advantage as I made my way toward the *Star Wars* books. I knew exactly where Grendel was, napping in a cubbyhole Jason had carved out for him on the fourth row, about shoulder level, just under the *Conan the Barbarian* series. Out of the corner of my eye—it was never a good idea to go eyeball to eyeball with Grendel unless you had your own blood supply—I saw him perk up and roll into a crouch. I was wearing a pair of ski gloves, and just as he was about to swat at me, I grabbed him. There was much screeching as I ran to the back of the store and tossed him out the back door next to the garbage cans.

I loaded up an armful of the *Star Wars* books and looked at the spines. Troy Denning. It took me a while to fit him into the

D's in the main Sci-Fi section next to a Cory Doctorow novel. James Luceno, K. W. Jeter, Roger MacBride Allen, Timothy Zahn. All these *Star Wars* authors found new homes among their alphabetical brethren. And when I was done, I moved a few of the *Z*'s down to the empty shelf to camouflage my effort.

"Are you sure you want to do this?" Hugo asked.

"More than I want to look like Salma Hayek."

"And you're sure this frustration isn't about losing *Lady Chatterley's Lover*?"

"I don't want to talk about it."

I'd spent the last twenty-four hours looking everywhere for the book. Hugo and I couldn't find it anywhere in the Dragonfly or my apartment. And no matter how hard I tried, I couldn't remember where I'd had it last. I'd always made a point of putting it in my backpack. And now it was gone, probably after the Meetup, the flush of customers in the store, during which my backpack had been out in the open for any-one to get to. Stupid, stupid, stupid. Now Henry and Catherine were in someone else's hands, lost to me. I wish the thief had taken my wallet instead.

Hugo had stepped over to Cuppa Joe to fetch us a couple of blended mochas, and I'd started on the *Doctor Who* books when a whiff of expensive perfume drifted in with the afternoon breeze. I turned around and saw a girl of about twenty, whose face glowed with a delighted anticipation you'd expect she reserved for a puppy or a member of Cold-play. She fingered the ends of her straight blond hair, which was held back from her face by a faded bandana. Under the frayed ends of her denim skirt, I noticed a brand-new pair of sandals that, if memory served, I'd seen on Zappos.com for around $400. It took a lot of money and effort to look that granola.

"Do you work here?" she asked.

"*Work* is a rather relative word around here," I said, struggling to squeeze a book into its new home. "You could say I'm empowered to help you."

"I'm looking for Jason."

"He's not here today. Is there something I can do for you?"

"No," she said, still gazing around the store. "I just wanted to see Jason."

I took a good look at her. Toned arms and a flat stomach from what I assumed to be years of dance lessons. A tan too deep for the Bay Area, where the beaches saw more fog than sun, so I guessed a recent trip with the parents to Mexico or the Caribbean. The soft hands and new manicure with sparkle pink nail polish led me to conclude the trip wasn't to build homes for the poor. Even the *Che* T-shirt knotted just above her pierced navel couldn't hide the smell of money. How did Jason get on the radar of a girl like this?

"I can give him a message," I said.

"I'll leave him a note," she said.

She pulled out a small pad from a drooping canvas bag proclaiming *Free Tibet* in graffiti lettering. As she held the pad up against the wall to write, I tried not to look over her shoulder. Well, I actually didn't try that hard.

Dear Frederick,

I have, sir, traveled to your kingdom to see for myself all of the riches you have described. It is indeed a marvel to behold. But I have not ventured into the forest yet, not without a guide. I will return when you can show me the way.

Nimue

Frederick? Kingdom? Riches?

When she was done, she folded the note once, twice, and then she continued to fold it into an origami swan. Setting the creature in her palm, she held it out to me, like a princess bestowing a gift on a peasant.

"You want me to give this to Jason, right?" I asked.

"Yes, Jason."

"Short guy. Bit of a limp."

"That's him."

I took the swan and she fluttered her fingers at me in a wave good-bye, and then out the door she went, almost knocking over Hugo, who was returning with our drinks. I followed her with my eyes as she walked by Cuppa Joe, where the Overly Tattooed & Pierced parked in front nearly fell out of their seats.

"Hugo! *She* was looking for Jason."

"Our Jason?" Hugo replied. "Short, bit of a limp?"

"Yep."

"The universe is miraculous."

What peculiar formulas of the universe had brought her and Jason together? I wondered. Were they dating? I couldn't imagine Jason dating anyone. He might have to stop being snarky for five minutes and his whole being would implode. Now I considered what it must be like for someone like Jason to impress a girl. I'd never asked about his limp or his hands.

Nor the odd shape of his head. I'd told myself it would be intrusive to ask, but the truth was I feared his answer. I didn't want to know his tale of woe. I needed him to remain my evil nemesis. But whatever it was that shrank his body and twisted his right leg inward, it couldn't have made any part of his life easy, least of all finding love. And even he deserved that. I tried to imagine Jason in love, smiling, happy. Was it possible? What was Henry like outside of his notes to Catherine? Was he an ogre under the bridge? Was that why he started writing the notes, because he wanted to show someone what was beautiful about him? Maybe this Nimue was a princess after all, here in the Dragonfly looking for her frog. I hoped he would be her prince. And more than that, I hoped she would be worth the defrogging.

I thought about this as I pulled out all the books I'd moved and put them back where Jason had them to begin with, back where they belonged.

·

That evening, Hugo and I hovered in Apollo's stacks, near the space in the middle of the store that had been cleared out for a reading by a local writer. Her memoir had just been published by a small Berkeley press, and Apollo had set up nearly twenty rows of chairs, but only a dozen or so women dressed in the latest from last month's Arts & Crap festival were gathered.

"So I sat, stranded in the desert, alone with the body that had betrayed me, away from the husband who had deserted me, the children who now ignored me, and reminders of the fulfilling career that had gone to a more youthful and vibrant woman. It was then that I first thought of suicide."

I felt a little funny applauding suicide, but the enthusiasm of Hugo and the others got to me and I joined in.

"How long have you known her?" I asked Hugo over the applause.

"Portia? Since the late eighties, I think. We met in a Five Ways to Delay Your Orgasm class at the Humanist Center. I was dating the instructor and was needed for a demonstration. I got to know Portia and the other students quite well in that class."

I'd asked Hugo many times to please convey certain events in his life using the PG-rated version. He often forgot. Or maybe this *was* the PG version.

"And you lost touch?" I asked.

"As people do," he said. "When I saw that she was going to be here…well…all those memories."

We waited for the line of people wanting their book signed disappeared before we walked up to the table to greet Miss Portia. She was well over six feet tall, and while not heavy, she was round like a fertility idol, with a cotton candy cloud of hair dyed a color of red found nowhere in nature. She buried Hugo in a hug that would have suffocated a small child.

"I didn't think I'd ever see you set foot in this store," she said, holding him by the shoulders, looking him over like she'd found a designer shirt in the bargain bin. "Your aura hygiene is so much better than in the old days. You've been purging your toxins, haven't you?"

Hugo introduced me and she placed her hands on the sides of my face as if anointing me for some office.

"My dear," she said. "I hope you find as much wisdom in Hugo's lovemaking as I did when I was your age."

"Portia," Hugo said. "Maggie's not—"

"Oh Hugo, she's lovely," said Portia, squeezing my cheeks into a blowfish face. "You will grow, my girl. You will blossom as you never thought you could. The goddess will awaken in you and all your future lovers will rejoice in your special time with Hugo."

"Oh, Portia," Hugo said, suddenly quite chipper. "That's so kind of you to say."

"It's true," she said, squeezing a little harder on my cheeks. "She's a very lucky young woman. Very lucky and very, very young. Exactly how young is she?"

"Portia," Hugo said, gently pulling her hands from my face. "Maggie and I aren't..."

I think Hugo went on to set her straight but I'm not sure because I had some kind of catatonic break for about two minutes, either from the thought of Hugo and me as lovers or from lack of oxygen. It was a toss-up.

The next thing I remember was Portia reading a poem from her book to Hugo as the Apollo employees snapped the chairs shut around us. "'I nibbled the nimble nectar of our music / And danced with love's ghost / Our sugar-coated courtship sang ripe / With passion's dazzling pleasure.'"

When she was done, she and Hugo were smiling at each other and he was patting her hand. He believed she had written it about him. And whether it was true, she seemed happy to let him think so. They were remembering a different time, if not necessarily a better one, when they were younger and perhaps softer around their edges.

I imagined the future Rajhit, when his parents finally won out and got him married off and back into the corporate world. I imagined him in a suit and with cropped hair at an amber-toned restaurant with his someday wife and in-laws and his mind fading out of the conversation to think about our night together or other nights to come. I was thinking we had at least two months together, tops. Maybe even three. This little game we had going—no contact info, no dates—was brilliant. There was always surprise, always desire. Not daily betrayals that wear away at you and flatten you out. I was going to be the woman he longed for when his mind snuck away from his life, not the one he was sneaking away from. I would never be the betrayed or the other woman. I would be the if-only woman.

Hugo and Miss Portia linked arms, looking a little dazed and a lot happy. They said their good-byes to me while never taking their eyes off each other, and left Apollo, looking as taken with each other as that pixie cut girl and the redhead had on their first meeting at Hugo's. And I was on my own again, wondering at the equations of motion that propel us all forward and back to each other again.

I looked around at all the people moving around Apollo, books in hand, checking out the stationery and journals as a Nina Simone song played softly on the speaker above. *I want a little sugar in my bowl. I want a little sweetness down in my soul.*

I sat on a small footstool near the literary journals, where I was sure to be alone. As Nina sang, I scanned the journals, remembering the literary journal from my own undergrad years. I didn't write for it, but I managed the website, which was a big deal back then. Every quarter, with the new journal fresh off the press, all the students on staff would devour those stories with names like "The Venus Glove," "Mandrake," and "Red River." They were stories to be read aloud around a table of friends in a Waffle House at two in the morning while eating smothered hash browns and pouring bourbon from a flask into our coffee. I reached out and pulled a stack of journals from the rack, read a few lines, and picked out three of them to buy, even though they each cost more than I made an hour. Just holding them reassembled a version of me I'd forgotten.

Something in my deepest core gaped open. I missed Henry and Catherine. I missed the book. I missed their notes. I had all the pictures on the website, but it wasn't the same. I missed running my fingers over the imprint of ink on the paper. I missed touching the same pages they had. I hated the thought of it in someone else's hands, and the realization that I would probably never see it again made me ache.

"Isn't it illegal for you to be in here?" I looked up to see Rajhit bending down next to me, some rolled-up magazines in his hand.

I looked up at him and saw his smile fade into something else when he saw my face still caught up in the memory of those raw late nights. His eyes lost their mischief and grew softer and serious, and he stooped down to one knee so that he had to look up at me a little where I sat on the stool. He reached over and ran his finger along the tops of the journals I held against me, nearly touching my skin.

"What are you reading?" he asked.

I lay the journals on my lap and he came closer so that he could open the covers and read the story titles. As he let out a long breath, I leaned over and kissed him.

As I started to pull back, he stopped me by sliding his hand over mine, the one holding the journals. He stood, looked around, and nudged me toward him as he backed into the small corner behind the *P*'s. And then he kissed me, not the gentle, playful kisses of our night together. This time, his kisses were daring, as if they could scale mountaintops. He leaned into me so that all I could feel was his body and the books behind me. I pulled him tighter, absorbing him into my skin so it would feel like this always.

"My place?" I whispered in his ear.

He shook his head. "The Dragonfly," he whispered back.

CHAPTER SEVEN

The Faithful

Do we pass each other every day? How can I not
know you? Not see your words on your face?
                                    —Henry

I was still half asleep at eight the next morning when I unlocked the door to the Dragonfly. I'd been trying to come in
early, mostly to deal with the eBay orders before the store
opened at ten, but this was the first time I'd actually made it
happen. The night before, when I'd arrived home from that
late visit to the Dragonfly with Rajhit, I'd found a note on my
door from Hugo, asking me to get there early, promising his
raspberry scones and his famous little quiches with bacon and
red pepper if I did.

"Ah! Maggie," Hugo said, appearing from the stacks and
catching me mid-yawn. "We can begin now."

When my mouth closed and my eyes opened I saw that
Hugo was holding an old dented saucepan in one hand and a
wooden spoon in the other, both of which I'd seen on a top
of a shelf in the office and assumed were there by accident.
But clearly this wasn't the case, which made me nervous. Behind him was Jason, holding a box of matches and two bound

sticks of some kind of grayish green dried plant and looking like someone had just told him we were soon to be invaded by *Twilight* fans.

"What's going on?" I asked.

"We have to touch the books," Jason said.

"Now there's more to it than that," Hugo said, banging the pan with the spoon. "We're infusing the books with our energy."

"We have to touch the books," Jason said again, reaching out and flapping his fingers across a row of mysteries.

"So we touch them with pans and spoons?" I asked.

"No, no," Hugo said. "The pan and the spoon are to energize the air."

"Won't the air get energized with the books?" I asked.

Hugo's arms dropped to his side and his shoulders sagged. "Well, now you're just not making any sense." With that, I just kept my mouth shut and went with it.

For the next half hour or so, Hugo walked through the stacks, beating his pan with his spoon while Jason and I followed him like a couple of altar boys with our sage sticks lit and smoking up the place.

"The thing with used books," Hugo explained, "is that they bring their pasts with them. They haven't just popped off a printer's press and then stacked themselves in a box to be sent to a store. They are abandoned here by people who no longer want them. Orphans in a Dickens novel. They are discarded as people move on with their lives. They're too heavy to move or they take up too much space. That's how they end up here. We have to release them of their former lives so they can move on to those who do want them."

Jason had the same look on his face as Grendel did when I blocked his sun. It seemed that for this one moment, Jason and I were allies.

"They're books, Hugo," I said. "People buy them or they don't. I don't think the books have much say in it."

Jason punched my arm and held his finger up to his lips. So much for our allegiance.

Hugo stopped and turned to me, hands on hips, still gripping the handles of the pan and spoon. "You've been very interested in numbers lately, so tell me. How many more romance novels have we sold since you cleaned up that section?"

"I don't have strong data from before," I said.

"How many more?"

"Thirty percent, more or less."

Jason took a step back, and I think his mouth fell open a bit before he caught himself and closed it. I tried not to smile. I didn't want him to think I cared that he was impressed.

"That proves my point," Hugo said.

"That proves that people buy more when they can find what they're looking for," I said.

"But what about what they *aren't* looking for?" Hugo asked. "It's the books that need to be discovered that we're concerned with today. You gave them your energy. People are drawn to them now." He turned, giving the pan a good smack with the wooden spoon. "This is why we energize the air with the pan. This is why we cleanse it with the sage. And after that, what do we do, Jason?"

"We touch the books," Jason said, not even bothering to conceal the grumble.

"All of them?" I asked Jason in a whisper, a little worried now about my morning.

"Just the most misfit of the misfits," he said. "We pick a different section each month."

"Exactly," Hugo said, having reached the office and the end of our energizing and cleansing of the stacks. "Now I'm going to warm up the scones and quiches in the toaster oven while you two decide on this month's section."

He was barely through the door when I turned to Jason and said, "The Westerns."

Jason's eyes grew wide. "There's a Westerns section?"

I took Jason into the little U-shaped pathway at the end of Romance and one short Drama shelf down from History and showed him the one lonely bookcase of cowboy books. There wasn't much here, mostly thin old dime-store Zane Greys and Louis L'Amours, with dry-cleaned cowboys on the covers and green tinting on the edges of the pages. Few came in, few went out. They didn't suit the tastes of a neighborhood that would implode if the free citywide WiFi shut down for fifteen minutes. But I had an affection for these books, with their titles like *Riders of the Purple Sage* and *The Last Trail*, and would borrow one every once in a while, just to dust off the abandonment from them.

"They're all out of order," Jason said.

"The whole store is out of order," I said.

"Except for the Romance section."

"And Sci-Fi/Fantasy."

We paused for a minute, looking at the crammed shelves, trying not to acknowledge that we'd just given each other what could be construed as compliments.

"So how does this work?" I asked. "Do we just run our fingers over them?"

Jason shrugged. "At a minimum. Hugo likes it better if you actually take the book off the shelf though, get to know it."

"We should get a database," I said. "With an ISBN scanner. We could look up inventory and track it. Tell people what we have in stock and don't. Then we'd really know the books."

"Okay, sure," Jason said. "And then we'd have scanners and security stickers and those things by the door that sound an alarm every time someone farts. We don't need a friggin' database to tell us what's here. I know what's here."

"You didn't even know there was a Westerns section," I said.

"We don't need a database. We just need to give a shit."

And then he was gone. Looked like I was giving a shit all on my own.

The Westerns occupied just one bookcase, but because most of the books were so short, there were a lot of them. Even so, it wouldn't take me long to show these guys a little love and make Hugo happy.

I'd started clearing out one shelf to make a workspace to start at least organizing the books by author when I heard the wobbly wheel of a cart turn the Poetry corner. Jason tapped down the cart's wheel brake and unloaded some poster board, markers, and a five-year-old calendar with pictures of the old West on it.

"It came in with a box a couple of weeks ago," Jason said. "We can use the pictures to makes signs that will let people know we have a Westerns section."

We worked for an hour or so, while Hugo served us quiche and scones. I couldn't tell if Hugo was more pleased by the two of us working together with minimal bickering or his belief that we'd taken his theory to heart and were, indeed, touching the books. The thing is, I liked these books. Or rather, I liked the idea of these books, the twenty-five-cent price printed on the cover, the determined faces on the cowboys, the sheer number of the novels Zane Grey and Louis L'Amour produced in their lifetimes.

"I loved these books when I was a kid," Jason said absently.

There were many things I would have expected Jason to say back in the catacombs of the Dragonfly. That he loved these books as a mini-Jason wouldn't have even made the top one hundred.

"I used to read them in the school library," he said. "While I waited for someone to pick me up."

With the image of a young Jason swinging his feet in his library seat to the gunfire of a Zane Grey, I felt the numbness of my own childhood spread through me. I thought about sneaking books upstairs, reading with a flashlight under the covers and a towel along the bottom of the door to hide any light. I remembered the loneliness of hiding who you are from your parents. It was like coming out when I told my parents about what I wanted to study in school. There were threats to not pay my tuition. Looking back, I almost wish they hadn't. Maybe if I'd had to work harder for what I wanted, I wouldn't have walked away from it so easily when the whiff of stock options drifted my way.

"Maggie!" It was Dizzy's voice.

"We're back here!" I yelled.

"Back where?"

"Marco!" I called.

Dizzy Marco-Poloed his way back to us.

"Whoa," he said, looking around. "There's a shitload of books back here."

There wasn't even a bookstore in the town where Dizzy and I grew up, but we would take the books we'd checked out from the library and ride our bikes down to Sweetwater Pond, sit on the edge with a couple of bottles of Coke and a bag of boiled peanuts, and read. Dizzy and me, our whole growing up, we only made sense when we were together.

"Look at this," he said, taking *The Lonesome Gods* from my hand. "You read it like seventy-eight times."

"Whoa," said Jason, looking at me. "How old are you?"

I poked him in the arm.

"There's only one thing that pissed her mom off more than her holing up for an afternoon reading," Dizzy said, "and that's reading something as low-rent as those bodice-rippers and cowboy books."

"Cut it out," I muttered.

"We could do it for a book group meeting," he said.

"Do what?" I asked, putting the book back on the shelf.

"*The Lonesome Gods*. The members take turns hosting, right? You love this book. You should pick this when it's your turn."

"I don't…"

"Come on," he said. "Louis L'Amour is a dead white guy. He's a classic American author. That qualifies, doesn't it? You want to make an impression on Avi? Do something daring. Pick something that's not in Wikipedia's entry for best hundred books of all time. Avi'll eat it up with a spoon."

"She doesn't want to," Jason said.

"Why not?" Dizzy said to me. "You love the book. You just said."

"Dumbass, you don't nominate your favorite book to a book club," Jason said.

"Why not?" Dizzy asked.

"What if they don't like it?" Jason said.

He was right. One's favorite book should be protected, safe from the opinions of others, packed away in one's heart with lilac-scented tissue paper or perhaps copious amounts of Bubble Wrap.

"Okay, okay, whatever," Dizzy said. "But here's the deal. I just got a call from Avi. Patricia whoever the fuck isn't going to be able to host our next meeting. Avi was trying to get in touch with you to see if we'd do it, but you're in the dungeon of cell coverage. So she called me."

"She wanted *us* to host it?" I asked.

"Yeah, well, we're a package deal, right? You and me? Only we can't do it at my place or yours, but I thought I could rent a back room at a restaurant."

"We'll do it here," I said.

"Here?" Dizzy and Jason both said, turning to me with looks that said "in this dump?" on Dizzy's face and "in this sacred space?" on Jason's.

"We can make it work," I said. "The place needs a good cleaning anyway."

"Lemony fresh here we come," Jason groaned.

"Avi will love it," I said, ignoring him.

"How do you know?" Dizzy asked.

"I just know."

"What about the catering?" Dizzy asked.

I handed him one of Hugo's scones and watched him try not to let his eyes roll back in his head.

"We can take care of that, too," I said. "What's the book anyway?"

"It's two weeks away and you don't know what the book is?" he asked, madly trying to catch scone crumbs pouring from his mouth.

"Do you?" I asked.

"It's on the website," he said, pulling out his phone. "I'm not *talking* on the phone," he said before Jason could object. "*Madame Bovary*?"

"Perfect." I said. "French food and a tawdry book."

"Is there a miniseries?" he asked.

"Book!" Jason said, standing on his toes to get in Dizzy's face. "It's a book!"

We'd started to walk toward the front of the store, where I was sure we'd find a copy on the summer reading table we'd set up when I saw Dizzy grab a few of the Westerns off a stack sitting on Jason's cart.

"Can I buy these?" he asked. "Are they ready?"

"Every book in the store is ready," Jason said, lifting the stack from his hands and grabbing a Max Brand as he led him out of the section. "And this one's on the house for putting up with her."

"I'm totally writing about this place on Yelp," said Dizzy.

·

Rajhit's condo was a town house two blocks from Castro Street. According to the flyer in the box below the FOR SALE sign, it featured bamboo floors in the ground floor kitchen and living room, three bedrooms, upstairs laundry, a walk-in closet, all stainless steel appliances, a patch of yard in the front, and a small workshop in the back. Inside, it was empty, except for the living room, which housed a futon, a bike repair stand, which was now suspending my bike in the air, and a small graveyard of bike parts on a canvas tarp in the corner. I peered at a picture on the refrigerator of him and his parents, which showed that at one time this place had been filled with furniture that would make my mother drool. But now everything was gone. And Rajhit seemed happy about it. Though we hadn't discussed the FOR SALE sign.

I was sitting on the futon wearing a knee-length sundress I'd bought at a secondhand shop, and reading *A Duke of Her Own*, while Rajhit gave my bike a tune-up. I liked watching him work on bikes, his face full of solicitous concentration as if he were trying to get the machine to tell him its troubles. He measured the chain wear. He listened to it as he turned the pedal. He applied oil as if it were a potion. These tasks weren't boring to him. They were healing.

"Why do you read them?" he asked.

I looked down at the cover, which showed a woman with her gown half open in the back.

"You mean romance novels?"

"You seem more…" He shrugged, spinning the back wheel against his hand.

"The literary type?"

He smiled at me from behind the spinning spokes. I set the book down in my lap.

"They're fun. The heroines are strong-willed, independent, determined. They command pirate ships and fight in duels and spy on heads of state. It's a good time."

"And the sex has nothing to do with it."

"Oh, the sex has a lot to do with it."

I stood and walked over to my bike, standing barefoot on his expensive floors. The bike and at least three feet were between us, but I still felt my body pull toward him.

"Have you ever been in love?" Rajhit asked.

"That came from nowhere."

"I'm not saying anything," he said, eyes still on the back wheel, seeing if it was straight as it spun. "I'm asking. Have you ever been in love?"

"Sure, I guess. Probably."

"If you were, I'm fairly certain you'd know."

"There's absolutely no guarantee of that."

He stopped the wheel and began freeing the bike from the stand. He sat on the saddle and hooked his arm around my waist, pulling me to him.

"Have you ever told someone you loved him?" he asked.

I thought about the words and how they should feel in my mouth. They should be bigger words, something ungainly and hard to say. Something you have to take a class to learn how to say.

"No," I said. "You?"

He shrugged, so I had my answer.

"So," I said, wrapping a slip of his hair around my finger. "My turn. How many other women are riding around town on one of your bikes?"

"What?"

"It's no big deal. I'm not living with any delusions. I know about Deborah, and I'm assuming there have been others."

His furrowed his brow. "You've been talking to Jason."

"Well, Jason talked to me."

"Maggie, we're grown-ups. We both have a history."

"I know. That's what I'm saying."

"I don't think it is."

He closed his eyes for a second and took a deep breath.

"This...," he said, gesturing back and forth between us, "you and me. It's not been exactly conventional."

"No, it hasn't," I said, hoping this was getting us back to where we were before.

"You know, I'd like to have your number," he said.

We held out for about ten seconds before we started to laugh. Considering all the things we'd done to each other's bodies in the last weeks, it really did seem whackadoodle that we were still tethered together only by chance and circumstance. I pulled out my phone from my pocket and started to ask him for his number so I could text him mine, but there was something about having *Rajhit* and *texting* in the same thought that made me stop.

Yeah sure, we could exchange numbers, e-mail addresses, Facebook/Twitter/iChat IDs, and any other numerous account names. But then what? He'd call, we'd make plans. He'd pick me up at an agreed-upon time. I'd spend the hour before getting ready, worrying if I looked okay. We could make small talk over chicken Parmesan, then sit in the dark with the rest of Mountain View and pretend we thought the dialogue in the action movie we were watching was worth losing our hearing for. We could worry about when to call each other (too soon is desperate, too late is rude). We could plan more dates and make more plans and hold hands while we walk through Pottery Barn, and he could try to impress me with how much he knows about Shakespeare. Or we could just…

I leaned into him and slid my hand around the back of his head, pulling his lips down to mine. This. This is what I wanted. The wonder of this. The anticipation of this. The surprise of this. And then his hands were on my arms, holding me just out of kissing range.

"You're trying to change the subject," he said.

"I'm trying to get seriously physical with you."

"Believe me, I appreciate it. It's just I'd like to move on from the games."

"Games?"

He shook his head. "I don't mean bad games, like we're messing with each other's heads. I mean the fun and games we've been doing. But at some point…"

I stepped away from him. I didn't go far, just to the other side of the handlebars. I felt like I needed to look at him straight on. I could see mild concern in his face and knew it was reflected in mine.

"I'm not good at this," I said. "And I'm okay with that. I don't think everyone has to be. I think it's okay there are some people who aren't. I'm making everyone else look good."

He rolled forward a bit until the front tire was between my knees and he was close enough to kiss me if he wanted to. But he didn't.

"That's not the woman I know," he said.

"We don't really know each other," I said. "Not yet, anyway."

"I think we do," he said, worry gathering on his face. "After everything."

"Look," I said. "I'm a big fan of people falling in love.

Huge. I say, good for them. I wish I knew how it worked. I really do. When Hugo found me that book, when I saw all those notes between Henry and Catherine. I don't know. I just kept reading them over and over, trying to figure it out. I mean, here it was, right? The process. Not a made-up story. A real story. It was right in my hands. And I look at those notes all the time and I try to figure it out. But I can't. Everyone seems to get it. But I don't. And you know? I'm okay with that. Maybe that book disappeared for a reason. Maybe it found its way back to Henry and Catherine. It should be with them. It felt a little wrong that it was with me, the one who couldn't understand it."

I realized he hadn't tried to interrupt me or to argue with me and I'd been too wrapped up in my own rant to pay attention. But now that I was paying attention, I saw what I'd done. He was silent, still, vacant. He didn't argue or try to convince me. He'd gone someplace I didn't exist.

My eyes started to burn and I knew what was coming. I muttered something about having to go to the bathroom and ran upstairs. I stayed there for a while, leaning against the sink. I wasn't really sure what had just happened, but there had to be a way to stop it from going so very wrong. But I'd already started feeling the absence of him.

I walked back into the hall, where the door to his bedroom was open. Like the rest of the place, there wasn't much in there—a bed I'd never been in, an alarm clock next to it, and a battered old book. The book. My book. Henry and Catherine's book.

It sat at an angle on the bedside table, half hanging off the edge as if he'd placed it there after reading it one night. He'd had it this whole time. He'd taken it. Didn't even ask me. Just took it. And right then, I'd wished I'd just left things after that first night, just left them the way they were, all sweet and tender and pure. But no. I had to get greedy. I wanted more of him and I sank my teeth into that desire until I hit the bitter core.

There was a price for passion. I heard it in my mother's voice every time she called me when she was alone in that big house. I wondered what she felt like at the first betrayal. Maybe it wasn't even a woman at first, maybe something small like lying about working late when he went out drinking with his friends. When did she first know? And when did she know that it had gone further?

I grabbed the book and went downstairs.

Back in the living room, it didn't look like he'd moved since I left. I didn't care.

"*This* was in your bedroom," I said, holding the book out to him, grasping the pages together with both hands.

He looked up at me like he hadn't realized I'd left the room.

"The book. Henry and Catherine's book. You took it. I've been going crazy trying to find it. And you've had it all along. You just took it. Stole it."

As recognition of what I was saying filled his face, he started to speak several times. His hands moved toward me but stopped.

"Maggie, I just wanted…," he said. "The notes, I just wanted us to be…"

"What? You wanted us to be them? Henry and Catherine? Well, we aren't. They probably never met and good for them if they didn't. They'll never have to have a moment like this one."

I waited for him to say something, anything. But he just stared at me, his mouth slightly open.

"Keep the damn thing," I said and shoved the book at him. Though he tried to grab for it, his efforts just flung it into the air.

I grabbed my bike from the stand and tried to turn the bike in the direction of the door, but my foot got caught in the canvas tarp he'd put down underneath it to protect the floor. I tumbled onto the floor, surrounded by the pages covered in Henry's and Catherine's notes. Rajhit held me from behind by my shoulders and asked me if I was okay. I looked down at the floor. I could see a scratch, a deep groove in the beautiful wood. I rubbed my hand over it as if I could erase it. He held my wrist, moving it away, moving me away.

"It's not your fault," he said. "It's not your fault."

.

"Believe it or not, someday," Jason said, rattling a pair of dice in his hand, "George Lucas will die and someone with dump trucks full of money will pull up in front of the houses of his heirs and say, 'Here, take all of this money and remake Episodes I, II, and III. We're begging you. They just suck. There are no words for how badly they suck.'"

Seated behind the counter, verifying the shipping address for an eBay buyer of a first edition of *Valley of the Dolls*, I glanced up at the roar of dismay and joy at Jason's roll. It was the second Friday of the month, which meant it was Jason's board game all-nighter at the Dragonfly. Tonight it was Axis & Allies, and Jason had furnished half a dozen bags of artery-clogging snacks and enough caffeinated sodas to light up San Francisco. His friends were a mishmash of IT guys, coders, an intellectual property lawyer, a financial advisor, the Nimue girl, other booksellers, and, oddly enough, Dizzy. Apparently he and Jason bonded over a game of Magic: The Gathering at Cuppa Joe, and Jason invited him to game night at the Dragonfly. "He's like tournament level," Jason told me. "How could you possibly be friends with someone so cool?"

They had all appeared at closing, already jacked up on vindaloo and pearl iced teas and looking for a book fix before hitting the down-and-dirty with the Third Reich. I'd never admitted this to Jason, but these were the customers I loved. They rarely traded in anything and bought books by the truckload, burning through their acquisitions with the heat of a Viking 18,000 BTU range, a rate that made my bag-a-week romance novel habit look like an Easy-Bake Oven. How in the world they found time to read between watching all those reruns of *Doctor Who*, igniting online message board wars about which doctor was the best, and still working sixty-hour weeks in the cubicle farms around the Valley was a mystery to me. Because they actually did read the books they bought, instead of skimming over the trivial stuff and getting to the good parts like I did. They remembered impossibly complex names, alliances, languages, cultures, and family trees. And they liked only about a quarter of what they read. They were in a constant search for that one, that special book that would satisfy their desire for mind-blowing plots, jaw-dropping wizardry, and emotional knife-twisting all at once. And when they found it, they treated the author like a god, traveling across the country and sometimes oceans to attend conventions to meet anyone attached to the stories they loved. They lived in fear of sequels being scrapped by the nonbelievers running the publishing houses, or the author dying before finishing the series. Laugh if you like. Call them pathetic even. But I'd like to see Jonathan Franzen inspire that kind of passion.

In this culture, knowledge was everything, and Jason was the grand pooh-bah, an interplanetary, multidimensional, dragon-slaying, Celtic-punk-rocking Harold Bloom of all things involving swords and lasers. They all came to Jason. I'd sat in that very same spot two days before and watched him pull a title out of the air for a customer with only "there's a man in a wheelchair in a chateau" and "the cover has a picture of a big house on a hill and a girl and boy running away from it" to go on. In less than two minutes, the customer had the book in her hands. As I rang her up, her eyes glistened as she kept saying over and over, "I loved this book as a kid. I never thought I'd find it." At ArGoNet, I saved my customers millions of dollars. But I never made one of them cry from the joy of it.

"I always thought Luke should have gone to the dark side," said Sasha, the redhead from Hugo's party, who I'd discovered worked in the Children's section at Apollo. "Then Leia could be the one who would save the Republic."

"I always thought Luke should have put all those Ewoks in a row, then taken one of those gliders and rammed down the line of them," said Dizzy, lying on his back by the game board, taunting Grendel with his hand.

Jason started to squeal, mimicking the cries of perishing Ewoks in their death throes. His knobby little body shook and he rolled over on his side, holding his stomach.

"Even better," said Doug, the tall IT guy with a Louis XIV mullet who kept telling his anxious cell phone to fuck off. "You could strap each foot to an Ewok and then you'd have slippers that could walk for you."

"Ewalkers," said Jason.

"Esocks," said Dizzy.

Dizzy Frankenstein-walked around the front of the store like he had Ewoks on his feet. Everyone laughed. Everyone except Dae-Jung, the custodian of Apollo's Sci-Fi section.

"I like the Ewoks," Dae-Jung said, rubbing the front of his brown T-shirt over the printed words *Can't sleep, clowns will eat me*. Only I was close enough to hear him, as he was browsing through a table of Connie Willis novels near me. He had a habit of getting up and walking around until it was his turn to roll instead of sitting with the others.

"I like the Ewoks, too," I said, even though it was mostly untrue. But I liked Dae-Jung. I didn't want him to feel all Pluto-ed out in this solar system. He smiled and shrugged his shoulders a little as he turned back to the book he was perusing.

Nimue had started showing up at the Dragonfly more and more often, "helping" Jason shelve books in the depths of the stacks. I'd glimpsed them one day over the top of a row of books in the Presidents section, the faces of all those leaders of the free world staring down on them from the spines. Her arms had encircled his neck, fingers interlaced, the way you're instructed by other girls to kiss a boy in middle school.

And, of course, the canoodling back in the stacks also made me think of the absent Rajhit. I hadn't heard from him in a week, since the scene at his place. I'd pictured the book there with him a thousand times since, and I tried hard to think of why he took it. It was just so weird, how he kept repeating that it wasn't my fault.

"You're so sweet to remember my sushi," Nimue said, staring into the plastic tray Sasha handed her from the grocery bag. "No brown rice? They usually have the brown rice California rolls at Whole Foods."

For the most part, Sasha's face stayed frozen in indifference, but I saw one eyebrow arch upward with annoyance and she lifted the Safeway bag to show Nimue the logo.

"Oh, I see. It's no problem. I don't suppose they had low-sodium soy sauce there, did they? Regular soy sauce always makes me feel so bloated."

This time Sasha's face didn't look so passive.

"There's some in the mini fridge in Hugo's office," I said before she could reply.

"Oh, great. Thanks!" Nimue started to rub her wooden chopsticks together while it became apparent to me that she expected me to go fetch the soy sauce for her.

"It's in the mini fridge," I repeated. This time she got my meaning and pulled herself out from behind Jason and glided back into the stacks as if she were doing me a favor.

Sasha was by the counter now with money for the last *Gunslinger* novel.

"What's the deal with Jason and her?" I whispered.

Sasha looked back over her shoulder, then leaned in toward me over the counter.

"It's penance dating."

Dae-Jung, under the delusion he was being stealthy, sidestepped over from the Connie Willis table. "We don't know that."

"Please," Sasha said. "It's her idea of volunteer work. She's always with the biggest stud muffin knight she can find. But then she gets a crap rep for being a bitch after giving roadhead to that squire her knight sent to pick her up for the Twelfth Night weekend. So what does she do now? She snuggles up to Jason. You know...melt the bard with a heart of steel. He never wrote love poems until she came along. Only battle epics."

These words she spoke, they sounded like English and yet...So many questions swirled around in my mind. Knights? Squires? Twelfth Night? Stud muffin? I started with the most perplexing of all. "Jason wrote a poem?"

"Poems. He's got lots of them," Dae-Jung said. "They're really good. He's a bard in our kingdom."

I was still processing the plural of *poem* when the rest of what he said sank in.

"He's a who in your what?"

"He's a bard in the Kingdom of the Mists," Sasha said. "It's an SCA thing. Society for Creative Anachronism."

"You're telling me that not only does Jason write poetry, but he also...well, I'm not quite sure what a bard does. Are there tights involved?"

"We call them leggings," she said with an impressive eye roll. "Bards write, perform. Sometimes they're musicians. Sometimes they sing. Jason's a poet. He's really great. You should ask to read some of his stuff."

Jason wouldn't even let me go near his Heinlein. There was no way he was going to let me read his poetry.

"No one expects it to last," Sasha said. "But she'll get social cred for the effort and be inserting herself back in line for queen before the end of the summer."

"Look! Look! It's your people!" Dae-Jung held out *Doomsday Book* toward me, then dropped it on the counter like it was going to eat his arm.

"What are you talking about?" I asked.

"Your people!"

"My people are from South Carolina."

"Not family people. Book-writing people. No, not people who write books. The people who write in books."

I snatched up the book and frantically flipped through the pages. Had Henry and Catherine written in another book? It made no sense. *Doomsday Book* didn't come out until the nineties.

"It's there," Dae-Jung said, pointing to the title page. The rest of the group had gathered around me, even Nimue, who draped herself over Jason's shoulders.

"*'To a lover unknown,'*" I read. *"'I have been inwardly guided this day to leave this note for you in hopes that you will find me. Come be the muse for my man song and we will both sing to the Goddess for her blessing, just like Henry and Catherine. Love in all being, Ralph.'"*

Everyone was silent for a moment, until Sasha asked the question that lingered in all our minds.

"What's a 'man song'?"

Dizzy placed his hands on his hips, stuck out his chest, and shook his shaggy red mane.

"You play your man song on your man flute. It is an ancient art only the fiercest of manly men can perform. Be forewarned, it makes gym bunnies throw their kilts over their heads in glee."

"Sometimes I want to crack open your head and look at the pictures inside," said Jason.

Dizzy held up his hand. "Caution, my friend. Many a soul has gone forth there only to return forever scarred."

"This Ralph guy picked *Doomsday Book*?" Dae-Jung asked, taking the book from me. "Don't most of the people die of plague in that book? He couldn't have picked up *To Say Nothing of the Dog*, which at least has romance in it."

Dizzy held up *Daughters of Darkness* from a cart by the counter. "Christ, I found another one. *'I know you're out there. I know you're looking for me. I'll be lurking about in these stacks, waiting for you to come. I'll be watching. Careful, I bite. —Georgie.'* Yeah, well, that's all very…um…" He looked behind him into the stacks. "Okay, it's a little scary. But sexy scary. Anyone got a pen? I'm writing him back."

"That book's about lesbian vampires, lamb chop," Dae-Jung said, taking the book from Dizzy and putting it back in the cart.

"You can't blame them for trying," Nimue said. "I mean, to find your love in a book? How amazing is that? Books are so sexy. Bookstores are sexy. And people who work in bookstores, don't even get me started."

She turned and gave Jason a fashion magazine smile. Behind her, Sasha stuck her finger down her throat. But Jason looked as if Nimue had just unspooled his twine.

"Maybe there's more," Jason said, looking up at her, completely besotted.

Everyone turned slowly, peering into the stacks as if they were indeed the enchanted forest Jason had described to Nimue, with magical chipmunks in the shadows sputtering glitter out their tuchuses. Without a word, each of us started toward the stacks slowly, as if a sudden movement might scare the notes away.

It didn't take me long to find one. It was in *Possession* by A. S. Byatt, basically a personal ad from a woman named Sarah who was looking for someone who would make her laugh and lie on the sofa with her and listen to *This American Life*. A note in another book was a quote from a Neruda poem. And another said that the writer would be in the Shakespeare section every Friday afternoon at two, waiting for someone, anyone, to show up.

I put the books back where I found them. I stood in the middle of the aisle. I could see the image I'd visualized that day with Rajhit in the stacks: that the roof was off the Dragonfly and that I was looking down at all the movement in the stacks. I could see Jason, Nimue, Dizzy, and everyone else inching through the stacks, sifting through books to find those tender confessions of longing. I could feel all the stories around me. Not just the stories conjured by the authors, or even the note writers, but the stories of the books themselves. Someone had bought each one of these books brand-new and fresh out of the box. There was something about the book—the cover, a random page, the summary on the book jacket—that compelled him or her to buy it. But that was only the beginning of its journey. And whatever that journey was, the Dragonfly was only a stop along the way. And now the books all around me were conveyors of hopes that we are not alone.

I knelt down, sitting back on my heels, fingers on my temples, trying to understand what I'd unleashed. But all I could think about was Rajhit. I just wanted to erase the last week and reset at that moment right before whatever changed changed. I wanted to go back and say something else, something that would keep us from that "it's not your fault" moment. Or say something that would make it my fault, because then I could fix it. My mind grasped for something to do, something to say to him. I could leave him a note. Yes, a note. A note in a book. Not like Henry and Catherine with all the gushing and the fireworks. We would be us, starting over with our own book. But what book? I had to find the perfect one. And I wouldn't be leaving it in the Dragonfly. I'd take it to his place and leave it at the door, tuck it inside the screen.

And then I stopped. What would the note say? "Miss you!" with a heart dotting the *i*? "Meet me in the park at noon?" "Call me?" with my sought-after digits? Thoughts of what he would think, what others would think, even what I would think. God, I sucked at this.

I got up and dusted off my momentary lack of dignity. I started to turn to go back to my eBay sales, back to where I was before all of this began, when I was myself. And then I saw them. Dizzy and Dae-Jung. They were at the end of the aisle, a good twenty feet of fiction away from me. Dae-Jung was leaning back against the row of books facing me, Dizzy next to him, turned toward him. They were looking down at a book, in that way that people do when they really want to be looking at each other.

CHAPTER EIGHT

Fortunes and Foils

Old love, new loves. We are never the same with
one as we are with the other.

—Catherine

As he pulled his Volvo into the driveway, the headlights
blinded me and I raised the hand holding the glass of bourbon
to block the beams. Hugo paused at the bottom step to our
front porch, then sat down on the top one.

"You've barely been in the store this week. Anything I
should know about?" I asked.

"Nothing comes to mind," Hugo said. He nodded toward
the glass in my hand. "Anything you want to tell me about?"

"Nothing comes to mind." I drained it.

I'd left game night at the Dragonfly and walked home. The
night air was heavy after a hot day, a rare warm summer
evening. It seemed to be a waste not to drink my way through it.

"I am a coldhearted witch who is impenetrable to the mysteries of love," I said.

Tears welled and rolled down my cheeks as I looked at
him. I rubbed my eyes and felt Hugo's hand on my shoulder. I
leaned toward him and rested my head on his knee.

"What's this all about?" he asked, brushing back the hair from my face. "This isn't about romance novels."

I shook my head.

"Have you eaten tonight?"

I held my stomach. It ached for food. But I wanted to hurt a little more.

We sat there in silence, Hugo rubbing his hand in a circle on my back like I was six and had stubbed my toe.

"When I was in my twenties," he said, "I spent a couple of years in Paris. Okay, I followed a woman to Paris. She left, but I stayed."

"This is going to have a happy ending, right? I need a happy ending."

"Yes, I fell in love with another woman there."

"Oh good."

"Older. Married. Two children."

"For heaven's sake, Hugo."

"We met in the Mélodies Graphiques, a stationery store on Rue du Pont Louis-Philippe. I could not stop thinking about her. I went to the store every day, hoping I would see her again. One day, I looked in the guest book, thinking I might find her signature from the day she was in. As I'm leafing through it, I see a message. *Meet me at La Vinchey*. I knew it was her. It was a restaurant in the Latin Quarter. But the date was two days before. I had missed her. I went to the restaurant and asked after her, but they didn't know of the woman I meant. I was despondent. Then one day, I'm walking through a park, taking pictures, not at all close to the shop or the restaurant, when I see her. She's sitting on a bench, reading a John le Carré novel, of all things. I sat next to her. And it began from there."

"You were lovers?"

"For several months. She would leave messages where she could meet in the guest book of that stationery shop. I had no money. I think that's what she liked about me. That and my Idaho manners. But one day the notes stopped. I came to the shop every day and sometimes multiple times a day. Then one day, the man who owns the shop says to me, 'Stop asking so many questions and listen for the answers. It's time to go home now.'"

I waited for more, the big finish. But he sat quietly.

"Not that I don't appreciate your sharing your personal tragedy there, Hugo, but I'm wondering how that little story's supposed to make me feel better."

"I'm sorry," he said. "Is that what we're doing?"

"There are no limits for how much you suck at this," I said.

"This is not exactly my forte," he said. "Usually when there's a woman who's unhappy in my presence, I do things that you and I don't do."

I pushed myself to an upright position and patted his knee, my knobby pillow, with an alcohol-heavy hand. "And why is that? Not that I'm offering an invitation. But you go all Casanova on anyone else you meet with a vagina and a heartbeat."

His beard stretched across his face as he smiled. He reached out and tweaked my chin.

"You're just much, much too precious."

I felt a good cry coming. I didn't want to cry. With as much bourbon as I had in me, it was going to hurt. I lay my head back down on his knee.

"I don't like who I am," I said.

I felt his hand on the back of my head. "Then I'll have to like you enough for both of us."

I told him about my fight with Rajhit. After I'd gotten it all out, Hugo stood and held a hand out to help me up. We went into his apartment and soon udon noodles were soaking up the bourbon in my stomach. Hugo wrapped a blanket around my shoulders, the faded moose-patterned one he'd had since his days as a Boy Scout in Idaho.

"I brought you a present," he said.

He handed me a small hardcover. Another of the Waverly novels, *The Tale of Old Mortality*. It was part of the same set he'd been reading for weeks, an 1898 edition in fairy forest green and mischievous gold lettering.

"Open it," he said.

Inside the front cover was written, "Betty Valentine, 514 Fifth Street, Indiana City, Iowa." The letters were long and narrow like figures in an art deco painting and below her name and address was a class schedule and a record of her grades in each. Betty was not an exceptional student. But she was a gifted artist. The next pages showcased pencil drawings of young women with long curly hair, their bodies bent over their laced toe shoes. Each one was labeled with a title such as "Exercise A" or "I'll Never Get This One Right." On these pages, their sapling limbs bent backward and forward, invulnerable to gravity. And on the copyright page, she'd penciled the faces of Betty's friends around the date 1897. Darlette, with big Betty Boop eyes and rosebud lips; Rosetta, with a curl slicked down against her forehead; Lodoak, with a pixie cut and a bow; Yamtia, with a beauty mark; and Ricardo, with a pointed chin and pointier sideburns. And on the blank page facing the preface, Betty abandoned the ladylike pirouettes and drew a chorus girl alone on a gilded stage with velvet curtains, lace trimming her open-backed costume, with one high heel lifted off the floor and an arm reaching high above to hold a feather boa and cover her face.

"Why the Waverley novels?" I asked. "I've been wondering."

"I've been wanting to read them for a long time now," he said. "It just seemed like the right time."

"Thank you," I said, holding the book close. "It's beautiful."

We sat in silence for a while listening to Miles Davis play "Bye Bye Blackbird" like a woman had ripped out his heart and backed up over it in a big powder blue Cadillac. And that made me think of another heartbreaker.

"Where do I know the name Nimue from anyway? It's been bugging me."

"Merlin," he said, his eyes still closed, his clasped hands now cupping the back of his head. "She stole all the poor old bastard's secrets, then trapped him in a cave until he went mad. He was so in love he didn't care."

"Jesus Christ on a cracker. Who the hell names their child after someone like that?"

"It's just her SCA name. The Society for—"

"Creative Anachronism. Yeah, I heard about that. How do you know so much about this anyway?"

"It all started in Berkeley in the late sixties…"

"I'm guessing there was a woman involved."

He sighed. "Roxanne de Bouvier was the name she gave herself. I met her in a physics class. She gave quantum entanglement a whole new meaning."

"Please stop there, I beg of you," I said. He chuckled and

I couldn't help but join him. When it came to women, his appreciation was endless, though I'd recently noticed a drop in the number of women who came by the store looking for him, asking about him, asking about other women looking for him. I still couldn't imagine Hugo losing his charm. The earth would have to start spinning in the opposite direction. No more signs of Miss Portia. Even Mrs. Callahn seemed to be keeping her distance.

"This isn't going to end well is it?" I asked. "Frederick and Nimue."

"Nope. Train wreck. Any day now."

"I don't suppose there's anything we can do to stop it."

He yawned, stretching his arms over his head and arching his back, looking a lot like Grendel in the process. "Not a thing."

When I got up to leave, I kissed him on the smooth top of his head and told him I'd see him at the store tomorrow. I tried to give him his moose blanket back, but he shook his head and told me to keep it. It was when I got to the door, the blanket rolled up under my arm, that the words came spilling out of me before I could stop them.

"How would you like a partner at the Dragonfly?"

·

The night of the SVWEABC meeting, the Dragonfly vibrated with the laughter of women. Hugo circled the front of the store offering dates wrapped in prosciutto with one hand and re-filling wineglasses with the other. Waves of giggling whispers followed him as he moved from group to group. He was infinitely pleased to have so many beautiful, smart women in his store at the same time, and I think the SVWEABC was just as pleased with him. I may have provided Hugo, the atheist that he was, a vision of what heaven would look like.

I caught sight of Avi, who toasted me with her wineglass from one of the chairs we'd borrowed from the funeral home down the street. Our preparation for tonight had all the organization and planning of a kindergarten invasion of a Baskin-Robbins. There was frantic dusting and vacuuming, and, right before the meeting, a strategic placement of a ficus tree from Cuppa Joe over a curious stain in the carpet. Hugo had hauled over the side table Mama sent me the day of my first SVWEABC meeting. It looked so natural between the two chairs that I wondered why I hadn't thought to bring it in before.

I stood on the edge of the scene and thought to myself what a marvelous thing it was to be right where I was at this exact time. Even Jason couldn't spoil my mood, though he was trying his best, bless his heart. He appeared at my side with a tall woman whom I remembered as Karen from the last meeting. She was dressed head to toe in black except for Tahitian pearls draped around her neck and a diamond ring big enough, if it caught the light just right, to redirect airline traffic.

"Uh, your friend here is interested in a novel about Vikings," Jason said.

"Sounds more like your area of expertise," I said, bending my head toward him and matching his low tone.

"I suggested *The Greenlanders*," he said.

"Been there," Karen added.

"But she says she's looking for more spice."

"And less scenery," Karen said.

"So, uh," Jason said, shrugging his shoulders, "more your area, maybe?"

"Bare chests on the cover?" I asked Karen.

"You're brilliant," she said, toasting me with her martini glass, which was curious considering I didn't remember bringing martini glasses, let alone vodka. But from the looks of her purse, she could have been carrying around a full bar in there.

"Sandra Hill," I said to Jason and pointed toward the Romance section. He looked at me blankly. "We got in a copy of *The Reluctant Viking* just the other day. Go. You won't get cooties, I promise."

Karen turned to follow him, but glanced back at me over her shoulder.

"Don't you just love men who know their books?" she said, following him with a swivel in her hips that made me a little concerned that I'd sent him back there alone with her.

Out of the corner of my eye, I saw a shadow dart across the floor. When I turned to look, there was Grendel running for the stacks, with the tail of the scarf I'd seen Avi stuff into her purse earlier trailing behind him like the cape of an evil villain. Many thoughts ran through my head. I could pretend I didn't see it. Or Avi could forget she brought it. Or maybe Grendel would rip it to shreds and then present it to her as a gift right as she was leaving. I had to go after him.

In the Fiction section, I managed to catch sight of Grendel turning the corner. When I followed, he was gone. But there was a creaky library ladder leaning against the wall-side shelves. At the top of the ladder I could see the tip of Avi's scarf dangling from a small space between two stacks of books stuffed at the top.

Trying not to think about what peril lay ahead, I started to climb up to Grendel's new lair. From the top came a low growl just loud enough to make me look up. Two green eyes stared down at me from the dark cave of books. This wasn't going to be easy.

I was two rungs up when I caught movement out of the corner of my eye and turned to see Rajhit walking down the aisle toward me.

"You're not going to climb up that thing, are you?" he asked.

I hadn't seen him in over a week, not since I'd left his apartment that day. I'd busied myself with this meeting to distract myself from thinking about him, but now I had to grip the ladder to keep my knees where they should be. He was fresh out of the shower. His damp hair was combed back, a few of the dry strands falling on the side of his head. I resisted the urge to brush them back.

"I've got to get up there," I said, pointing up at Grendel's hiding place.

"I'll hold it for you," he said. As I began to climb, he reached around me to hold the sides of the ladder. I could smell soap on his skin.

"I didn't know you were having a party," he said. "I wasn't going to bother you, but Hugo said he didn't think you'd mind."

"I don't mind," I said, reaching for the scarf. A low guttural growl came from the cave and I jerked my hand away.

"Are you sure you want to do that?" he asked.

"Maybe I'll just buy her a new one," I said. "It couldn't be any more than six months' salary, right?"

I turned on the ladder and stepped down it, facing him, into the expanse of his arms. I tried to pretend I couldn't feel his breath through my shirt.

"I'm sorry about the other day," he said.

I wanted to ask him what happened, but I didn't want the hurt to come out in my voice.

"Everything's changed so much, so fast," he said. "A few weeks ago, I was selling my place, then I was thinking of going to Amsterdam for a while to apprentice at an antique bike shop there. Travel. Maybe come back here and set up a shop of my own. But now I don't think I want to do that. At least not the leaving part."

A wave of laughter washed through the party, and I heard someone call my name. We didn't have much time.

"Why did you take it?" I asked.

"This whole Henry and Catherine thing," he said, looking down at his hand still on the ladder. "It's just gotten out of control."

He slid his backpack from his shoulder and handed me the book. It smelled of leather from a new cover he'd given it and all the pages were bound to the spine with fresh glue.

"I was misguided," he said, handing me the book. "I was going to leave you a note in it. I thought it would be romantic."

"I don't want to be them," I said.

"I know. I get it. I just got carried away with the whole Henry and Catherine thing. It's like online forums, message boards, gaming. People tell each other all sorts of things. They take on personas and the personas take them over."

"Like falling in love with a fellow Blood Elf in World of Warcraft?" I asked.

"Yeah, something like that. It can be freeing. You don't let the world define you. You can be removed from the person the world sees and be your true self."

"Or your true elf," I said.

"I don't want to be Henry and Catherine," he said. "I want to be Rajhit and Maggie. I want to be in this world. With you."

I heard my name again from the front of the store and knew that in a few minutes I'd be back among my guests, drinking wine and talking about our book, and this moment with Rajhit would be over. I hooked my fingers into the neck of his T-shirt, pulled him to me, and kissed him. It was a soft thank-you kiss at first, full of a certain compatible comfort. But then there was more. We held each other tighter, leaning back on the ladder, and I felt my cells fly in the air like confetti.

CHAPTER NINE

Doing Laps

I have abandoned my heart on these pages.
—Catherine

I opened the door to my apartment slowly, not wanting the hinge's teeth-jarring squeak to wake Rajhit, but the door was silent. Inside I found the dishes from last night's supper clean and in the drying rack, a pitcher of iced tea next to marinating steaks in the refrigerator, and, most blessedly of all, a clean bathroom. My heart leaped in the joyful abandon of a woman who didn't have to sponge her own toilet. Mama could keep her three-carat diamonds. Nothing said true love to me like sparkling white porcelain and a whiff of diluted vinegar on the floor. He'd prepped food. He'd cleaned. He'd fixed things. All in a I'm-just-a-normal-guy-who-wants-to-make-my-girlfriend-happy sort of way. With that thought, I froze in the hallway and listened to soft snoring beyond my bedroom door. Was I a girlfriend again?

We hadn't talked much since he came home with me the night after the SVWEABC meeting. He'd slept for nearly all of the three days since then, and in those small windows of time when he was awake, we were too busy with getting-back-together sex to discuss the inner meaning of our reunion. I hadn't asked how long he planned to stay. I found the ignorance liberating. No questions, I decided. If I asked, decisions and actions could be required. I was unprepared for such certainty.

I leaned against the doorway to my bedroom and watched Rajhit sleep, his long body curled under the smooth white sheet. I'd never seen him that still before. He'd always seemed in constant motion, never settling, the bed a ravaged nest the morning after he'd been in it. But now he lay in the same place I'd left him nine hours ago. It was hypnotically peaceful. I noticed my own breath matching his, the full lung expansion of slumber, as the long light of the late afternoon stretched across the room. *To breathe you in, to make you essential to me.*

His first day here, I'd come home to find two Macy's shopping bags in the corner of my bedroom holding a few shirts, jeans, shorts, a pair of leather Trek sandals, and boxers. He kept them there, clean clothes in one bag and dirty in another, never asking for a drawer or space in the closet. I didn't know whether he feared imposing on me or if he wanted to be ready for a fast getaway. He was a traveler with no concern for his missing luggage and who had "gone native" at his destination. Maybe that's what I was. His destination.

Next to the bed, I slipped out of the thrift store dress I was wearing and slid between what I discovered were fresh sheets. I pressed myself against his back, feeling his sleepy warmth against my breasts. He sighed, swimming to the surface, away from his dreams. I reached around and tickled him along the line of hair that started below his belly button and headed due south.

"You're home," he said.

"Just now."

"I got steaks."

"I saw. And iced tea."

"I put sugar in it."

I squeezed him tight. "As God intended."

"You have an unnatural relationship with iced tea."

I kissed him between his shoulder blades and slid my hand farther down, feeling him growing hard beneath my fingers.

"And the bathroom's clean," I said.

"Gnomes," he said. "Noisy little devils. Kept flushing the toilet and giggling."

He rolled over and kissed me. His kisses were different than they were that first night, richer, fuller, deeper. Different from the way I'd been kissed before. It was like visiting a city where you used to live, where things were familiar but you couldn't quite figure out the new expressway.

His lips moved to my neck, and he whispered, "I missed you."

I wasn't sure whether he meant today or while we were apart. *Don't think too much*, I reminded myself, *just let this happen.* I guided one of his hands to my breast and his mouth followed. I encircled his head in my arms and arched into his mouth, feeling I could never get enough of myself inside him. He moved down my body, between my legs. His hair felt like feathers against my inner thighs. I giggled. One of his hands ran up my side and I grasped it, entwining our fingers, squeezing our palms together, and it surprised me that this felt the most intimate of all.

I closed my eyes, sinking into the playful pleasures of his

tongue, and tried to ignore the tiny thought, a gnat in my brain, that wondered when all this would end. Then he was on top of me again, kissing me, and I tasted my self, my innermost self, on his lips.

.

The single greatest bookstore that has ever existed was called Shakespeare and Company. It was born in Paris just in time for the 1920s and was closed during the German occupation in 1941 when, according to legend, the owner, Sylvia Beach, refused to sell a German officer her last copy of *Finnegans Wake*. Miss Sylvia was the binding of the Lost Generation. Thornton Wilder spent time in Shakespeare and Company, as did F. Scott Fitzgerald and Gertrude Stein. Ernest Hemingway wrote about Miss Sylvia and her shop in *A Moveable Feast*. At Shakespeare and Company, books were sold and others borrowed for a modest lending library fee, and writers congregated in its orbit. Miss Sylvia nurtured their egos and their spirits and sometimes provided a roof over their heads in the small room upstairs. She financed the first publication of Joyce's *Ulysses* by selling pre-orders to her friends and patrons around Europe. And though she declined to take on its publication—she did not think it Lawrence's best work, and she did not want to be known as a publisher of erotica—Miss Sylvia's Shakespeare and Company sold *Lady Chatterley's Lover* when it was banned in England and the United States.

Hugo had hung a framed photograph of Miss Sylvia behind the counter of the Dragonfly, of her standing in the doorway of Shakespeare and Company with James Joyce. Sometimes I wondered what she would think of the Dragonfly. I could see her sitting next to Hugo in the store window, amused at all of my bustling about, trying to make the Dragonfly palatable for the Google generation.

My days at the Dragonfly went much like this. Unlock the store around nine. Drink my cheap drip coffee from Cuppa Joe and put out the tables in the front of the store with the bargain books, the ones that lured the passersby into our stacks. Around ten, when Hugo arrived and made tea, a few customers would trickle in and Hugo would help them while I tried to find places for the books we took in the day before. Hugo usually kept the *New York Times* crossword at the front counter and worked on it throughout the day, with customers offering input along the way. Around noon, Jason would appear and I'd take a long lunch so that I could stretch out my time until ten that night and close. The afternoons were a lot busier, and we'd have a steady stream of people until dinner, when it could get outright crowded. We needed at least two more people to help out in the store, but Robert and I agreed we needed more of a financial cushion before we could bring anyone on. And in the meantime, the books kept coming in and going out.

I wasn't the only one who was making changes in the store. Since I'd cleared out a space by the window, Grendel had taken to having his afternoon nap there, so Hugo built a display of cat books around him. Jason had a tall pile he refused to move that he was calling his "project." After I'd done my Romance section makeover for the second time, thanks to Jason, I'd started in on the sloping pile of hardcovers by the cash register. Even Avi contributed, donating an OPEN sign, based on one used by her favorite sweet shop in London, which consisted of four lettered tiles that clipped together. Each evening we moved the N from O-P-E-N to form N-O-P-E.

As I sat on the floor and separated Henry James from James Patterson, Miss Sylvia looked down on me with the knowing look of a sharp truth. Miss Sylvia turned down the opportunity to publish *Lady Chatterley's Lover* for several reasons, but the most basic reason was she lacked the funds. Bookstores are stores, and stores need income to survive. The Dragonfly, like Shakespeare and Company, balanced on an unraveling high wire, and I was the one running around the circus floor with a butterfly net.

.

"You asked me not to send you furniture," Mama said.

In the backyard, I sat with my blue Solo cup of bourbon, alone, looking through the window at Rajhit reading a book in my bed.

"Not usually, but this time is different," I said. "I'd like for you to send me a chair. I know my asking for it takes the fun out of it for you, but you have a need to send me furniture, and I happen to be in need of a new chair."

"Are you drunk?"

I looked down to the bottom of my Solo cup.

"Not yet. You?"

Ice cubes in a jelly jar were my only reply. My mother was alone again in a silence that needed to be filled. I thought of Rajhit inside, alone in my bed. I knew I should tell her about him. But I wanted to keep him to myself for a while longer.

"Mama, do you still love Daddy?" I asked, and immediately regretted it.

"Of course I do," she said. "He married me, didn't he? Gave me a child, a beautiful house, everything I wanted."

"Yes, ma'am. He sure did."

"What a question to ask you mother," she said. "What's wrong with you?"

"I'm sorry. That was rude."

I wondered if she was in the blue cotton housedress that snapped up the front, the one she wore only when Daddy wasn't home.

"What kind of chair do you need?"

"One that's good for reading," I said. "And won't show much dirt. And a floor lamp if it's not too much trouble. I'll give you the address."

"I know your address, Margaret Victoria."

"It's not for my place."

"What have you done now?"

CHAPTER TEN

The Sweet Spot

It is our imperfections that make us more worthy
of love.

—Henry

Jason stood in the platform window of the Dragonfly, staring
at the new chair sitting between the two older ones. He bent
over and sniffed the fabric, which still smelled like the plastic
wrap the deliverymen had removed that morning. It was the
perfect reading chair. Wide enough to curl up into, but still narrow enough to provide easy access to armrests so you could
hold your book at the right angle. The fabric was a warm wheat
color with a faint pattern that would hide drips from teacups
and ICEEs. It really was a beautiful chair. Mama did good.

When Hugo told me he would talk to Jason about my becoming a partner in the store, I did no short amount of fret-
ting. Though Jason and I were getting along, our truce was a
delicate thing. It was one thing to be his peer. It was another to
be his boss. Then I got the idea to enlist Mama's help. We'd finally have three chairs in the store, and Mama got to send me
some furniture. Make Jason happy; make Mama happy. This
chair was the stone with the names of two birds on it.

After the ArGoNet sale, my stock wasn't worth a ton, but it was enough to satisfy both Hugo and Robert, the superhero accountant. I didn't tell Rajhit about this. I didn't talk to Avi or Dizzy. It felt good to make a decision on my own. Ever since I decided to become Hugo's partner, I felt like I'd slid into a groove cut out for me. My days felt crisp and new. I was in motion again.

After giving the chair another good sniff, Jason turned and slowly lowered his skinny backside into the seat. He bounced up and down a bit and then slid back into its cushioned depths, trying not to look too pleased.

"So Hugo talked to you," I said, sitting next to him. "About my partnership in the store."

He shrugged. "Are you seeking my blessing or something?"

"No, I'm a partner here, whether you like it or not."

"So this chair isn't a bribe?" he asked.

"Oh, it's a bribe, all right," I said. "I don't expect you to be happy about this. I'm just trying to reduce the amount of violence."

He slouched down a bit and pulled his knees up so he sat cross-legged in the chair. He stretched his hands out over the armrest. Grendel appeared and rubbed up against it, purring savagely.

"Can I have a raise?" he asked.

"If we increase sales ten percent over the next three months, we can talk."

He seemed satisfied with that. He opened a book and started to read while I went to the counter to run over some numbers to give to Robert when he came in the next day. I would give Jason a raise. He was worth it. Sci-Fi/Fantasy kept this place afloat. Someday, I might even give myself a raise, but until then, Jason's $12.50 an hour would make his paycheck bigger than mine.

The bell over the door rang out, and I looked up to see Gloria's familiar fusilli curls. On this particular Tuesday, though, she wasn't alone. A man followed her. He was not much taller than her, his hair a little grayer, his eyes nearly shut and looking at nothing. He was blind. She pushed open the door with her right hand while holding his hand with her left. He carried her NPR tote bag for her.

"Good morning," I said, hoping to be introduced, but she gave me the same ill-humored look she always did. She bent her arm to lock her and her companion's entwined fingers close to her body, like their joined hands were a football, and trudged back into the stacks.

I looked around. Jason was still breaking in the new chair. The front of the store was quiet. I followed Gloria into the stacks.

It was Tuesday, so Mysteries was her target. I kept my distance, pulling a few books off the shelf here and there and taking a look at them. I told myself I was doing as Hugo liked and touching the books, but I could only think about Gloria and her husband—for I was certain he was her husband.

As she scanned the shelves, she said something to him loud enough for only him to hear. He laughed. I couldn't remember ever hearing Gloria say much of anything, and I certainly couldn't imagine her saying anything funny. But perhaps we are our truest selves with the ones who love us. And there was something about the laugh, the muffled quality, the way his eyes warmed. This was *their* laugh, their alone laugh. When she stood, two books in hand, he reached for her face. When his fingers found her cheek, she patted them against her skin, in that absent way of habit. The small tenderness was like breathing or eating, necessary and essential.

To make you essential to me.

I was intruding. I turned away, a bit ashamed for spying, a bit happier seeing them, knowing that even silent, sour Gloria could be someone's great love.

.

That night, I couldn't sleep. I lay in my bed next to Rajhit, listening to his soft snores. Headlights from a passing car scampered across the walls through the sheer curtains. I rolled to my side, finding again the arrangement of my body when it'd been only an hour or so ago when my back was curved against him, his arms reaching around me, his teeth gently pressing on that bone where my shoulders met, our limbs entwined like jasmine branches swaying in the wind.

We were becoming familiar with each other now, building on the repertoires we'd learned from other lovers, still in that tender phase before maybe-if-we-start-I'll-get-in-the-mood sex or well-I-am-awake sex or I-guess-we-haven't-done-this-in-a-while sex. Sex with Rajhit was fun and joyous and lying there pressed against him again, just for a moment, I curled up under the illusion that it would always be like this. And, at the same time, I was battening down my emotional hatches. This would end. It had to. The alternative was even more unthinkable.

But it was the moment after the sex that was keeping me

awake. We were lying facing each other. He had pillowed his head on his bent arm and was stroking the side of my thigh with the other. And then there were his eyes, looking straight into mine. I pushed back the instinct to say something, to make a joke, to break the silence, to break our gaze. We were looking at each other. Not watching, not glancing up between bites of dinner, not listening, not thinking of what we would say next. Looking at each other, vacant and full at the same time. And then I felt a word on my tongue.

Love. The word seemed to unroll itself through my limbs. Love. I could say it. Right at that moment. I could. It didn't mean forever. People fall in love, they fall out of love. This wasn't any different. There would be an unspoken "for now" on the end of it. He would understand that. I could taste the words, flavored with sea salt from the distances they'd traveled through other people's lives to finally be in mine. But I pressed my lips together, knowing that even the smallest of sighs would give it enough room to come tumbling out. *You cannot put the glass back in the pane after it is broken,* Catherine had written back to Henry. What is said cannot be unsaid. So I said nothing. And then the desire to say it came back again. I would this time. But his hand stilled and fell between us. And that's how I ended up wide awake and listening to him snore.

I slid out of bed and walked into my dark kitchen. I poured myself a glass of bourbon. I downed it and poured myself another. My phone buzzed on the counter and the screen lit up with a text message. It was from a budgeting app I'd downloaded. "We love you! Do you love us? Rate us on the App Store." Great. Anonymous engineers could say it, and I couldn't. I gave them one star.

I felt it. I was pretty sure I felt it. You'd think with all the novels I'd read in my life, with all those people falling in love, I'd be more certain of the symptoms in myself. But maybe that was the problem. Maybe I wasn't really in love. Maybe I was just going through the motions, trying something everyone else already had tried, like going to a Chili's.

In the dark and the quiet, I mouthed the words. I. Love. You. That wasn't so hard. I did it again. Nothing happened. It was still dark and quiet and the bourbon bottle was still mostly full. So far, so good. I snuck down the hall to peek in the bedroom door. He was still asleep. I went back to the kitchen and tried again, this time with sound. "I love you," I said to the night. Then I ran down the hall again to be sure he was still asleep.

Back in the kitchen, I practiced some more. This was getting easier. The words picked up momentum, racing out of my mouth like a toddler finding his legs. I felt proud of myself. I went back to the App Store and changed my rating of the budgeting app to five stars.

I reached for *Lady Chatterley's Lover* on the edge of the counter. I held the book shut, cupped in my hands like a Magic 8 Ball, closed my eyes, said "I love you," and dropped the book on the counter.

Are we waiting for our most perfect selves, for all our scars to disappear, for the rearrangement of time and science to erase our defects? With more time before we meet, will we be able to excavate greater kindnesses or contentments from our souls? No, it is not for our perfections that we are loved. It is our imperfections that make us more worthy of love. —Henry

I heard low voices outside. Peeking out the kitchen window, I saw Hugo sitting on the top steps between our apartments. Mrs. Callahn was in the yard, leaning against the tree, her voice quiet in the dark. Then she walked up to him and took a sip from the mug he was holding. I started to leave the window, thinking I would get dressed and join them. But there was something about the way Hugo looked up at her, desperate and weary, like a knight who had traveled too far on his quest and couldn't remember the way home. After a few words I couldn't make out, she reached out and tenderly placed her hand on his bent head. I felt as though I'd never seen two people be truly alone together before.

I let the curtain drop and went back to bed. Even after the bourbon, I felt a current of nerves just beneath my skin. In my mind, I turned the picture of Hugo and Mrs. Callahn over and over, trying to understand what I'd seen.

I lay next to Rajhit, propped up on my elbow. I leaned over and whispered in his ear everything I wanted him to know.

CHAPTER ELEVEN

Breaking the Glass

This cannot be undone. You cannot put the glass
back in the pane after it is broken.

—Catherine

Sitting in Pioneer Park, I looked up from my book and
watched the people scuttling by. Though the apartment complex across the street was quiet—all the Googlers had already
shuttled away to their campus to plot to change the way we did
everything—the park still buzzed with people rushing back to
their offices, takeout in one hand, phone in the other.

Five weeks. That's all it had taken to reassemble my life. I'd
gone from not wanting to admit I was spending time in the
Dragonfly to being its co-caretaker. Five weeks ago, I'd been
desperately pursuing Avi for her help in finding a job. Now she
and I had tea, drinkable tea, in the office of the Dragonfly as
we went over financial statements with Robert and looked for
ways to firm up the store's financial ground. Five weeks ago,
talking to Jason was like enduring a pesky itch in a place it
would be impolite to scratch in public. Now he and I seemed
to have struck a truce. He'd warmed up to the website I created
and was now manning our blog under the name Lummox.

He answered questions about books (yes, we have *Harry Potter* in Spanish), our new hours (10 a.m. to 10 p.m.), and whom one would have to kill to get into the Friday night game night (the list was long). And they asked if we'd ever found out anything about Henry and Catherine (nope...nada...zippo). Five weeks ago, I was still nursing, if not an injured heart, then a disappointed one. And now I sat under my favorite tree on Hugo's moose blanket, just a few paces from where Henry had waited for Catherine, feeling my senses ripen because I knew Rajhit was close by.

Pioneer Park was just a couple of blocks from the Dragonfly, wedged right in between city hall and the library with side street access so you'd know about it only if you were going to check out books. A small plaque at the entrance to the park nearby told us all this place was originally a nondenominational cemetery donated by Maria Trinidad Peralta de Castro in 1861. But now it was filled with grassy knolls and overfed squirrels. Wide wood benches lined its pathways and oak trees looked down on the buildings around them as if they were company who had stayed past their welcome.

My favorite tree was a large oak with one branch slung low to the ground so, with a little help, it was sittable. As I waited for Rajhit with two lamb shawarmas, I'd spread out on a blanket, shoes off, my toes in the grass, and read a Laurie Colwin novel. (How could I have made it so far in life without Laurie Colwin?) Rajhit was late, not by much, but still a bit late. *Lunch in the park?* I'd left a note in the pocket of his jeans the night before, and when I got to the Dragonfly this morning, a single word on the torn corner of a yellow legal pad was pinned to the inside of my backpack. *Yes.*

I stood and stretched and stepped across the nearby path to the fountain. Henry and Catherine's fountain. *Sunday is the first day of summer. Meet me in Pioneer Park, by the fountain, noon.* This was the one note I'd kept to myself, a little bit of Henry and Catherine that was all mine.

I'd read Henry's and Catherine's notes over and over again, looking for patterns, trying to identify that one moment in which they knew their lives were linked. For the life of me, I couldn't see it. I felt like I was looking at one of those modern paintings that was all one color, and seeking all the emotions the artist left on the canvas. Instead I just saw a block of purple, and I felt stupid.

The fountain was tucked away in a small Japanese garden close to the back entrance of the library. It was small, modern-looking (no peeing cherubs, thank goodness). I walked the gravel path around it. This was the spot where Henry met Catherine on that first day of summer, in a time when men wore suits and hats to baseball games and women wore pearls in the afternoon and carried clutch purses in white-gloved hands. I imagined Henry there, played by Van Johnson...no, Montgomery Clift, pacing anxiously, trying not to look at his watch. A woman would walk toward him and he would hope that this one would stop at the fountain and he would have at last found Catherine. He would try not to stare, not to grin, not to seem a fool in this small town, at least not until he was sure it was indeed her. But one by one, they would pass him by and he would watch them go with a tip of his hat. Then a slim Elizabeth Taylor would turn the corner and he would know. They both would know. They would be shy at first, having revealed so much of themselves already and now losing the courage of anonymity. And then he would take her hand and, well, all would be spoken.

I wondered if there was anything left of them on the ground they'd walked on in the park. Maybe I could organize an archeological dig. I would find DNA evidence that we could feed into a supercomputer, one of those fictional ones in the movies that make impossible leaps of logic to get the hero the data he needs. I could piece them together and give the Dragonfly's followers what they craved.

But I didn't want to know what happened to Henry and Catherine. I wanted the knowledge of their fate to be slipped into a bottle and tossed at sea. They weren't characters in one of my paperback romances. Chances were that if they had gotten together, they were somewhere nursing the wounds of decades of betrayals—some small, some big. Against my better judgment, I hoped they weathered them and had found some happiness together.

I shook my head, trying to clear out those thoughts. *Rajhit. Rajhit.* This was me and him, not my parents, not Henry and Catherine, not me and Bryan. This was me and Rajhit. I focused on the water, the sound of it pouring into itself, the sparkles in the sunlight. I circled it slowly, chanting our names under my breath, focusing my thoughts on where they belonged. *Maggie and Rajhit. Maggie and Rajhit.* "We decide who we are," he'd said to me. "There's only me and you."

As I came back around to the front of the fountain again, the heat of the day was starting to get to me. I bent down to dip my hand in the water and splash a bit on my face. And that's when I saw the small plaque bolted to the fountain.

DONATED BY MOUNTAIN VIEW'S SISTER CITY IWATA, JAPAN. DEDICATED FEBRUARY 2009.

I stood. I must have misread it. It was hot. I was bent over. Must have been a little dizzy. I stooped down and read it again and then again.

DEDICATED FEBRUARY 2009.

February 2009? Five months ago? That must have been just the date of the dedication. The fountain had to have been here for longer, like decades, for Catherine and Henry to have met here. I looked more closely at the fountain. Fresh-cut granite, clean lines along the ground, no moss and hardly any dirt on it. Then I noticed a small black wire running into the back of it. My eye followed it to a solar panel in the bushes that must be running the pump. The fountain was new.

Help. I needed help. A woman walked by in a brown City Parks uniform, carrying a litter harpoon like a walking stick. Under a wide-brimmed ranger hat, silver hair framed her tulip face, which was adorned with bright pink lipstick. A badge on the front of her shirt read "Gray Badgers Volunteer Ranger."

"Excuse me," I called after her. She turned, her face beaming. "Can you please tell me how long that fountain has been there?"

"A few months, I guess, more or less," she said. "Lovely ceremony. Not many people, but the cookies were from that new Indian bakery on El Camino Real. The one that doesn't use eggs."

"And there wasn't another fountain in the park before then? Maybe in the sixties?"

"Oh, no, dear. There's never been a fountain here before. This was still a cemetery then. My children used to play hide-and-seek here on Halloween night. Better than egging people's doors, I thought. My husband, Albert, though…"

She was still talking, but I wasn't listening. I was chewing over what I'd just learned. The fountain was installed in February. There wasn't anything here before then. There was no fountain until *February of this year.* The park was a cemetery in 1961. I pulled out my phone and scanned through the pictures, looking at the ones I'd taken of the notes. There was one of the title page of the book, the one with the date on it. *1961.* I'd always wondered which of them had written the date on the title page. And as I zoomed in on the date in the photo, I finally knew the answer. Neither of them. The ink was different. The handwriting was different. Neither of them had written the date. Henry and Catherine weren't writing the notes nearly fifty years ago. They were writing them this summer.

"…but after Albert died, I didn't give a rat's ass what he thought anymore…" The Gray Badger was still talking.

"I'm sorry, but can you tell me when the first day of summer was this year?" I asked.

"First day of summer, first day of summer," she muttered, tapping her temple with her gloved hand. "Oh, wait. We can check the calendar." She pulled a small leather backpack to the front of her.

"It's okay," I said. "I've got my phone."

"Hold this, dear," she said, ignoring me as she passed me two lipsticks, a packet of tissue, and a coupon book to hold while she dug around in the well of the bag. "Ah, here we are." She pulled out a booklet calendar and riffled through the pages. "There, June twenty-first. Of course. Summer solstice. I remember now. We had a lovely ceremony, just me and the girls you understand, out on Brenda's property up in the Santa Cruz Mountains. Built a big fire, danced around naked, gave blessings to the Goddess Gaia. At least, I think it was Gaia. Anyway, wonderful night. Not like the old days though, when we were all couples. That was a time. Are you all right?"

I had to sit down. My heart felt like it was going to beat right out of my chest. I thanked her and sat on the bench facing the fountain. Two small children were running around it, swiping their hands through the streams, laughing, flinging handfuls of water at each other. I tried to piece everything together.

Okay, I told myself, you can figure this out. The first day of summer was June 21. The SVWEABC meeting was…when? I woke up my phone again and checked the blog. June 20. So Hugo brought me *Lady Chatterley's Lover* out of the Dragonfly the night before, the nineteenth. How many days before the first day of summer did Henry leave the note? Four? Five? A week? Had Catherine had enough time to see it before Hugo brought it to me? What is enough? And if not?

"For fuck's sake, why couldn't they do Match.com like normal people," I said a little too loudly. The kids playing in the fountain stopped and stared at me. "Yes," I said to them. "I'm a bad woman who ruins people's lives and curses in public." I waited for the maternal units to swoop down on me, but they seemed too busy gossiping on a blanket nearby.

I had to put *Lady Chatterley's Lover* back where Hugo had found it that night. Maybe it wasn't too late. Maybe Catherine came to the store every day hoping the book would reappear. I tried to remember the Dragonfly customers from before its renaissance. There hadn't been that many. It shouldn't be hard. Was there a woman who came in a lot? Hugo would remember. I had to talk to him. And for heaven's sake, I had to take down the website. I had to take down everything. I thought of those notes—those dear, tender notes—I'd broadcast to the entire world.

I jumped up, ready to grab my things, but then I saw Rajhit walking toward me. Rajhit. He would help. I wasn't on my own. Rajhit would help. He saw my face and walked faster over to the bench.

"What's wrong?" he asked, his hands on my arms, guiding me to sit back down. I felt like he was holding all my parts from spilling out.

"I have to go back to the Dragonfly," I said. My hand grabbed at the front of his shirt.

"Sure," he said, but not moving, his face more worried. "Tell me what's wrong first. Are you okay? Did something happen?"

"I have to put the book back," I said. "I have to talk to Hugo."

"He's not there," Rajhit said. "I ran into him as I passed by the store. Said he had an appointment. Maggie, please, tell me what's wrong."

"Henry and Catherine," I said. "They're real. I mean they're here. Today. Those notes weren't from 1961. They were from this year. Just a few weeks ago. They're out there. And I don't know if she saw it. His last note. What if she didn't? What if she just thinks he abandoned her? I cannot believe this is happening. What did I do?"

His hands loosened around my arms, and I watched his face as his next breath came much harder than the one before. Why wasn't he more surprised? He just looked so sad. And in that moment, I knew everything was worse than I thought.

"How do you know?" he asked.

I stood and took him to the plaque on the fountain.

"We have to go," I said, pulling at his arm, but he stood still, holding on to my hand to keep me with him.

"Maggie, wait," he said, not looking up at me.

There was something in the vacant way he held my hand that made me stop. And when I turned to look at him, I knew I was in the moment right before everything was going to change.

"I'm Henry," he said.

He looked up at me, holding my hand in both of his while I felt the blood in my body scatter, not knowing which way to go. The moment hung in the air like a paper airplane that had flown too high before resolving itself to gravity. He tugged on my arm to guide me back to the bench. All the park sounds around us disappeared.

"But I'm not Catherine," I said, trying to fit all of the new values into the same old equation.

"I thought you were," he said. "That night in the backyard with the cigars. The book had disappeared, Catherine never showed up at the fountain. And then there you were, the day we were supposed to meet, with the book, and I thought, *She knows who I am*. But you didn't say anything, so I asked you about the title. *Tenderness*. And you said exactly what she had said, and I thought, *Here she's been this whole time*."

My brain raked through scattered bits of memory. That

night with the cigars, the Laundromat, the party at Hugo's. There had to be something there, something that I could show him. *See, this is why you should have known I wasn't Catherine. This is why you shouldn't have... just shouldn't have.*

"I put their notes all over the Web," I said. "You let me do that. You let me put *her* notes out there."

"I thought you were asking me if it was okay, that night in the Laundromat. I thought you didn't say anything because you wanted to keep up the pretense, another game. I was captivated."

He made a small move of his hand toward mine, but stopped himself.

"That day you were tuning up my bike," I said. "When I found the book at your place. That's when you knew the truth."

He nodded.

"She's out there," I said. "Thinking you deserted her. Thinking you gave the book to me to exploit for the Dragonfly. Oh God."

"I tried to find her," he said. "I put a letter back where..."

"Where you and she used to write to each other."

"Where the book used to be. But she never came for it."

"Your letter to her," I said, not at all gently.

"You're acting like I cheated on you. I didn't."

"No, you're not cheating on me. You're cheating on *her* with me. You *loved* her," I said, shoving the word at him.

"I love you."

"Because you thought I was her."

He dropped his head in his hands. I watched his shoulders rise and fall.

"When I thought you were Catherine," he said, "I was grateful. I couldn't believe how lucky I was."

I felt a breeze on my neck. The kids were splashing in the fountain again. A lizard sprinted under a shrub.

"I couldn't have written those notes."

"You don't know that."

"I do. I know that I never would have written back to you. I know that."

"But you would now."

He was right. I would now. I would now because I was a besotted creature with no free will. I would have written to him because my heart quickened whenever I heard him on my doorstep. I would have written because I brimmed with wonder every time I opened my eyes to see him. I would have written because of all he means to me. Only none of it was real. The person I was when I was with him existed only because he thought I was Catherine.

"It's all a lie," I said, forcing the air through my lungs to push out the words.

"Please don't say that," he said. "Please, Catherine."

We both stopped breathing. He loosened his grip on me and I stood, stepping away, floating from his grasp like a balloon released from a child's hand. We looked at each other, knowing what had been said could never be unsaid, and I felt the physics of things come undone.

CHAPTER TWELVE

Unexpected Ripples

It is no use to look ahead for what is coming. It will come all the same.

—Henry

"It was Jason's idea," I said. "Hugo didn't approve at first. Too negative. But Jason played the whole yin-yang angle on him, telling him that if we make recommendations for books we love, we should also warn people about books we hate."

I stood in the middle of a small group gathered around the teppanyaki chef making dinner in Avi's outdoor kitchen that, with its marble countertops and wet bar, looked like a Weber with a God complex. The chef poured oil into a volcano made by stacking sliced rings of onion and flames shot up toward the sky. The wine-lubricated crowd applauded. I didn't know how much Avi was paying for the catering, but she might have been better off picking up the tab after an evening at Benihana.

"So why have signs up in the store warning people against buying your product?" asked a silver-haired man named Larry who worked for Avi's venture capital firm and had been by my side all night asking questions about the Dragonfly.

"Not warning them against the books. Just suggesting they

might make a nice gift for someone you don't really like, like your mother-in-law or a neighbor whose dog pees on your hydrangeas. Jason looks at it as a public service."

The group around me laughed. I was here, with CEOs and venture capitalists. In my life at ArGoNet, I never would have met these people. I was high up the food chain, but I wasn't an executive. Board members, investors? None of them knew who I was. It took the Dragonfly to get me here. Because of the Dragonfly, these people laughed at my tales of bookstore labor. I was unique. I was hip. I wasn't one of them or trying to be, and it gave me the freedom to be comfortable around them. This is what I missed out on in high school.

When Avi invited me to this dinner, I turned her down. I didn't want to go a party. I just wanted to pour a highball, crawl under the covers, and not think about Rajhit. I'd been working twelve hours a day at the Dragonfly with no breaks, no reading, hardly any eating. Just work. Work would put me back together. For the first couple of days, I worried that maybe Rajhit would come by. I was a quivering mass of "I don't want to see you." But he didn't, and the sun came up and went down every day regardless of what had happened, as if being lied to was just a cute little hiccup on the road to a rom-com happy ending. Fuck the sun. Fuck rom-coms. I hurt in a way I'd spent my entire life trying not to hurt. Rajhit had burrowed himself into my marrow, injected himself into my veins. And I'd let him. So I was pissed at myself as much as I was pissed at him. And I told no one why. Not even Dizzy. It was my hurt, and mine alone. Well, mine and Catherine's anyway.

Hugo and Jason could tell something was up and kept their

distance, but Avi kept calling and telling me how all these people wanted to meet me and hear about the Dragonfly. I didn't want to go. I told her ten times over I didn't want to go. Until it hit me. Software start-ups look for capital among people like this all the time. Why not the Dragonfly? Maybe one of these vulture capitalists would want to buy themselves some community credibility. So here I was like a late-night infomercial host, talking up the Dragonfly like it sliced, diced, and made julienne fries and these people were insomniacs with high-limit credit cards.

"And what about Apollo Books and Music?" Larry asked. "What do you know about them?"

"No matter what branch you go to, their restroom is always located in the Children's section."

I basked again in another round of laughter. They were eating out of my hand. I was goddamn charming.

"Apollo Books and Music is owned by the McNeil family," I said. "They have twenty-five stores in Northern California and Western Nevada. Books, CDs, and DVDs. And their stores are too big. Thirty thousand feet to sell books? Please. There's a reason only about half of the store is books. They need all that nonbook crap to stay afloat, I guess. And DVDs and CDs in the era of iTunes? No way. I'm convinced all we have to do is wait them out."

"We?" Larry asked.

"Well, the Dragonfly."

"You think you can topple them?"

"I think we can do anything."

I wasn't going to say it here, in front of all these people I was hoping would invest in the Dragonfly, but I honestly didn't have a problem with where people bought their books. Apollo, Amazon, Barnes & Noble, ebooks, the Dragonfly. Who cared? I didn't think the problem was where people were buying their books, but that people weren't buying enough books. We still needed storefronts, just to remind people we were there, with people inside who knew what they were talking about. There was no way the Dragonfly would ever put Apollo out of business, and I didn't think it should. But that didn't stop me from displaying the kind of entrepreneurial bravado I'd seen a thousand executives do a thousand times. I half-expected the party guests to pull out corporate-speak bingo cards and start marking off squares.

As the food was served, I looked over the rim of my wineglass at Dizzy, whom Avi had insisted I bring, talking to two men in polo shirts. He was drawing something on a napkin and moving his hands around as he talked. I didn't have to be within earshot to know that he was talking about code. His face was bright and joyous and his smile a little crooked like it got when he was high on algorithms. And he laughed that death-defying laugh of his. My heart felt a little lighter watching my friend. Avi had promised me when she invited us to this evening that he would have people to talk to. I was grateful that it was true.

I scooped another glass of wine from a passing tray and went to sit in one of the teak wood loungers lining the infinity pool. Beneath the murmur of the pool's waterfall, I could hear a soft soundtrack of fusion jazz and the conversation of people who didn't have to worry about how to pay the electric bill. It was one of the few nights around the San Francisco Bay when you could sit outside without a jacket. It wouldn't have surprised me if Avi had special-ordered the tropical temperature along with the sushi appetizers. I liked this. I wanted more of this.

I heard the click of high heels and opened my eyes to see Avi slipping out of her slingbacks and draping herself in the chair next to me. She held her glass near the rim, as if daring it to slip to the ground. It wouldn't matter if it did. There were dozens more waiting on the caterer's trays. At Avi's, there was always more of everything.

"Enjoying yourself?" she asked.

"Miraval is for suckers."

She reached over the side of her chair and held a hand out to me, taking mine in a way that was almost sisterly.

"I'm so glad you agreed to come," she said.

"Thank you. And I don't just mean for tonight," I said.

"I hope I've been a friend."

"The best," I said. "The kind with good advice and a house I consider a vacation destination."

She laughed and sat up on the edge of her chair, leaning forward over her clasped hands.

"I was waiting until later to share something with you, but I can't wait. Come with me."

We picked up our shoes and carried them in one hand and our wineglasses in the other, giggling like two schoolgirls sneaking into the principal's office to raid the confiscated pot supply. Inside the house, I followed her down the hall into a room that was obviously her home office. Like everything else in Avi's home, the room felt feminine, but powerful. It was the room of a woman who knew exactly who she was and her place in the world. A chenille-covered Fortress of Fuck You. *Someday*, I told myself. *Someday*.

She waved me toward the sofa on the opposite side of the room from her desk, where she picked up a leather portfolio. She wrapped her arms around it, sat on the edge of her desk, and grinned at me.

"I've always thought," she said, "that the moment right before you get what you want is often better than when you actually get it. I want you to live in this moment right now. What I'm about to give you is not a gift. It's something you've earned. But this moment is my gift to you. I want you to feel it, so you can remember it always."

The air got still around me. Looking back, I wonder sometimes why my mind didn't start spinning around to all the possibilities of what was about to happen. But there was always something about Avi, something seductive and exciting, something that just made me want the next moment to happen, no matter the cost.

She held out the portfolio to me. I held it with all the anticipation her words had conjured. I opened it. Tucked inside the right pocket was a letter addressed to me. It was an offer letter. The salary figure, bolded in the first paragraph, far surpassed what I had ever hoped to make at ArGoNet. The logo at the top of the letterhead was revamped but still recognizable. It was Apollo Books.

Avi knelt in front me, sitting back on her heels, smiling up at my confusion.

"We bought them," she said. "Me, Larry, a few other partners. We put in our own money to form a buyers' group and got some additional capital from one of the funds in the firm. You met Jim earlier tonight. He manages the fund."

"You bought Apollo."

"Yes. And we want you to help us run it. Make it so much more than what it is today. It's a chain, sure, but only because they have the number of stores they have. Really, it's just a family business and they're still running it that way, and losing money by the fistfuls. But we're going to take it to a level where we can compete with the larger chains. And you're going to help us."

In my stomach, a beehive of questions buzzed. I couldn't grab hold of one fast enough to get it out before another one flew by.

"I knew that first day we met you were special," Avi said. "Nothing makes me happier than finding talent in unusual places. In just a few months, you turned that little store into a valuable property. Well, as valuable as a used bookstore can be, I suppose. But the point is, we believe in you. And we want Apollo to be so much more than a book and music store. We want to get into new media. We want to take it to a new age, meditation rooms, gathering places where people can come and discuss ideas, debate, philosophize. The culture of book lovers you've created at the Dragonfly can grow over and over again. Publishers will be begging you to put their books up front. And they'll pay handsomely for it. You can give exposure to the authors you think people should know about. You'll affect the thinking and reasoning of all our customers. You'll be one of the most influential women on the West Coast."

Her words were so beautiful, unlike anything I could have imagined. I was going to make a really good living selling books and in clean, new bookstores that I could take my mother to. I wasn't going to have to live on macaroni and cheese anymore. I'd never taste instant ramen again. I was going to have a car and health insurance and books whenever I wanted them. New books.

"What about the Dragonfly?" I asked.

"Put it behind you. Better yet, bring what you love about it with you. It's brilliant, don't you see? Smaller community stores. Just like you said. Hugo, Jason. They can work in any store they like. They're fantastic. Hire a hundred more like them. You've hit on the perfect formula. Now it's time to replicate it a hundred times over."

An image popped into my mind of Jason and Hugo in matching polo shirts.

"They're people. I can't just copy and paste them."

Avi stood and walked to her desk. She paused for a moment and then turned back to me.

"Maggie, I have some news for you," she said, like she was telling a toddler the price for a tooth under the pillow just dropped. "To finance the deal, we had to sell off some real estate holdings. It was highway robbery what the buyer got for the properties, but one must do what one must do in these times."

"What does this have to do with…" And then I knew. The envelope that Hugo wouldn't let me see. The one from our property manager.

"You own the building," I said.

"Yes," she said. "Well, our group did. It was part of the real estate assets Larry brought to the venture. I know you love that little shop, Maggie. I love it, too. It's darling. And people will transfer their affections to the new Apollo soon enough, I'm sure of it. It's a small price to pay for getting everything you want, isn't it? Maggie?"

I was looking at her, I knew I was, possibly even nodding. But this had all hollowed me out, and I just wanted to roll over on my side, cover myself with Hugo's moose blanket, and go to sleep. No more Dragonfly. It was gone.

Avi picked up a paperweight—some kind of award with lettering carved in frosted glass—and turned it over in her hands, looking at it and not me.

"Maggie, I hope you're not the kind of person who's unable to appreciate a brilliant opportunity when it is presented to her."

For quite possibly the first time in my life, my mouth was stuck behind my brain. Too many thoughts rammed into one another. I imagined the moment after I accepted and the feeling of being a sellout. I imagined the moment of turning it down and feeling like a fool. So I said nothing and floated in the in-between. In another world where the Dragonfly would live on, I could see myself in this job, as if the Dragonfly were a counterweight to a life I'd live without it. If the Dragonfly existed, then I could exist somewhere outside the Dragonfly. But if it was gone, then what?

She pushed open a smile and pulled me out of my seat. Then she guided me toward the picture window. Outside I saw Dizzy, talking to a larger group, all captivated by what had become a series of napkin drawings.

"He's coming, too," she said. "We've bought ArGoNet as well, and we're turning it into our new social media division. Silver Needle Holdings needs him. He can redesign the software from the ground up. Build his team however he wants.

He's been buried long enough in mediocre business models. The two of you together. Nothing can stop you."

She let go of me and retrieved the portfolio from the sofa.

"And you missed the best part." She slid the brochure from the sleeve inside and handed it to me. It was an ad.

APOLLO BOOKS

ESSENTIAL TO YOU

·

The morning after Avi's party, I'd come into the Dragonfly early as had been my wont since the Rajhit breakup. It was a place of quiet with a to-do list long enough to save me from my thoughts. After Avi's surprise announcement, I had even more not to think about, so I'd gotten in extra early. I was looking forward to time alone and quiet. But when I arrived, there sat Dizzy on the sidewalk with his laptop open, wearing a hoodie from some company we'd worked for years ago, two Cuppa Joe cups beside him. Eight o'clock in the morning and he was already wired on caffeine and ambition. I doubted if he'd even gone to bed.

"Oh hey," he said when I kicked him. "Mocha?"

I took the coffee and opened the door. He followed me and started to change the tiles of the store sign from N-O-P-E to O-P-E-N, but I waved him off. Dizzy liked moving the tiles of the sign. But I didn't want customers this early. And a mean little part of me didn't want to please Dizzy.

"Can you believe it?" he said. "The holy swiggin' infrastructure from scratch. Do you know how many times that kind of opportunity comes along? Monks get laid more often. Okay. Buddhist monks. Okay. One Buddhist monk living alone under a volcano with no goats gets laid more often. It's like someone offering you a chain of bookstores to run any way you felt like it."

"That's kind of what they did," I said, motioning for him to hold it down. Even though we were alone in the Dragonfly, I glanced back into the stacks as if the books could absorb his words and tell on me when Jason and Hugo arrived. The Dragonfly was over. And it was my fault.

He turned his laptop around and showed me the screen filled with boxes and shapes that looked like sixties pop art. It was a revised schema for the ArGoNet system, all shiny in primary colors. It really was a software architect's dream, going back and reinventing what you'd done before. You knew all the past failures. You could avoid them.

The thing is, no one sets out to write code that turns to crap. At first, the visionary creates something that meets a need. The product managers research how it will work in the market and makes a business case for features and writes requirements. Then a software architect designs how it will work, and software engineers write the code. After design meetings and code reviews and large pizza delivery bills, testers test it. The testers then argue that the software did not meet the requirements while the engineers argue back that it works as designed. Bugs are filed. More meetings burn up everyone's time. The technical writers say they don't care how it works, they just want someone to make a decision. Everyone walks away thinking they've agreed to something different. User interface designers figure out how many clicks it takes to get to the center of the

Tootsie Pop. Marketing goes all Hulk Hogan on one another over where the advertising dollars go. And if all goes well, the planets align, and everyone eats their spinach, the disappointment after product launch will be brief.

And then the next time comes. A new version is planned with unleashed optimism. *We'll fix all the things that didn't go right the last time out. We won't make the same mistakes again. We'll get it right this time.* But compromises come early and fast. There are technical cliffs too steep to scale. "A" can't be done, so everyone accepts a "B" and then an anemic "C." By the time the "We launched!" pizza party comes along and the T-shirts with the project name that only fifty people in the world know about are passed around, everyone drinks expensive beer and cheap wine and tries to not look terrified about what users might say. Plans for the next version are already in front of you, seductive as silky promises in the minutes before midnight. This time you will be able to construct your masterpiece. This time will be different.

"It's a great big steaming stream of awesome, sugar-britches," Dizzy said. "For you, too. I never would have believed I'd find a project like this with a bookstore company. And you did this. None of it would have happened if you hadn't impressed Avi at that masturbating cock sack of a book club. Christ! Then the store! Of all the bass-ackward, thundershit ways to back into a searing mountain of gold. It's not just me they want, it's you, too. And not like last time. They really think you can do this."

"There was doubt last time?"

"Well, I mean, it was a big thing for you, right? You were in a library before and then, well…those other companies and then ArGoNet. That was a huge jump."

He tossed his empty cup into the wastebasket and smothered me in a bear hug, his excitement making him lose all concern for my ability to breathe.

"What if I don't want it?" I asked, my words muffled against his hoodie. "What if I want to…" I almost said *stay with the Dragonfly.* But the Dragonfly would be no more. "What if I want something else?"

I didn't really know I meant it until I said it. It felt good to say it. And I was scared and all the fears of not taking the best offer I was ever going to get came flooding back. I looked at my friend, hoping he would understand. I was tired of Dizzy being Code Warrior. I wanted him to just be my friend, that grown-up Bart Simpson with a super-size brain and a big squishy heart. But my words skipped over him like a flat stone on a flat lake.

"You'll take the job," he said. "It's the smart thing. And you're smart, so…"

"It's not smart," I said. "It's convenient."

"Jesus!" Dizzy slapped the top down on his laptop and spun around at me. "What do you want? You mope around for months about getting kicked out of ArGoNet and now it's back and it's even better. You'll be making more money than you have any right to. You're going to be the face of a new company. And you're telling me you don't want that. You don't want everything handed to you on a silver fucking platter like in a fairy tale. You're telling me you want to stay here in this shitty little bookstore instead of building a life for yourself. And what about that guy? Yeah, you think I don't know you're not seeing him anymore? The one you were so crazy about? What'd you do, Maggie? Just stop seeing him because he was too great? Just tell me, because we're all dying to know, what the fuck is going to make you happy?"

I hadn't even had a chance to turn the lights on yet, and already someone was asking me for answers I didn't have. Dizzy and I stood there looking at each other in the gray quiet of the Dragonfly. People passed by outside. A dog barked at our door, remembering we kept treats behind the counter. The clock on the wall behind me clicked another second away. And then his phone rang.

Dizzy mashed his earpiece into his ear and answered his phone, just as the door opened and Jason entered, pushing his bike through the door. He looked annoyed to find me here, but I thought maybe Dizzy would put him in a good mood. Or at least they could distract each other and leave me the hell alone. But in my eagerness for them to forget about me, I forgot about two things. Dizzy was on his cell phone, and I hadn't told him not to say anything about the job offer.

"Yeah, yeah, new data center," Dizzy said in his phone. "The guys we're dealing with now couldn't open an umbrella in a rainstorm."

"Dude, no cell phones," Jason said.

Dizzy looked around and opened his arms as if to say, "There's no one here. Who cares?"

Jason came over to the counter and gave me a "what the hell" wide-eyed look. I gave him an indulgent "give him a break" shrug while I tried to figure out how to get Dizzy out of the store.

"Yeah, yeah, she's on board," Dizzy said, turning around to look at me.

I shook my head, trying to tell him to stop talking, darting a glance at Jason, who was looking at me curiously.

"Get off the cell phone, man," Jason said, keeping a suspicious eye on me.

Dizzy swatted at him. "I'm sure Maggie can start next week. She's just got a little cleaning up to do."

"Take it outside," Jason said, thrusting his finger at the door.

"Hold on a minute," Dizzy said. He tapped the earpiece to put the call on hold and turned to Jason. "Listen, I'm with her," he said pointing to me, obviously not realizing that carried no water with Jason. "I'm working on a deal with Apollo Books worth millions. Until you can convince me that my phone call is keeping you from that kind of business, I'll finish the damn phone call." He tapped the earpiece again. "Sorry about that…"

Bottled fury churned in Jason's face. I recognized it. I'd seen it enough in Dizzy's face through most of our school days when he was locker-stuffing fodder for bullies twice his size and half his IQ. And now he was one of them.

I stomped around the counter, past Jason, and snatched Dizzy's phone off his belt. I could hear the voice on the other end of the line. I turned off the phone's connection to Dizzy's headset, then put it on speaker. Dizzy jerked around to see me walking toward the door with the phone. I could hear the guy on the other end talking about negotiating tactics and term sheets.

"Hey," I said into the phone as I walked out onto the sidewalk. "Did you know Dizzy dressed as Mae West for Halloween his senior year? There will be pics on Facebook momentarily."

"Who is this?" asked the guy on the other end.

"And he got three twenty on his Verbal the first time he took the SAT," I said.

I felt a hand on my arm. Dizzy had caught up with me. He reached for the phone, but my reach had a good two inches on him and I held the device away from him toward the traffic that was rolling down Castro Street. I could hear the voice on the other end, "Dizzy? Dizzy? What the hell is going on?"

"Mags, quit kidding around," Dizzy said, jumping for the phone, but I spun around and held him off. "What the hell are you doing?"

"Apologize," I said.

"Okay, okay, I'm sorry. Please fucking forgive me. Now give me back the goddamn phone!"

"Not to me. To Jason."

He was still reaching for the phone, trying to find a weak spot in my defense.

"Sorry, man!" he said over his shoulder.

I turned to look at him and he stopped struggling when I stopped trying to keep the phone from him. Jason stood just outside the Dragonfly's door, trying to figure out if he should do something.

"Why did you bring me out here with you?" I asked Dizzy.

"What are you talking about?"

"You had the world by the tail," I said. "You didn't need me."

"No, but you needed me. Jesus Christ on a cracker, Mags. You were sofa surfing. You couldn't even manage the bar bill. You were sleeping with stoners. What was I supposed to do?"

I turned back toward the traffic and tossed the phone under the wheels of a passing Prius. Dizzy stood beside me as we watched the black tires roll over it. The crunch sounded so satisfying, like crushing an empty can, and I felt the thrill of someone who had just gone one step too far.

"So you're mad at me for telling you the truth," Dizzy said.

"I'm mad because you think that's the truth."

Dizzy had to wait for a couple of more cars before he could scoop up what was left. It was mostly just a Pop-Tart-shaped collage of plastic and circuits.

"Someday," I said, "you will thank me for that. Until that day comes, you keep your ass away from my store."

I walked back to the Dragonfly. Jason jumped back to give me space to get in the door. I dropped down in a chair and held my head in my hands. Tears as thick as cake batter rolled down my face.

Jason sat on the edge of his chair, his hands folded between his knees until Grendel dropped from his place in the window display and jumped into Jason's lap.

"Do you really have a job with Apollo?" Jason asked.

"I have an offer."

"Is it a good one?"

"Yeah."

He shrugged and swung his feet, which didn't touch the floor. Grendel stuck his head under the crook of Jason's arm.

"Are you going to take it?"

I wanted to tell him about the lease, that there wouldn't be a Dragonfly soon, that there was no place for me if I didn't take it. But I wanted to talk to Hugo first. So I just shrugged and cried some more. Jason fidgeted with that awful ignorance of what to do.

"Rajhit and I broke up," I said.

He nodded.

"Blueberry bagel?"

He was gone for longer than I thought he would be. But when he returned with the Posh Bagel bag clenched in his hand, he was also balancing two Big Gulps.

"Blue ICEE or red ICEE?" he asked.

I took the blue.

·

A silky mist draped over the early evening as I squinted through the windshield of Hugo's Volvo at the park's signs. It was dark, and it was the Santa Cruz Mountains. I had no idea what I was doing. Finally, through the trees, my head-lights caught patches of LEGO-colored pavilions, and I knew I'd found the place.

It was a special day for both Hugo and Jason. It turns out that Hugo, to no one's real surprise, had attended the party back in Berkeley in the sixties that started the whole SCA. So he was now being celebrated as Anno Societatis I, a member of the first year of the society. That morning, I'd nearly lost it as he came strutting out in an Elizabethan nobleman's outfit Jason had procured for him.

"I think it rather suits me," he said as he lifted a gold goblet up toward me to the rounds of applause from our store full of customers. "I shall wear it every day."

It had all been Nimue's idea. Once she found out Hugo had been to that infamous party in Berkeley, she invited him to events constantly, but he always gallantly declined. And when I say gallantly, I mean he bowed, called her "m'lady," and everything. Sometimes I think she kept asking him just so he'd say no like this. But it was Jason who finally got him into some leggings. Tonight, there would be a ceremony for those who had contributed to the Kingdom of the Mists in the last year. A new king would be knighted after the war and he would honor those who served in his new kingdom. This included Jason, or Frederick the Bard as he was known. Hugo wouldn't miss that. Neither would I.

I pulled into an open parking space and took a deep breath. Jason knew about the job offer but not about the Dragonfly losing its lease. Hugo knew about the lease but not the job offer. No one knew about Rajhit's being Henry. All of these secrets felt like bricks in my stomach.

I checked my phone one more time. I hadn't heard from Dizzy since our fight. According to Facebook, he'd left yesterday to meet with a development group up in Portland. Silver Needle Holdings wanted to move all the development team up there to reduce expenses. Not many of the ArGoNet coders wanted to go, so Dizzy was in heavy recruitment mode. It was going to take a lot more than the skeleton crew he was left with to put together the vision Avi and her team had in mind. And then there was Avi. She was on board the Silver Needle ship thinking I was in the cocktail lounge, where she would join me later, when in reality I was still on the dock, sitting on a pile of rope and sweating all over my ticket.

I left the car and, flashlight in hand, trod up the path toward the pavilions, the music, and the scent of roasting meat, hoping no mountain lions were hungry. When I passed a woman dressed like the St. Pauli Girl necking with a guy who looked like he belonged on the cover of one of my romances, I knew

I had to be close. After asking a few people for directions, I finally found the encampment where Jason and Hugo were staying.

"It's been quite a day," Hugo said. "A World War Two reenactment group scheduled the field for the same day, so they all joined in. We had Lancelots and G.I. Joes going at it all afternoon."

"And a king was chosen this morning," Nimue reminded him. "That's important, too." Nimue described in great detail the heralding poem Jason wrote for the newly crowned king. But there was something in her tone that made me feel like she was more interested in the king than the poem.

"It happens sometimes," Jason said about the conflict with the field that day. "We try to be careful with scheduling the grounds and all, but organization isn't our greatest feature. We had a squire in the kingdom once who was also a project manager at Oracle. Tried to get all our *i*'s dotted and *t*'s crossed. Had a spreadsheet posted on Google Docs with everything planned out for everyone to see. But no one ever read it."

"Sounds dreadful," I said.

"It turned out to be for him," he said. "After he got cranky when no one met their deadlines, they put him on a raft in the middle of the night and he woke up in the middle of Loch Lomond."

Sasha and Dae-Jung were there, too, introducing me to a dress and accessories they'd borrowed from a friend about my size. The two of them walked me over to the park's restrooms, where they had to explain to me how to put the outfit together. The restroom was full of maids and ladies primping and fluffing and generally tucking in and pushing out. There wasn't a stall for me, so I sucked it up and stood behind the wooden barrier in front of the door that blocked the casual viewer from getting a look inside.

"Think of it as a dressing screen like in the old movies," Dae-Jung said from the other side of the barrier after Sasha got called back to fix an issue with a camp stove. "If it weren't for being in the outdoors and in front of a public restroom, it could be quite elegant."

I liked Dae-Jung. And I knew he and Dizzy had been seeing a lot of each other. And I knew that he probably knew about me and Dizzy fighting. So as I stepped into my dress, just wearing my underwear, pretty much out in front of God and everyone, I went back and forth as to whether I should ask this nearly perfect stranger about my best friend.

"I don't think Dizzy and I are seeing each other anymore," he said, solving my dilemma.

"You okay?" I said after a pause.

"He says he's moving to Portland. Didn't even bring up what that means for us. Not that we've been together long, but he didn't even make it sound like he wanted to try to keep things going. That was last week, and I haven't heard from him since. So I guess that's that."

I was dressed enough to come around the barrier and find Dae-Jung in his squire's garb, learning back against the wall and trying not to care about getting dumped.

"That happened to me not too long ago," I said. "Only I'd been with the guy a couple of years."

"What did you do next?" he asked.

"Another guy came along."

"And you're with him now?" he asked, pulling away.

"Well, no."

"You're not very good at this, are you?"

"Doesn't look like it," I said.

Dae-Jung stood and hugged me. "Dizzy's kind of an ass, isn't he?"

"There are times," I said.

He took a step back and looked me over, then helped me with the belt that wrapped around my waist and hung down the side. My dress was a deep green with a scoop neckline, not so very different from the one the heroine wore on the cover of *The Defiant*. I brushed my hair back and pulled the white cotton veil over the crown of my head and fastened it with the silver circlet. And though the train was a little awkward and the circlet had a habit of wandering, I had to admit that I got a kick out of dressing like a Renaissance lady for an evening. There was something about putting on that dress, ornate and splendid, that reminded me how pretty I could feel. As I looked at myself in the murky restroom mirror, an idea came to me. I handed Dae-Jung my phone.

"Take a picture of me," I said. "I'm going to put it on Facebook and horrify my mother."

When we got back to the tent, Jason was there waiting for us in full costume and holding a lute, looking every inch the Renaissance troubadour. We all walked together to the ceremony as everyone except Hugo and me sang a saucy drinking song they all knew the lyrics to. The ceremony was everything you'd imagine from a group of people who spend every nonworking hour designing armor and embroidering dresses. The pomp and circumstance made a British royal wedding seem like a small cozy affair. And there Jason was, in front of everyone, bowing before his king, accepting his praise, without saying a word. I did not know exactly what world this was, the one with a silent and respectful Jason, but I knew I liked it.

On the way back to our camp, we stopped at a prancing bonfire to watch a dance filled with swooping bows and some of the most shameless displays of flirtation I've ever seen, even including those I'd encountered in my native South. And in the middle of all this was Nimue, dancing with her new king, playing the coy maid. Sasha and I stuck our fingers down our throats in mutual disgust.

Hugo and I found a log to sit on to watch. A friar handed us two tankards of hard pear cider. The air was rich with patchouli oil, henna, and burning oak. Four minstrels started a jig and the dancers dropped their stately poses to jump about and swing one another round and round in gleeful abandon. I threaded my arm through Hugo's and leaned on his shoulder, letting myself sink into the strangeness and wonder of it all.

"What a bunch of geeks," I said. "And they buy so many books. God love every one of them."

"You're a geek, too, Maggie," he said.

"Not like this. This is commitment. This is telling the world to go fuck off and leave you alone. It's great."

I felt Hugo's head lean on top of mine and we sat in the silence of things unsaid. The musicians took a break, and more ale appeared. Someone passed around smoked meats and dates. Hugo and I sat up to eat. And after we drained our mugs, I felt his hand on my arm. When I turned, he was looking at the ground, and I could see he was pulling in his thoughts like a net of fish. For a whisper of a moment, I thought he knew all about Avi's offer. I thought all of my indecision would be over. Hugo would understand. He would either give me his blessing to go or tell me why I should stay. I sat and waited, my heartbeats pushing through the numbness of the ale.

"The Dragonfly is losing its lease," he said. "I don't think I can start over again somewhere else. Not at this point in my life."

It was the first time I'd ever thought of Hugo as old. His eyes crinkled as he looked at me with heartache and grief.

"I thought I could fix it," he said. "But the building is being sold. They're putting in a Cheesecake Factory. It'll be like someone plunked down a Vegas casino in Mayberry."

My stomach quivered as his words sank into me, and all I could think of was how to take this off his shoulders.

"We should close the store," I said.

"You and Jason could start over. I'd give you my part of the store."

"I have a job offer," I said before I even knew the words were there.

He smiled, his eyes glistening, and held my hands in his. He hadn't known, but he gave me my answer anyway, and I watched him sink into the relief of someone who had his decisions made for him. My eye caught Jason on the other side of the fire, laughing and looking at Nimue to share the joke, only to find her staring off elsewhere. My thoughts jumped ahead to see a hollowed-out Dragonfly with boxes piled high and dark shapes on the carpet where the shelves had been. I began to feel the full loss of everything. We sat like that for a time, Hugo and I, among so many who loved the Dragonfly, alone and safe in our knowledge of its demise. Our customers would be fine. Years from now, they would still talk about the Dragonfly, and about Hugo, Jason, and maybe even me. But there's no shortage of places to buy books. They'd all move on. And the Dragonfly would just be one of those places like their favorite bar in college or the long-ago disappeared taqueria that used to serve those great waffles.

"I wanted more for you and Jason," Hugo said. "I wanted the Dragonfly to be more."

"We all wanted a great many things," I said, and leaned against him again, feeling his arm around me.

"Go find your inner geek, Maggie," he said. "And don't settle for anyone who doesn't love you for it."

My father was not a bad man. There was always food on the table and clothes on my back. I had a great education and paid for none of it myself. I wanted for nothing, except for moments like this. ———

Hugo and I sat like that for a while until he decided to turn in. I walked to our camp with him, and we spent another few quiet moments swaddled in our decisions. After saying good night, I wandered around the campfires that were still ablaze, fueled by laughter and loud boasts. I wasn't thinking of the Dragonfly or Apollo or Hugo. I wanted to think of Jason and what a Dragonfly-less life would be for him, but there was just no room left in my brain. My heart hurt and my thoughts were tired. I just wanted to wander until all I could do was sleep.

Then, through the music and all the drunken whooping, I heard it. A laugh. Dizzy's laugh.

I admit my first instinct was to hide. I had a stabbing awareness of how I was dressed. I'd completely forgotten about my costume until this moment, but I didn't want Dizzy to see me in it. Things were bad enough between the two of us. I couldn't imagine the grief that waited ahead of me. Then I remembered that the reason I felt so comfortable was that everyone else was dressed like me. That means Dizzy was dressed like me. Well, not in a dress. Hopefully. Whatever awkwardness I felt was trumped by my curiosity about what Dizzy was wearing.

I followed the sound of his laughter through the camp until I spotted him, sitting in a group around a fire, in WWII olive greens, helmet and rifle in his lap, toasting with a pewter tankard. I can't imagine what I must have looked like, in my costume, walking out of the darkness and into the light of the campfire, some sort of Shakespearean specter come to haunt him. But when he saw me, he dropped his rifle and fell backward off the log he was sitting on. The two young knights sitting on either side of him laughed and swung their tankards in the air while they pulled him upright on the log with an aplomb that made me think they'd righted many people on logs before.

Sitting upright again, he dropped his head away from me, trying to block his face from my view. I circled around his group and by the time he was prairie-dogging in his seat to look for where I'd gone, I was standing right behind him. In a gesture that had, over the years, become as automatic as brushing my teeth, I swiped the cap off his head and swatted him with it.

Through the wild laughter around us, Dizzy slowly turned his head and looked up at me. I motioned for him to follow me.

"How long have you been doing this?" I asked.

He shrugged. "First time. Dae-Jung thought I might like it. He knew a guy."

"He's here, you know," I said.

He pretended he didn't hear me.

I motioned to a log and we sat, looking down on the camp. He took out his flask from his back pocket and handed it to me before he took a sip. Dizzy could be a dickwad, but that didn't mean he wasn't a gentleman. I took it and drank. Thank goodness it was bourbon and not wine.

"You posted on Facebook that you were in Portland," I said.

He dug the butt of his rifle into the ground near his feet.

"I didn't want anyone to know what I was doing this weekend."

"The Dragonfly is closing," I said.

It was like someone plugged him back in. He grinned and came as close as Dizzy could to bouncing.

"You're coming to Portland. I knew it! You're going to come to Portland. We are going to be fucking awesome! It'll be just like it used to be."

And that's what made my decision for me. Not wisdom from Hugo or temptations from Avi or even my own decrepit bank account. Dizzy showed me what nothing else could, that I wasn't the person I'd been at the beginning of the summer. I didn't want to be fucking awesome. I wanted to matter. I shook my head and watched Dizzy deflate.

"You're not going to take your dream job?" he asked.

I shook my head again.

"Then what the fuck are you going to do? You have another offer?"

I shrugged. "Maybe I'll open another bookstore. I've got the inventory."

"I can't believe you came all the way to California to own a shitty used bookstore," he said.

"I came all the way to California to be with my best friend."

I felt him look at me from the side, and that's when it happened. The heartbeat that separated the time when Dizzy was my best friend from the time when he wasn't. And it took the two of us dressing up like people we weren't for me to see it. He would go to Portland and I would stay here. We'd text, we'd video chat, and I would love him forever. But we'd never be as we once were. None of the major events in my friendship with Dizzy had ever been sealed with words. We had never declared our friendship or our affection for each other. It was just there. It still was. Just not the same. This was our parting. We were swimming in different rivers now.

He handed me back his flask. I drank and started to feel the warm lava of the bourbon spreading through my body, and for some reason I thought of the James Joyce story "The Dead" with Gretta mesmerized by that last song of the night in the drawing room filling her with nostalgia for her tender self.

"I kind of like you like this," I said. "All World War Two guy, I mean. Very manly."

"You're one to be talking, shallot lady," he said.

"I think you mean Lady of Shalott."

"Yeah, something like that."

At first the red flashing lights in the distance seemed part of the night, blinking to its rhythms. But then my mind focused through the cider and the cannabis in the air.

"Looks like there's a problem," Dizzy said, pointing to the lights. "Maybe we should head back."

We started down the incline and fell into pace with others headed toward the approaching ambulance. In the distance, above the heightened voices, I thought I heard my name, but I wasn't sure. As we got closer to the lights, I saw Jason running toward me. If he was looking for me, that meant…

I ran in the direction of the ambulance, Dizzy close behind me, toward the paramedics pressing rhythmically down on Hugo's chest.

CHAPTER THIRTEEN

Breaking the Frozen Earth

What is worse? To have this and never lay eyes on
you? Or to never have had this at all?

—Henry

We were in the ER waiting room, just after midnight, when we
first heard the word *stroke*. Other people, anxious to hear about
their loved ones, gave us a wide berth. At first I thought it was
to keep their distance from our bad news, not wanting our ill
fortune to infect them. But when I picked up the train of my
dress to keep it safe from the wheels of Hugo's gurney, I remembered that we—Jason, me, and friends—were still in our
Renaissance clothes and Dizzy was in his fatigues. It seemed
odd that our clothes should worry them. The security guard
had confiscated the swords and guns at the door, after all.

In the ICU, I gave instructions to our friends. Call Robert.
Get us a change of clothes. Put a sign on the door of the
Dragonfly. Hope filled everyone's hearts as they rushed to their
missions. If there was something to do, then all would be well.
They left us, our knights and ladies, spurs for pretend horses
clinking on the tiles. Jason and I were alone, left to stare at
Hugo through a glass window in the ICU.

"What's going to happen?" Jason asked.

"I don't know," I said, looking at him reflected in the glass, watching for cracks in his face.

"When will we know?"

"The doctor said he'll come by around noon with the test results. We'll know more then."

"What if something happens before then?"

"Another doctor will come."

"Are you sure?" It seemed an odd question to me, one too naïve for Jason. I turned away from his reflection to look at the real him. I started to tell him, "Yes, I'm sure. That's the way it works." But I stopped, realizing that Jason had probably had a lot more experience with hospitals and doctors than I had, and his fear was probably from experience.

"I'll make sure of it. I promise," I said.

In the ICU waiting room, I took off my cloak and offered it to Jason as a pillow. He needed to lie down. The rows of chairs had no arms, and we were allowed to stretch out here, unlike in the ER, where discomfort seemed mandatory. The nighttime janitor mopped the floor, and I could smell institutional disinfectant in the dirty soapy water. I entered a reminder on my phone to bring Hugo's incense for his room. I posted on the store's Facebook page, Twitter feed, and website that the store would be closed for a few days. More news was to come. We would open again as soon as we could.

·

The doctor came as promised. The next day there was still a murmur of hope. They let us in to see him, one at a time, fifteen minutes every couple of hours. I massaged Hugo's feet. Robert stood beside his friend and stared at the monitors, as if they were a balance sheet he could not puzzle together. Robert's wife, Charlene, came and in the waiting area they held hands, heads bent in prayer. When it was Jason's time to visit him, he sat at the foot of Hugo's bed and read him Jack London stories aloud. I could hear his voice, muffled through the glass. He read well, slowly and determined, as if he were trying to coax a fearful animal close to the fire. It was comforting listening to him. But it wasn't landscapes crunchy with snow and the lonesome howl of wolves that filled my head. Instead, I saw a nineteen-year-old Hugo in a navy surplus coat roaming the foggy docks of San Francisco with *The Call of the Wild* stuffed in his pocket, its soft cover curled from constant reading. Looking at Hugo's face, I imagined his drooping mouth was a faint smile and that he, too, was thinking of that young man.

On my phone, I noticed that my mother had called a couple of times and left voice mails. I couldn't deal with her now. Later. Everything was now later.

·

It was never a question that someone should always be there, so we decided to take shifts at the hospital. I took the night shift. At first it was easier being there than in my apartment. But by the third night, lack of sleep caught up to me and I couldn't keep my eyes open. I don't know when I fell asleep, but when I woke, I found Hugo's moose blanket draped over me.

I sat up and looked around. The only other person in the waiting room was sitting in the seat next to me, and for a few foggy moments when I first woke, I just stared at my mother.

"Your hair is a mess," she said, reaching out to me and fingering the ends of my hair. "So many split ends."

I just sat there, not knowing whether to be happy or annoyed that she was here. Too tired to decide, I dropped my head forward, resting my forehead on her shoulder and clutching the moose blanket up to my chin.

"I saw your post on Facebook," she said. "About the store closing. I was worried."

"You follow the Dragonfly on Facebook?"

"You had me send the chair there," she said. "Goodness knows I'd never get any information out of you. What choice did I have? Then someone posted about Hugo's stroke."

"And you came?" I asked, when the answer was obviously yes.

She reached over and patted my hand, almost slapping at it, without looking at me.

"I thought I could help," she said. "I posted a note on the Facebook page asking if someone could come get me from the airport. And some kind of hippie Indian boy came. He was wearing green rubber flip-flops but he was driving an Infiniti. He must have borrowed it."

I started to cry, and she leaned her beautiful head down against mine. I could smell the lavender soap she'd used all my life, the starch on her cotton shirt and slacks, and her hair spray cavorting with Chanel No. 5.

"He took me to your apartment. We'll talk later about why he has a key," she said. "He said you would want this thing with deer on it, so I brought it. I figured no one would keep something this ugly unless it was important."

·

Word of Hugo's condition spread. The front of the Dragonfly was awash in flowers and cards, including an enormous arrangement from Apollo Books & Music. I called Avi the next day to thank her, but neglected to mention that I had taken the bouquet to the children's ward at the hospital. It seemed wrong to leave a gift from the enemy camp in his room, though Robert did point out the indignation might be just the ticket to get Hugo out of bed again.

My mother had Dizzy scavenge Mountain View for "normal food" so there was always something at home and snacks to offer Hugo's visitors in the waiting room. The rest of the time, wherever I was, she was with me, reading *Southern Living* on her iPad or the Barbara Taylor Bradford novel Jason brought her from the Dragonfly.

"You know, I don't usually read much, but I like this," she said to Jason, holding out the book from her and examining it like a vintage ring in an antique shop.

"Jason has a talent for picking the right book for someone," I said.

Someone else's mother might have talked to Jason more about this and his life and background. She might have delicately extracted details from him to piece together his history and how things had come to be the way they had for him. She might have offered motherly comfort and possibly some advice for making his way through the world. But as I saw

Georgine looking down at Jason's hands, I could smell what was coming next. My mother was fixing to be blunt.

"What happened to you anyway?" she asked Jason, nodding her head in the direction of his hands and leg.

To my surprise, Jason didn't flinch. He held up one of his pinched hands so she could see it better and she cupped it in hers, rubbing her thumbs over it like it was a seashell she'd found on the beach. I'd never even seen Nimue touch one of his hands before, and yet there was my mother.

"Cerebral palsy," he said. "It's just a medical bullshit term for they-don't-know-what-the-fuck."

"Language, young man," she said.

"Sorry."

"Go on now. Don't pout."

He shrugged and kicked the chair in front of him.

"They're pretty sure it was the drugs my mom did when she was pregnant," Jason said. "She stopped the drugs. She got mean. They took me away."

Mama nodded in a quiet way. She was a pain in the ass, but in some ways she was also a miracle.

"Baby, don't you fret," she said. "They always treat you worse when they feel guilty."

·

Jason was halfway through "To Build a Fire" when Hugo had his second stroke. When the monitors started to wail, Jason bolted upright and sat frozen until a nurse pulled him off Hugo's bed. I rushed into the room and grabbed him, wrapping my arms around him from behind so he couldn't see the fear in my face. The doctor said we should prepare ourselves and asked again if there was a DNR. I didn't know. Robert nodded. Jason left and didn't come back. Mama stood outside the glass and watched me as I held Hugo in my arms and counted each breath until it was over.

.

Dizzy drove me and Mama home, in a rental car so Mama wouldn't smell like French fry grease. While Mama went through a checklist of what we needed to decide, I stared out the back window thinking that the last time I'd seen everything we passed by Hugo had been alive.

I was anxious, feeling like I'd forgotten something. But I hadn't forgotten. It was the leaving of Hugo that had emptied me. I tried to picture what they wouldn't let us see. Moving the body from the room. The transport to the crematorium. These were mysteries, the things we paid other people to do for us. In centuries past, it would have been the family who tended to him in death, just as in life. But faceless, nameless people did what I could not. And what would bring me comfort now was just a job to them.

At home, on the sofa, the rims of my eyes felt raw and dry, a cold ache behind them like a constant ice cream headache. No tears left. I looked down and caught myself scratching my arm on top of the red marks I'd made earlier. Why did grief feel like ants under my skin?

At my apartment, Mama talked on and on about the right thread count as she put the new sheets she'd bought me on my bed. In the kitchen, Dizzy made grilled bologna sandwiches. I stepped outside for air and checked my phone. A dozen calls to Jason and nothing back. He knew Hugo was gone. He had to. I was worried. He should be with us.

In the side yard next to Hugo's apartment, I heard noises. I walked to the Japanese maple so I could see around the corner. Through the dark, I could see Mrs. Callahn, yanking tomato plants out of the pots and stuffing them into large garbage bags. Without a word, I went back inside.

Lady Chatterley's Lover lay on the breakfast bar. Pen in hand, I turned toward the end of the book, just past where the notes had ended, and wrote:

My dear friends,
   Our beloved Hugo is gone.

Yours, Maggie

．

The mail at the Dragonfly had backed up in the week since we'd closed. A few bills, more sympathy cards. Flowers lay in front of the door. Crayon drawings were taped to the glass. I gathered up a handful of mail and held it against me as I unlocked the door.

"You're going to have a time cleaning all this up," Mama said, holding a pink gerbera daisy while she waited for me to open the door.

"People mean well, Mama."

By the time I managed to get in the door and lock it behind me, my mother was already standing by the counter—her right hand resting on it as if it were a ballet barre. She scanned the Dragonfly's landscape. For the first time in a long time, I saw the store as a stranger must see it. Even after weeks of cleaning and organizing and sign-posting and rearranging, in my mother's eyes, it must have still looked like a great big pile of books and a cash register.

In her silence, I could almost hear her calculating what they'd spent on my education, how many years I'd worked since getting out of school, the things she thought I'd sacrificed to have this life. And now she was seeing that life. She was in a cream pantsuit with a clay-colored silk blouse and matching pumps. Not a hair out of place, no wrinkle daring to appear on either her clothes or her face. Next to her, everything in the Dragonfly looked grubby, even her daughter.

"I know it's not…," I said. "I mean…it's a venture."

My mother turned around and looked at me. My mother didn't believe in ventures just like she didn't believe in the Easter Bunny or plaid pants. She believed in certainty, even to the point of delusion.

"I can make tea," I said.

"It's too early for a glass of tea."

"I meant hot tea." I looked at the mugs by the electric kettle and the only clean one was Hugo's.

"I'll go to that place next door for coffee," she said.

Alone, I started to go through the mail. Most of it I skipped until I saw a card with the CIA Bathroom's names on the return address.

Dear Maggie and Jason,
There are cards we could send that are already prepared for

times like this so we do not have to be. There are books we could recommend to you and groups you could join to help you process your feelings. None of it works. This is grief. It will hurt and hurt until one day it will hurt a little less. Think of that day.

Yours,
Mike, Mike, and John

I put their note back in its envelope and taped it to the counter to remind me to read it every day.

I was sorting through the rest of the stack when Jason walked into the store. We stood frozen in surprise, staring at each other. He was the first to move. He bolted past me and into the stacks. I went after him.

"Jason!"

I caught a flash of him turning the corner at Self-Help and followed him around the corner.

"Where have you been? I called everywhere. I was worried. Were you with Nimue?"

He stopped suddenly, and I almost ran into the back of him. He turned and looked at me, his face hard. I took a step back. He turned again and walked into the office, slamming the door behind him.

"Jason!" I called, knocking on the door. "Jason, talk to me!"

Through the door, I heard the desk chair roll and creak as he sat down.

"Jason, come on. I haven't seen you in days."

But it was silent beyond the door. So I kicked it, hard. Pain darted up my leg.

"Crap!" I yelled at either Jason or the door. I wasn't sure which.

The door jerked open, and he stared up at me. Then he scooted past me and headed back toward the front of the store.

"He's gone!" he screamed over his shoulder.

"He's gone? You think I don't know that? I held him while he died. Where the hell were you!? Huh? Where the hell were you? I sat there and watched him die. Where were you?"

"I'm not talking about..." He turned to me, his breathing heavy. "I'm not talking about Hugo."

"What?" How could he be talking about anyone else? How could he not be consumed with this?

"Grendel, you asshole." Like an idiot, I looked around as if the cat would just appear. "He's been gone for two weeks, and you haven't even noticed."

The cat. Hugo was dead, and Jason was thinking about the cat. Whatever thread of sanity I'd been able to keep intact over the last week snapped. I felt that quivery release in my chest when you first know you're falling and can't stop and the chill from knowing that you don't care. A hard landing was better than holding on this long.

"I want you out," I said.

"Out of what?"

"Out of the Dragonfly. Robert will send you your severance."

"You can't do that," he said.

"The Dragonfly is mine now," I said. "I can do what I want."

Someone was tapping on the door, asking to be let in. The door was unlocked but we still had the sign set to N-O-P-E. Jason and I, our attention drawn from each other, turned to see Gloria, standing at the door in green Keds and a *Too many books, too little time* sweatshirt, waving at us and pointing to the inside of the store, asking to be let in. Jason picked up the nearest book to him and threw it at the door. She tapped her watch and pointed at the posted hours. This time, I threw a book at her. Then Jason and I laid out a barrage of flying paperbacks along the front window after her as she scurried down the sidewalk past my mother. When it was over, Jason sat in the new chair, holding on to the armrests like the chair was getting ready for liftoff.

"What's going on here?" Mama said, coming in the door, a cup of coffee in each hand and her purse swinging from her arm.

"We were fine without you," Jason said to me. "Everything would have been fine without you."

"Children, don't," Mama said, setting the coffee down. "Quarreling isn't going to fix anything."

I looked at Jason. She was right. I couldn't fix this.

"Dae-Jung says you're taking that job," he said.

"What job?" Mama moved to my side, looking at me expectantly. "What kind of job? In an office? Will you have a secretary?"

"He says that Dizzy told him Avi got the idea to buy Apollo because of you," Jason continued. "He says that that's why the building is being sold. That's why we're losing our lease. That's why the Dragonfly is closing. Because of you."

"Is that what he's saying?" I asked.

"That's what I'm saying," Jason said.

His face was red and his whole body tight. I could feel his anger from ten feet away.

"Am I really fired?" he asked.

"Fired?" my mother said. "Who said anything about anyone getting fired? Of course you're not fired."

"A lot can happen while you're out getting coffee, Mama."

"Am I?" he asked.

"Geez," I said. "No, of course not. I have no idea what words are coming out of my mouth anymore."

That seemed to defuse him, and he leaned back in his chair. It was the first time I'd ever seen him sit in a chair properly instead of drooping over the sides with his legs swinging. The chair looked much too big for his small body. He shifted and reached down into the seat, pulling at something he'd sat on. He held up a broken Waverley novel, *Kenilworth*. I joined him on the stage, sitting cross-legged on the floor by the chair. He handed me the book.

"Hugo died," Jason said.

"Yeah, he did."

"Grendel's gone."

"I see that now."

"She's going to break up with me," he said. "She's just waiting for the memorial. Like that's the end of it and she won't be a bad person. Like everything will be okay after the memorial. I assume we're doing something like that."

"It's a thing people do."

I didn't try to argue with him, tell him lies to make him feel better. It wouldn't have worked anyway. If it did, I'd have told myself a few.

·

"Just one more," Robert said, turning the paper to face me on the window table in Cuppa Joe, careful to avoid the wet ring left by my mug of tea. I nibbled on a sweetened rice biscuit as I pretended to look over the document. Robert sipped his plain green tea. He had advised me to wait on the paperwork. There was time. But I wanted it over. Final, with nothing hovering over me. Hugo left the store to Jason and me equally. But my partnership had thrown off the balance. Robert, with the help of a lawyer, was fixing it. I remember how adult I felt when I signed the papers for the store with Hugo. Now I just felt old.

I'd come here by myself, telling Mama she'd be bored by all this paperwork. It was true, but I also needed to get away from her. After Jason's outburst about the Apollo job, she found the offer package in my apartment and from that moment on, she hadn't been able to stop bugging me about it. She'd never been excited about any of my software jobs. She couldn't get her brain wrapped around what I did there. But this? This had potential. This had status. This had money attached. This she could understand.

I looked up from my paper-signing to find Robert watching me instead of my pen. He'd been hovering around the Dragonfly for the last week. And he wasn't the only one. Jason hadn't seemed to leave, and I'd found a sleeping bag in the office. It was almost as if he were trying to catch Grendel or Hugo lurking about.

"I'm fine," I said.

"We need to talk about the memorial service."

"Not yet," I said.

"I know it's hard, but people expect it," Robert said.

He was right. We'd already had lots of requests at the store.

It was getting harder to put people off. I was getting to the point where I wanted one, to share the grief, to risk not being brave. But I remembered what Jason said about Nimue waiting to dump him until after the service.

"Not yet," I said.

The last few days had been a blur as I tried to retrieve a whiff of normal when nothing was normal anymore. In the movies, they show this time in a montage of scenes with a syrupy pop ballad in the background, images of people finding items left behind by the ones they lost. It's all over in the space of a couple of minutes, time-warped recovery, because everyone would walk out if it were anything else. No one wants to pay money to experience that kind of pain.

"He wouldn't want you to be sad," Robert said.

"Well, he's dead so he doesn't get a say anymore." I was sorry as soon as I said it, but I hurt too bad to take it back. "How long did you know?"

"Know what?"

"Know that he was sick. He was sick a while, wasn't he? He stopped smoking. He stopped smoking everything. The shorter hours at the store. Seeing old friends like Portia. He saw this coming."

Robert nodded. "Heart disease. He told me a couple of years ago. He knew he was on borrowed time. He was just going to coast until the end. With the financials being what they were, he thought he and the Dragonfly would go out about the same time. Then you and Jason started to make a go of the store. He started looking at it more as a legacy, something to leave you. That's when we changed his will to leave it to you both."

"How's Charlene?" I asked, trying to talk about something else. The subject of Hugo was just too hard.

"She prays for you. We both do."

"I don't believe in that. Neither did Hugo."

"Doesn't matter. We pray for you anyway."

He let his hand linger on my shoulder before he left, and I didn't watch him go.

It was a warm night and Mrs. Callahn had opened the tall windows in front of the store to let in the breeze from the bay. But it was past closing now and she slid the windows shut and locked them.

I'd never been alone in Cuppa Joe before. Having lost her lease as well, Mrs. Callahn was starting to pack up. The shop seemed empty and pathetic without other people. It was just a big tan room that smelled of coffee, stark and barren. No pictures on the walls. No plants. Just mismatched furniture and a long coffee bar. I felt like I was there for the first time.

"What are you going to do now?" Mrs. Callahn asked. "Out of business again."

"We'll see. Jason may keep it going. I'm not sure I have the heart for it."

She sat in the chair across from me and sipped a coffee in a tall glass that made it look like a Guinness. I wondered how she slept at night.

"What about you?" I asked. "You moving Cuppa Joe?"

She shook her head. "Eighteen years is long enough. Time to move on. Start over. You should do the same." She pointed at my open backpack and *Lady Chatterley's Lover* sitting near the top. "What are you going to do about that?"

I didn't understand. What was there to do? Did she know about Rajhit?

"Such foolishness," she said, sliding the book from my backpack. "Such foolish, foolish hope." She laid the book on the table, not opening it. She laid her hand flat and pressed her palm against the cover. I was no longer in the room for her. "'Sunday is the first day of summer. Meet me in Pioneer Park, by the fountain, noon.' So foolish."

Sunday is the first day of summer. Meet me in Pioneer Park, by the fountain, noon. She knew about that note. Only three people knew about that note. Me, Rajhit, and—

"You're Catherine."

We stared at each other. I could see her face twisting into fabrications, things she could say that would make me believe otherwise, but I knew the truth and there was no getting around it.

She shoved the book across the table at me. "This never happened. You left right after Robert did, and this never happened."

I held the book against me and tried to think of all the things I'd wanted to say to Catherine if I ever found her, but I was coming up blank. All I could do was dumbly repeat, "You're Catherine."

She stood and turned away from me, going behind the counter, folding dish towels.

"Leave," she said.

"I'm not going to tell anyone," I said. "I wouldn't do that."

She didn't look at me, just kept folding. But I wasn't going anywhere.

"I know who Henry is," I said.

She stopped.

"Do you want to know?" I asked.

She shook her head. Her eyes closed and her face grew solid as if she were trying to call up a force field around her.

I stood and walked slowly to the counter, not wanting her to bolt. "I've been wondering about you all this time, ever since I found out that the notes weren't from 1961."

"You should not have published them anyway," she said. "That was wrong. Very wrong."

"You're right about that," I said. "I'm sorry."

Her head bent so I couldn't see her face, but I did see two tears drop to the counter.

"We should not have been fighting," she said.

"Who?" I asked.

"Hugo and me. He said we should put eggshells right on the soil of tomato plants. I told him no. It needs to compost first. But he insisted. He took me back to the gardening section in the Dragonfly to show me a book. He pointed to a book back there, but then Jason called him. 'Read this,' he said. 'I need you to read this.' He pointed to a book. And after he was gone, I looked at the book I thought he'd pointed to."

And then I knew. Hugo. She thought Henry was Hugo. He'd gone by that name for a while in college. What was it? Something about a girl liking it more than Hugo, thinking Hugo sounded like a communist. He knew Mrs. Callahn in school. Henry. She thought Hugo was Henry. And if she thought he was Henry...then the notes...

"You were in love with Hugo," I said. "You thought Henry in the notes was Hugo writing to you."

And with that, her eyes, soft with sorrow, met mine.

"But Henry kept talking about not knowing you," I said. "You've known Hugo for forty years."

"I thought it was some kind of romantic game, leaving those notes for me, using a different name. I thought he needed this to erase all our history, so we could see each other with new eyes."

I moved a little closer, tried to guide her back to the chair, but she remained standing, as if her feet had grown roots into the floor.

"The first day of summer," she said. "I watched him from across the street. I did not want to be the first to arrive. So I watched. When he left, I was going to wait five minutes and then go. But he never left. He just sat in his chair and read. Noon came. Then twelve thirty. One. He stood and stretched and came here for lunch. I came back and made him a grilled cheese sandwich."

I pictured her, sitting over at Apollo, watching him in the window. An hour she waited. Each minute going by, another breath of hope gone. And then to come back and make him lunch, with him never knowing what she'd just been through.

"I had all of these words in me that I never said, not to anyone. I wanted men to respect me, even fear me a little. They come and they go. I wanted more of my life than to be someone's wife. I liked being alone. But I did not like being lonely. Hugo was always kind. I started to think maybe his kindness meant something more. And then I found the notes. We started writing."

"I'm sorry," I said. I didn't know what else to say. I was sorry, for everything I'd done, for love she would never have, even for meddling in the world of the Dragonfly. I did this.

I turned to go, stopping at the table to pick up the papers Robert had left and my backpack. *Lady Chatterley's Lover* sat on the table. I walked to the door without it. I had become accustomed to letting things go.

CHAPTER FOURTEEN

Nepenthe

Sometimes I crave a calm heart, strong and sure.
—Catherine

Hugo Carl Spandorff, a longtime and beloved Mountain View neighbor and business owner, died September 12. A native of Idaho, Hugo came to the Bay Area as a young man and earned degrees in literature and math from the University of California, Berkeley. After coming to Mountain View in 1982, Hugo purchased McNeil's Bookstore and rechristened it Dragonfly Used Books. He was an active member of several clubs, including the Mountain View Historical Association and Californians for Peace. He also enjoyed gardening. He was 59.

Plans for a memorial service are forthcoming.

.

Jason sat cross-legged in one of the reading chairs, wrinkling the legs of the new khakis he'd bought. They were too big for him and bunched at his waist under a brown leather belt. I should have asked Mama to help him pick some out. He held a paper plate full of potluck lasagna, though he hadn't been eating a lot since the breakup with Nimue, who had not waited until after the memorial service after all. She had come to the service, though, trying to convince everyone she was a concerned ex-girlfriend. While everyone else wore the color of flowers that Hugo loved, she appeared in melodramatic black, complete with a veil, like she was attending a state funeral instead of an informal memorial, in a dress that hung just short of her panty line. I had to fight the impulse to drop hot food into her bare lap. Instead, I let my mother do it.

"So that's it," Jason said. "No more Dragonfly."

"I didn't say that. I said I'd be willing to sell you my half of the business or be a silent partner. Whichever works better for you."

He set the plate on the stage and looked out the window over the flower arrangement of carnations the Chamber of Commerce had sent.

"So you're going to work for Apollo?"

"No. I'm not sure what I'm going to do. But whatever it is, I'm probably going to do it someplace other than here."

Hugo had left the duplex to Jason and me as well as the store. We'd already decided to sell it, which would give me enough money to live on for a long time. I indulged in a fantasy that I'd leave my key and a note and slither away. Get a backpack and a bus pass. Find a nice small town. Work as a waitress just for kicks. Be that mysterious girl with a past that everyone in town wonders about. Maybe the sheriff would fall in love with me, regardless of what he assumed to be my troubled past. "Only have as much stuff as you can pack in fifteen minutes, in case you need to get out of town in a hurry," Hugo told me once. I was starting to see the wisdom in that advice.

"I'll stay long enough to finish packing and find a new location," I said. "Even help you hire minions. You always wanted minions."

He laid the paper plate on the floor beside his chair. I almost protested, thinking Grendel would get at it. But I stopped myself in time. It had been four weeks and still no sign of the cat. Jason had been strangely quiet about it since that day he first told me the cat was missing. Actually, he'd been quiet about everything—Nimue, Grendel, Hugo. He seemed so adrift, shuffling around the Dragonfly like an old man who had lost his way home.

I thought he would be angry with me when I told him I was leaving. I thought he would yell and get all red and call me a quitter and a traitor. I was counting on it. I'd created the argument we would have in my head. I imagined how I would stay still, calm and stoic, and say things like, "I understand that you're angry and you have every right to be."

"You were here only because of Hugo."

"That's not true."

"Whatever."

I turned my head. Not being able to look at people I cared about was becoming too common. My mind dashed ahead to what might be next for me. A new job somewhere, a new life, new people who I would someday not be able to look at. I'd always thought of the hard times in my life as being like a book. The problem is resolved and then you move on. But it wasn't like that. The hard times didn't just end. The borders weren't that clear. They blend into the good times and link arms with more bad times. And our losses become bricks of silence around us.

"You'll be fine," I said.

"Stop acting like what you do doesn't matter to anybody, like this affects only you."

I reached around him and pulled him into a hug. I felt his arms tighten around me and heard him swallow hard. Then he pushed me away and, stopping to pick up his backpack, headed toward the door.

"You don't get to do that," he said. "Be all 'you're the best' so you get to leave feeling all good about everything. You don't get off that easy."

He slammed the door so hard that I didn't think the bell would ever stop ringing. And now I was alone with my mother.

"You're well rid of this place," Mama said, moving closer to me. "It's a burden you don't need, Margaret Victoria. Just put all this behind you."

I'm sure in her head, her voice sounded motherly, reassuring. If I'd been smart, I'd have kept my mouth shut. But as is always so true when I'm around my mother, I was in no way smart.

"It's more of a home to me than any place I've ever been."

I closed my eyes and regretted the words as soon as they were out of my mouth. Not because they weren't true, but because they were hurtful.

"Well, it's good to know how you really feel about me and your daddy," she said, her back straightening.

"I'm staying here," I said.

"But you just said . . ."

"I don't mean here at the Dragonfly. It's over."

"Then I see no reason why you don't just come home."

I looked up toward the front window at Hugo's empty chair, and I tried to think of what he would say at this moment. I focused on my next breath and waited for words from Hugo's mystical universe to fill my head. But they didn't show up.

"Really?" I said. "You see no reason why I wouldn't want to return to that house and live with you and Daddy?"

"I just want what's best for you," she said.

"No, I don't think so," I said. "You just want me to suffer like you do."

For a long unbreakable moment, our eyes met. I smelled Chanel No. 5 and dust and then it was there. The crayon scent of her lipstick, just like the day when I found out about my father. I saw her face as it was then, hard and blank, like armor, and my cheek burned with phantom pain.

"I have no doubt you love him," I said. "You love him more than the world he provides you. You love him more than you love me. More than yourself. But I also know your greatest love betrays you over and over again, and you do nothing about it."

I don't remember the look on my mother's face or if she slammed the door on the way out. The next thing I knew, I was on my knees, left with my own words in my head. A lifetime of silence was broken in a few seconds. Everything was gone now.

I looked around the store, and finally, my mother's version of the Dragonfly had started to fade from my eyes. I remembered the store swollen with people on a recent Saturday night. I remembered a group of boys—eleven, maybe twelve years old—pudgy cheeks, feet they hadn't grown into and thoughts only beginning to understand the importance of girls, scuffling about in the Graphic Novels section. They huddled over one book, pointing, laughing, one shoving the other on the shoulder. They raced to the counter to pay for the book by counting out coins and crumbled dollars from an Altoids tin. A woman in a floral dress holding a rhinestone leash attached to a Pomeranian browsed through Pets with the latest Patricia Cornwell in the crook of her arm. And then there was Hugo, his reading glasses on the tip of his nose, a novel in his lap. I walked over to a reading chair. I could still smell the faintest hint of his tobacco, and it was then that the tears came. At the time I thought we were keeping the Dragonfly alive. Now I realized we were keeping Hugo alive. But it wasn't enough.

I heard a tapping on the door and, wiping my eyes, got up expecting to see someone coming back to pick up a casserole dish. But I saw Rajhit. He was standing just outside the door, leaning his head on his arm against the glass. He looked at me, and his eyes were as weary as mine.

He stepped back away from the door as I unlocked it. For a moment, we stood there looking at each other in the open doorway, the evening pedestrians of Mountain View passing behind him on their way to dinner or drinks or to shop at Apollo.

I held out my hand to him and he took it. And then his arms were around me. Tears came after that. Hugo. The Dragonfly. Us. Then I took his hand and led him back into the stacks.

·

We sat in the Gardening section, me on my Kik-Step stool, Rajhit on the floor with his legs stretched across the aisle. In the dim quiet, everything around us looked forgotten.

"I didn't know if you'd want me at the memorial," he said. "I thought it might be too difficult. And with your mother here."

"Everything is more difficult with my mother here," I said. "You didn't have to stay away. You loved him, too."

He pulled his knees toward him and wrapped his arms around them. His hair was a bit longer. He'd bought new flip-flops, navy canvas with a Nike swoop on the sole.

"Thanks for picking her up from the airport," I said. "I should have gotten in touch to tell you that much earlier."

He shook his head. "You had a lot to deal with."

"Yeah, my mother is a handful."

"That's not what I meant."

"I know."

I leaned my head against the books beside me and tried not to look at him. I just wanted to feel him with me—no touching, no kisses, no sex—just be with him.

"I came to the hospital," he said. "When you weren't there. I spent time with him. I wanted you to know that."

It felt as if he were on the other side of a river and the stepping stones would appear if I just knew the right words. But I sat mute, feeling my sharp edges.

"I'm going to Amsterdam," he said. "The bike shop I've been talking to offered me an apprenticeship."

"How long will you be gone?"

He shrugged. "Don't know. My place sold. I've got some money to live on for a while. Thought I'd travel a bit."

"Eat. Pray. Fix Bikes."

"Something like that."

We got up and walked to the front of the store. With each step I changed my mind about whether I should tell him or not. But when we reached the front, I was standing on the side of telling.

"I found her," I said. "Catherine. I know who she is."

He shook his head and pressed his fingers lightly around mine.

"You are my Catherine." And then he was gone.

·

When the cab honked its horn outside of my apartment the next morning, it broke the heavy silence Mama and I were using to wage war.

She stood when she heard the horn and walked to the front door, leaving her luggage sitting in the middle of my living room. I picked up the bags and followed her.

Outside the sun was warm and golden, but with a promise of colder weather. Fall was coming. My Dragonfly summer was over.

I handed Mama's bags one by one to the cabbie, who placed them in the trunk and walked to the driver's door while my mother looked at him disdainfully, shocked he hadn't come around to open her door. I reached for the handle of the back passenger's side for my mother, but I didn't open it. In a few seconds, my mother would be gone. And I was ready for some space. It's just that I didn't want her to go like this.

We stood looking at each other.

"You don't have to go back yet," I said.

Her face didn't change, but her head cocked slightly to the side.

"You could stay...Well, not here obviously, but somewhere. I hear the Fairmont in San Jose is nice. Or San Francisco. I'm just saying that you don't have to go back."

I watched as Mama fought the smile that pulled at the corner of her mouth. She leaned toward me, tipped my chin up with her index finger, and pressed her lips against my cheek. Lilac, lipstick, Chanel No. 5. Then she whispered in my ear.

"*You* are my greatest love."

And with that, she reached for the door, opened it herself, and slipped into the backseat. The air around me still smelled of lilac as I stood in the street, a few golden sweet-gum leaves falling around me, and watched her ride away.

.

"When does the truck come?" Jason asked.

"When we tell them we're ready."

We were putting the books into storage, at least until we found an acceptable buyer, which was proving harder than I'd thought. Jason and I both agreed that we weren't going to let our books go to any of those online sellers who sell a book for a penny on eBay or Amazon and then make their money from the shipping. They didn't care about the books. They didn't care about the people who bought the books.

Sitting on the Kik-Step stool, I reached down and traced the dark rectangles in the carpet below me, the outline where shelves had been. Twenty years of browsers through the Dragonfly had created threadbare pathways that looked like chalk outlines of dead bodies in a Raymond Chandler novel. If my parents told me my childhood home was gone forever in the winds of a tornado, I wouldn't feel as bad as I did right then.

"I need air," I told Jason, who didn't hear me because he was already engrossed in one of the books from his stack.

I poured the last half of my beer into one of Hugo's tea mugs and stepped outside onto the sidewalk. I leaned back against the glass window of the Dragonfly and took a good look at Apollo. I hadn't spoken to Avi since I turned down her offer. Dizzy had moved up to Portland before the memorial. None of us had tried that hard to hide our disappointment with the other.

Apollo—the kingdom I'd abdicated—was moving on. Big signs in the windows announced that the store was moving to another location, and everything was on sale. Before Dae-Jung left for Portland with Dizzy (who'd asked him after all), he told me about Apollo's plan to move its branches into smaller stores so they would have a more neighborhoody feel to them. So we were packing. Apollo was packing. Mountain View would be left without a bookstore.

As I considered the behemoth of Apollo, my eye caught a movement in one of the sculpted potted shrubs that stood at attention at the sides of its courtyard entrance. It was black and furry and sitting in the dirt with its back against the rod of a pruned tree trunk. No, not sitting. Squatting. Pooping. It was a black cat pooping in Apollo's potted plants. Then I caught the outline of the ear with the bite taken out of it. It was Grendel.

Keeping my eye on the cat, I knocked on the Dragonfly's

window behind me. I didn't dare turn around, afraid I'd lose sight of Grendel. I just knocked harder until Jason came to the door.

"What!?"

I didn't turn my head. I didn't say anything. I just pointed.

Slowly, without saying anything to each other, we made our way across the street. I tried to keep my eye on him, but he was gone by the time we got to the planter.

"He's got to be here somewhere," Jason said.

We moved into the courtyard, dodging sale shoppers as we looked under tables and chairs and around planters and display stands. Then just as I walked up to a long planter stuffed with agapanthus, movement caught my eye. And when I peered through the arcing leaves, I saw a black nose twitching under the leaves at the far end.

He pulled his head back inside the bush and I heard the rustling getting farther away. Grendel was moving. I pulled off my sweater ever so gently and followed the noise.

There must have been something familiar in my voice or in my smell that told Grendel he was no longer among strangers, because to my amazement, he started walking toward me. Then I noticed that he was in a low crouch and there was a deep guttural growl coming out of him, and I realized he wasn't coming toward me. He was hunting me. I scampered away from the agapanthus just in time to avoid his charge. He chased me onto the tile and through a gaggle of middle school girls, and satisfied he'd run me off, he turned around to return to his lair. Only I was ready. I launched myself at him and scooped him up with my sweater. He struggled and it was all I could do to hang on to him. A paw got loose and I got the angry end of it but still I hung on. Grendel belonged with us, whether he liked it or not.

"You got him!"

Jason reached out for his cat, who was still attached to my finger, and for a moment there was this odd Chinese puzzle of Jason tugging on Grendel and Grendel still having his claw sunk into me and me yelling in pain and Jason yelling in joy and Grendel yowling like the world was coming to an end. Finally, the cat let go and I let Jason pull him into his arms.

That fucking cat. Living large over at Apollo while Jason was worried sick about him. While we were left with the disheveled strings of our lives, here that disloyal, traitorous cat was making himself at home across the street.

And then I saw it. Like I had before with the Dragonfly, I saw the top of Apollo lifted off the building so that I could look down on it and see it as no one else could. I could see the shelves brimming with books, not neatly ordered, but torpedoed across the store. I could see me and Jason at the front ringing up our customers, showing people to their sections. I could see Gloria and her husband and her NPR tote bag. I could see the CIA Bathroom sitting in big easy chairs, arguing, reminiscing, giving me a hard time. I could see it as clearly as I could see Grendel in Jason's arms. I knew then that I was going to love that cat forever.

CHAPTER FIFTEEN

Finding What Was Lost

There are times when this is all too much to bear.
—Catherine

Jason and I were having a round of Shakespeare Boggle, taking a break from the last bits of packing, when Avi came through the door. Later, Jason would say, "The air suddenly smelled corporate." And were it not for Jason, I would have had a completely civil and adult greeting with another human being. Instead, as I stood to say "hello," Jason jumped from his chair and assumed a Grendel-like position of defense. Grendel, for once, lay on his back in a sunny spot on top of a small stack of boxes, from where our human antics seemed to be amusing him.

"What do you want here?" he asked Avi.

Avi ignored his tone and cued up her designer smile. She was wearing an end-of-summer cream suit, with a whisper of the autumn that was nearly on us in her roasted orange blouse. For once, I didn't feel like the frumpy country cousin standing in front of her even in my holey jeans and Dragonfly T-shirt tied in a knot at my waist. It felt like she was the one who didn't fit.

"Stay gold, Ponyboy," I said. "I invited her."

Avi and I went down the block to the Starbucks where the Overly Tattooed & Pierced had also migrated. We ordered an extra large mocha with whipped cream (me) and Orange Zinger tea (her). As I picked up the orders and she settled in at a table, I saw Jason outside the front window motioning furiously to the Overly Tattooed & Pierced and saying things I couldn't hear but could guess pretty well.

Finger drawing an invisible line from Starbucks to the Dragonfly: *She just walked into our store!* Arms waving in the direction of our table: *And Maggie just followed her over like a zombie!* Finger pointing from his chest to the Dragonfly: *I've got to get back to watch the store.* Pointing to the Overly Tattooed & Pierced, and then bouncing palms down: *You guys stay here and look out for Maggie.*

I set Avi's tea in front of her and sat down at the table. I took a long slurp from my mocha, trying to look casual and wondering where to start.

She kept her eyes on me as she replaced the teacup in the saucer. A smile arced on her lips.

"It's not too late for you to be a part of the new Apollo Books, Maggie."

I gazed into the remnants of my mocha, clinging to the straw and the sides of the plastic cup. I wondered if someone there was an old gypsy woman who could read sticky coffee foam like tea leaves. For now, I'd have to depend on me.

"I appreciate you saying that," I said.

"I've been meditating on it and looking for a creative solution. The way I see it, you're not joining us because there's something missing from our offer. Something you want that we're not giving you."

The hum of voices around us seemed to crescendo and then disappear in a vacuum of sound, leaving a moment of silence like when the ocean pulls a broken wave back into the tide. Before I could spend another moment thinking about it, I blurted out, "How much do you want for the building here in Mountain View?"

She did not bother trying to hide her surprise.

"Why do you want to know?"

"Jason and I want to buy it for the Dragonfly."

She told me a figure that was way beyond the point at which money stopped being real to me. For me and Jason, money was something you held and handed to people from the till. It puttered—a jalopy made of spare parts—slowly from one person to another, making clinking noises when you dropped bits of it in tip jars. The figures we were talking of were too fast for sound. They were light-years traversed by rocket ships.

I swallowed my nerves and talked to her about how the retail real estate market was still on the low slope and how it would be great publicity for Apollo to give the Dragonfly a deal on the sale. Avi said something about having to discuss it with her partners and needing a property assessment but her words were white noise as my mind scrambled. There was no perfect job, at least not for me. There was no perfect love or even a perfect book. But I had a life I loved at the Dragonfly and I wanted to be tethered to it. I wanted to suffer the bad times and feel joy at the good.

"You'll be leaving the community without a bookstore," I said, making my final argument, just as I'd practiced.

"What are you offering?" Avi asked.

I told her a figure 15 percent below what we could pay after pooling together the money from Hugo's duplex and the small business loan Robert helped us acquire. She countered with another number and finally we agreed on a figure 5 percent below my threshold.

"I'm certain I can sell that to my partners," she said.

We walked to the sidewalk, and shook hands.

"You could have been great," she said.

"You too," I said.

·

There's a part of grief that's unexpected. After the days when you think you'll never be able to get out of bed again and after walking about feeling like your insides are hollow and your skin is made of paper, you start remembering. You remember not the death and seeing the one you love in a hospital bed with tubes. You remember what he was like before all of that, when he was well and you were whole. It's that remembering that catches up with you and then you know the person you lost isn't lost after all, but has become part of you and you're the better for it.

"What about that time he got all mad because he couldn't find organic lard?" Jason asked.

We all laughed, sitting around the blanket, the scent of fresh wood from the new bookshelves huddling beneath the aromas of our indoor picnic of samosas, vindaloo chicken, naan, and a rainbow of curried dishes. Jason, pretty much everyone from game night, the CIA Bathroom, and I still smelled of sweat and sawdust.

"It was some Southern thing for you, wasn't it?" Jason asked me.

"Hush puppies," I said. "He called the offices of *Southern Living* for the recipe because he wouldn't look it up online. But he could never bring himself to make them because he couldn't assure himself the hog lived in an organically cultured manner before giving his life for the cause of deep-frying."

They'd all come to the new Dragonfly to help make the shelves we'd need for our abundant inventory. Jason and I had been scouring estate sales, abandoned storage units, and anywhere else we could to stock a store five times the size of the previous Dragonfly. It was just too huge. I thought back to that conversation with Avi about how no bookstore needed thirty thousand square feet. So instead of filling it with inventory, we built walls to create study rooms, meeting rooms people could rent, and, of course, a coffee bar and café that we sublet out to a few of the Overly Tattooed & Pierced. We hired staff, including Sasha and her girlfriend with the pixie haircut, who we hoped would fill the store with their friends at night. The new Dragonfly cast out for a future.

Robert gave us a present of two framed pictures. One was of Hugo, standing in front of the old Dragonfly. It must have been right after he bought the store in the eighties. He looked so young. His hairline had only started its departure, his beard was nearly black. The other was of the three of us, Jason and Hugo in the two reading chairs, me on the floor leaning against Hugo's legs, all of us with our noses in a book. How Hugo would have loved seeing the new Dragonfly. I'm sure he would have felt a sense of victory at having run Apollo Books & Music out of town, and we would never try to disabuse him of that notion. He would have loved the new shelves, the new office. He would have loved this gathering of our family. He would have loved it all.

I think I'd always been scared of what love meant in my life because I was afraid of it controlling me, of what I would have to give up for it. But the truth is, for a love big enough, the sacrifices aren't sacrifices. They are necessities. The crime is making them for the wrong reasons.

As the others cleaned up from our indoor picnic, I went into the office to get some papers for Robert. Our first mail at the new address had arrived. Along with the bills and the catalogs, there was a book-size package addressed to me. I opened it and pulled out Henry and Catherine's *Lady Chatterley's Lover*. Inside was a notecard.

Time to move on.

—Miko Callahn

That night, I sat in my papasan chair by the window of the small apartment above the new Dragonfly where I'd moved after we sold Hugo's duplex. It was almost too cold to have the window open, but I liked hearing the last of the Castro Street visitors going home at night and the smell of the Thai restaurant across the street. After living next door to Hugo for years, the quiet and lack of luscious smells would have made me lonesome.

I opened *Lady Chatterley's Lover*. I reread all the notes, just as I had the first night I found them. Then I got up and went to my kitchen table with a sheet of paper and a pen. I held the paper steady and pressed ink into it, forming letters, forming words, forming my thoughts.

I didn't know what Rajhit's life was like in Amsterdam. I didn't know if he had found another love or if he still thought of me and our counterfeit affair. He existed around a corner I had not turned. But nonetheless, I wrote to his unknown heart. Because in the end, he was right. I was his Catherine after all.

After the letter was done, I folded it and addressed it to the shop in Amsterdam he'd told me about. Then in the night's light, I walked to the postal box across from the Dragonfly, opened the door, and dropped in the letter before I could stop myself. After working in software for a decade, I understood the bits and bytes of e-mail, Facebook posts, tweets, and texts, but dropping a piece of paper into a box and it appearing on the other side of the world a few days later? That was true magic.

CHAPTER SIXTEEN

Only Possibilities Last Forever

I must at last face all my questions.

—Maggie

I wake up to find Maya standing by my bed staring at me. She's started this habit lately, lifting the key to my place we keep in the office downstairs in the Dragonfly. She's been excited about starting kindergarten in a couple of weeks, but she's also been more clingy lately, like we might disappear while she's off learning her ABCs. Her mom, Aslay, just laughs and says it's all those children's books about orphans that Jason reads to her. "She'll learn," she says. "We're all staying put."

I get up and she brings me the phone when it rings. I sit on my bed and chat with Dizzy, who's coming to town today and taking me to lunch. We make plans to meet at the Nuevo-Indian restaurant in the space where Finnegans Wake used to be. He's trying to woo me to come work for his new start-up, which does something with mobile phones that I don't really understand. He didn't last a year at Apollo Books & Music. Turns out that rebuilding what he'd done before wasn't as exciting as the New & Shiny around the corner. Whatever his

THE MOMENT OF EVERYTHING

new company does, Dizzy is the FFS, future feature strategist. It's the most bullshit made-up title I've ever heard of, but Dizzy is excessively proud of it and I pretend I am, too. Sometimes it's enough just to see the people in your life happy.

By the time I hang up with Dizzy, Maya is pulling me toward the stairs. I tell her to get dressed. We have a big day ahead. After I open the store for the morning crew and tie up a few loose ends, Maya and I need to find her a new outfit and new shoes for the first day of school. Her mom and Jason think cutoffs and holey sneakers are perfectly fine for the big day. Jesus Christ on a cracker.

We head downstairs to the store, where Jason's sitting at the desk, checking our sales numbers for the last month. The late hours in the summer were good for us, but we're hoping the Christmas season will be better. Aslay is there, too. She's much more of a morning person. She's brought warm scones and fresh orange juice. She works at an organic bakery and is a little too militant about rice flour. But I like her. She and Jason met around last Thanksgiving, a couple of months after we reopened, when she came in looking for books for Maya. The two of them moved into a new apartment a couple of months ago. At twenty-six, Aslay is a few years older than Jason, but in a way that makes him seem older, too. They're planning a Christmas wedding at the Dragonfly. I want to tell them they're very young, that they haven't known each other long enough. I worry a little for all of them. But then, which of us are ever really ready for anything?

Maya stands on her knees in the chair next to Jason. She tells him about a turtle in her dream last night. He tells her about a bear cub who lives in an upside-down umbrella that hangs from the crescent moon. Aslay begs him again to write down these stories that swim around in his brain and he scribbles some lines in a spiral notepad we keep by the desk phone. Then the scones are buttered and my tea is ready and, when I sit down, I know it's going to be a good day.

When Maya and I walk into the main store, Sasha has already let in the morning crew and gotten the coffee bar going so that the whole place smells like coffee heaven. No burned beans at the Cuppa Joe Café at the Dragonfly. I can even drink it black, but Sasha has a Hammerhead Mocha waiting for me and a juice box for Maya when we arrive. Maya takes her hand to "help" her set out the fresh pastries.

"No doughnuts," I say. "She's already had breakfast."

They both pout and when they think I'm not looking, Sasha makes an exaggerated turn of her head and Maya pops a doughnut hole in her mouth.

"Maya," I say.

"Not a doughnut. It's the hole," she says, and I give her the "I'm not falling for that" look and hopefully that will be the end of it, because I'm getting ready for a meeting in the conference room with the morning staff about the new book trade tracking system Dizzy wrote for us as a side project. We're his beta testers. If all goes well, he's going to sell it in the App Store. Good for him. I'm just glad for the newish computers that came with his deal.

I still stick to my guns about a thirty-thousand-square-foot store being way too much space for a neighborhood bookstore. We rent out the conference rooms, offices, and cubicles in the upstairs to the Silicon Valley hopefuls thinking they have the next Facebook in the works on their hard drives. They love being with the books and being with the coffee and pastries more. We charge them just enough so that book sales have to cover only half our mortgage. Book sales may go up and down, but there's no shortage of dreams of the Next Big Thing in Silicon Valley.

Maya joins me at the checkout counter while I sort through a stack of mail, which is mostly bills. I'm just about through when Maya tugs on my shirt and holds out a postcard to me.

"I like this bicycle," she says.

I take the card. It has a picture of a bicycle parked in a field of yellow tulips. And I know who sent it before I turn it over.

It took two agonizing months for me to hear back after that first letter I wrote him. But when I saw my name on that envelope below the Dutch stamps, I just held it and ran my fingers over the imprint of the pen on the paper, paper he had touched. It was the first of many we wrote back and forth for the next ten months. No promise, no protestations of love. Just letters. Letters telling of our days. Getting-to-know-you letters. Letters only for us.

I turn over the bicycle postcard, expecting to see more colorful Dutch stamps, but there's nothing in the right corner but a small rectangle showing the sender where to put the stamp. Below that is just "Maggie." The card didn't come in the mail. On the left there's only "Meet me in Pioneer Park, under your favorite tree, tomorrow at noon." Rajhit is home. And I must at last face all my questions.

"What is it?" Maya asks, taking the card from me.

"A friend is in town."

"Dizzy?"

"No, another friend."

I slide the card into my bag between a notebook and a copy of *My Lord Wicked*. I have a day and two hours to fill before I see him. I look out the open door as the Dragonfly cranks to life. I will have plenty of work to fill the time.

Bookstores are romantic creatures. They seduce you with their wares and break your heart with their troubles. All great readers fantasize about owning one. They think spending a day around all those books will be the great fulfillment of their passion. They don't yet know about the sorting of what comes in, the tracking of what goes out, the backaches from carrying and shelving, and the little money that comes from any of it. All those readers just think about the wedding without giving much thought to the marriage. Books make for a heavy load, and there's no getting around it.

I worry about my future in the way I'm told I'm supposed to. Retirement, health care, insurance. Jason and I, as co-owners of the Dragonfly, struggle. When sales are good, we feast like thieves. In the slow times, we skimp by on peanut butter and jelly so we can make payroll for a dozen employees. There's always a moment, every day, that I wonder if I should have taken Avi up on her offer, if I could now be in a massage chair drinking piña coladas and deciding what books should be front and center in Apollo's aisles. And when I picture those virginally new books, I know I made the right decision. The books in Apollo are like people without pasts, without tales to tell. The books of the Dragonfly have been through many hands and will move on to others. They smell of human touch and all its possibilities.

As the day moves on and the light lingers, the Dragonfly brims with the purposeful lingering movement of those looking for what they don't yet know they need. The kind of people who come to the Dragonfly don't just own books; they need them, crave them, find it impossible to breathe without them. They come because they are in love with the store itself, with its handled wares and their untold tales. They come because they like wondering about the people who owned all these books before. They come because the people whose paths they cross are like the books they find, a bit worn around the edges, just waiting for the right person to open them up and take them home.

ACKNOWLEDGMENTS

Thank you to my agent, Stéphanie Abou, and my editor at Grand Central Publishing, Emily Griffin, who saw promise in my work and gave me the courage to make this novel all that I wanted it to be. Thank you to Ellen Sussman and Tom Parker, in whose writing workshops I not only learned the mechanics of storytelling but also met many other writers who have supported and encouraged me along the way. Two of those writers are Tracy Guzeman and Christine Chua, who kindly read many drafts of this novel, pushed me to make it better, and held my hand when it was time to let it go. Thanks to all the amazing members of my writing group—Gordon Jack, Eileen Brody, Rich Register, Cheyenne Richards, Mary Taugher, Beth Sears, Katy Motiey, John Foley, Lolly Winston, and Julie Knight—with whom I've survived many rounds of critiques and courses of questionable Chinese food. Sincere thanks to Robert Wendin for sending me taunting e-mails until I finished this novel. Thank you to Will Schuur for reminding me of what it's like to be in your twenties in Silicon Valley and for cooking all those delicious dinners. Thank you to Matthew Williams and Rebecca Laincz for all the late-night waffles and tales from the wild land of used bookstores. Thank you to my devoted and loving parents, Virginia and Harold Gilbertson—who are nothing like the parents in this novel—and to my brother John and his wife, Ethel, for all their love, support, and the use of their beautiful pond house—the best writing retreat on earth. And thank you to my husband, John, for helping me find the peace and quiet in my heart to be the writer I wanted to be.

READING GROUP GUIDE

THE
MOMENT
OF
EVERYTHING

BY SHELLY KING

QUESTIONS FOR
FURTHER DISCUSSION

1. "Books don't change lives, not like people think they do." Do you agree or disagree with the first line in Shelly King's novel? Do you think it's meant to be tongue-in-cheek? Did a book, or books, change Maggie's life?

2. At the beginning of the novel, Maggie's life is in a holding pattern after her layoff. Have you ever been laid off or fired? Does Maggie's experience, of feeling part of a corporate family and then being let go, resonate with you?

3. Have you ever read *Lady Chatterley's Lover*? Was it for a school assignment or leisure reading? Which of the book club members' interpretations ring the most true to you?

4. Though the Silicon Valley Women Executives Association Book Club is an extreme (and somewhat satirical) example of a reading group, have you encountered similar dynamics in any of your own reading groups? What do you think makes for a good reading group?

5. Have you ever written in a book?

6. How does Maggie's relationship with her mother change over the course of the novel? Do you fault Georgine for staying in her marriage? Why or why not?

7. Throughout the book, we meet characters who want to lose themselves in other worlds—from those who read romances to those who imagine they're Henry or Catherine and still others who participate in medieval re-creations. What does it say about these characters, and the world they all do live in, that they create and escape to these other worlds? Have you ever pretended to be someone else, either in real life or a virtual world?

8. By the end of the book, Maggie has lost two good friends for two very different reasons. Which of those reasons do you think is harder to get over? She's also made a very good friend in Jason—did that surprise you? Have you ever had an antagonistic relationship turn into a close friendship?

9. Who did you think Henry and Catherine would reveal themselves to be? Were you surprised by Maggie's discovery? Did you think her involvement in their love story was reasonable, or did she cross a line?

10. What do you think happens to Maggie and Rajhit after the novel ends?